Race into Murder

Karen Black

ISBN-13: 978-1975790127

This book is a work of fiction. Any resemblance to persons, living or dead, events, or locales is purely coincidental. The characters are productions of the author's imagination and are used fictitiously.

Race into Murder

Author, Karen Black

Editor, Robert L. Arend

Cover Design,
Dark Water Arts Designs

Cover Photo, Laura Barnes-Kadi

Publicity Photos,
Laura Barnes-Kadi, Mark Bellard

1

With an arch of his muscular neck, FraziersFury flared his nostrils and pawed at the sawdust-covered paddock. His steel-grey coat glistened in the southern California sun. It was the day of the Celestial Stakes at the Angelina Race Track and the three-year-old thoroughbred was ready to run.

FraziersFury understood what it meant to be saddled in the racetrack's paddock. He bucked and danced in excitement, and it took both his trainer, Jeff Frazier, and his groom to keep the colt under control as they walked around the circular paddock.

With some of the best young horses in the country competing, horsemen considered the Celestial Stakes a stepping stone to the Million Dollar Derby, one of the most highly anticipated races of the year.

Santos Velasquez was Fury's groom. He knew the animated young horse as well as anyone. At just over five feet tall, Santos had the broad shoulders and narrow waist of a man who kept himself in shape. He was exceptionally strong for his size and had no problem handling even the rankest horse. Although Fury's antics kept the groom busy, there was never any fear that he would lose control of the young animal. Santos had an uncanny ability with animals of all types and was an expert at controlling energetic young horses like Fury. His talent made him invaluable to Jeff.

"Fury sure is wound up," Santos said as they walked Fury to his stall for a final equipment check. "He reminds me of Esperanza. He was the first horse I broke. My father laughed when I said I would ride him. I was twelve years old. I got some big bruises, but once Esperanza understood what I wanted, he tried to comply. It was as if he understood my words and my thoughts. That big grey horse could run like the wind, but he was so efficient that it felt like slow motion. Fury moves like that. There is one difference. Fury is kinder than Esperanza was. I wish I was young enough, and thin enough, to race again. I would pay you to allow me to be his jockey. Look at him over there. He knows what's coming. He is ready to race."

Jeff chuckled. "He sure is. Carl has his hands full with that colt. I just hope he can keep him under wraps for the first half."

Fury had raced twice as a two-year-old, winning a Maiden Special Weight in a field of eleven his first time out. He moved up in class to an

Allowance race and finished second by a length after a difficult trip. Pleased with the result of his maiden race, Jeff moved Fury up in class. He entered the colt in the Obsidian and then the Rose Stakes; both rated Grade 3. Fury finished second and first respectively, earning national recognition and an offer from David Marsico, a well-known trainer who specialized in equine agreements for his clients.

Mr. Marsico wanted to purchase Fury for himself, however, he said he might consider a partnership agreement for a substantial sum, but only if he took over the training. Jeff's wife, Natalie, wasn't interested in selling, yet, at Marsico's insistence, Jeff agreed to meet to discuss the offer.

As a businessman, Jeff was ready to consider what the sale of the young horse would mean, not only to him as the trainer, but to Natalie, who was Fury's breeder and steadfast in her refusal to even consider the sale of her colt. Even if she would consider a sale, David Marsico would not have enough money to buy him. And since Natalie was Fury's sole owner, that was the end of the discussion.

Jeff and Natalie didn't have any children, so the horses were Natalie's babies. As a result, throughout their years together she had as much, or even more input into the daily regimen of the horses than Jeff, who also loved the horses, yet was a businessman first.

Fury was the couple's first home-bred stakes winner, and the paperwork listed Natalie as his owner. And though a race horse, Fury was also his owner's pet.

For Natalie, winning the Celestial Stakes—the most prestigious race in which she had ever entered a horse—would be a reflection on the married duo's ability to breed and train a sound and talented colt. For Jeff, a winning race was a reflection on their investment and being able to make a substantial profit. If Fury was unsuccessful on the racetrack, Natalie would have kept him as a western pleasure horse. Jeff had no qualms about admitting that he would sell any horse they had, for the right price; and winning races would increase Fury's value.

Natalie listened as Jeff gave the jockey, Carl Lawson, some final instructions.

"Get him out of the gate quickly," Jeff instructed Carl. "Try to keep him relaxed, and off the pace. I'd like to see him about four lengths back. If he absolutely demands the lead, don't use all of his energy in a battle trying to hold him back. It isn't my preference, but if you have to let him go, just do it; we'll see what he does on the front end. Given his attitude, I suspect he'll be tough to rate. He is definitely ready for this race. Do your best."

The jockey nodded. "Understood."

Carl was one of the taller jockeys who raced at Angelina. Long, smooth muscles stretched over his sixty-five-inch frame, like steel cables. He kept those muscles in shape with daily workouts, which gave him the strength to control a mount that weighed close to ten times as much as he did.

Carl was Fury's regular jockey and had ridden the horse in all of his races and formal workouts. When he was available, and that was most of the time, Carl was Fury's exercise rider, too. He had a rapport with the colt and knew that the young horse was ready to run.

The announcer's voice boomed over the loudspeakers, "Riders up!"

Jeff gave Carl a leg up as Natalie whispered in Fury's ear, "Run fast and come home safe, my beauty."

Carl turned Fury toward the track's entrance. The stunning grey colt pricked his ears, arched his neck, and with the slightest of bucks, danced his way onto the dirt oval. When he reached the track, however, Fury's antics stopped. It was as though he understood that it was time to work, and he focused on Carl's signals.

Carl Lawson had been riding for seven years. He had a good reputation and a decent win record. On occasion, he had ridden for some of the major trainers, but not their top prospects. The jockey had gotten some good press after Fury's win in the Rose Stakes, and he expected some additional recognition if Fury did well in the Celestial Stakes. When the California Horse Network interviewed him, Carl had given all the credit to Fury. The jockey was convinced that Fury was not only the best horse he'd ever ridden, but possibly the best three-year-old currently racing.

Frazier's Barn was where Carl had become acquainted with Jeff and Natalie. He became one of the couple's best friends, which led to him becoming Fury's exclusive jockey.

Natalie reached for Jeff's hand.

"He certainly seems ready to go," Jeff said, smiling at his wife.

Not taking her eyes away from the colt, Natalie said, "That he does."

Long, auburn hair brushed the side of her face and drew attention to her wide, lime-green eyes. Married for thirteen years, he thought she was the most beautiful woman he had ever seen.

Santos joined the couple, and the three friends crossed the paddock to the inside rail.

"I like to hang out with the trainer," Natalie reached for Jeff's hand. "It gets me a front row spot for the race." Jeff rolled his eyes as he squeezed her hand. Santos chuckled.

Jeff thought that Fury looked good warming up, but noticed the colt had broken out in a sweat. Fury was more anxious than in past races, and the trainer figured that it was probably because of the noisy crowd. Though lightly raced, Fury already had quite a following at Angelina, and the roar of the fans seemed to increase when Carl rode him onto the track.

Watching horse and rider, Natalie thought about the strength and determination jockeys needed to be able to do what they do; that horse racing is a dangerous occupation.

Jockeys make a living riding a half-ton mass of pure muscle that moves beneath them at 35 to 40 miles per hour, Natalie marveled. *The 120 pound riders balance on two little steel stirrups, holding onto a thin piece of leather, or a fist full of mane, yet somehow manage not to fall off.* After all the years working around the track, she still found those professionals amazing.

The announcer's voice filled the air. "The horses are in the starting gate."

For those few seconds, Natalie stopped breathing, exhaling only when the announcer bellowed, "And they're off, in the Celestial Stakes."

Natalie's home-bred colt moved quickly from the starting gate and onto the Angelina oval, spurring her excitement. She was midway into silently thanking the racing goddess for Fury's safe start when the announcer crumbled her exultation with his next report.

"After a clean start for all, FraziersFury is running 6th, with about eight lengths to make up."

Fury had bounded nicely out of the gate, but veered toward the rail, bumping, or being bumped, by the big bay horse in the process. Yet, neither seemed any worse for the wear while they thundered down the backstretch. Fury wasn't gaining ground, but didn't seem to be losing any. Carl had a tight grip on the reins and seated still as a statue. Fury seemed comfortable where he was. Eight lengths were farther back than Natalie would have liked, but she thought it was better than being in front too early.

"Come on Fury!" Natalie shouted, as if he could hear her and that would make a difference.

"The horses are approaching the top of the stretch," the track announcer called. "Nordstrom still holds the lead, with pilot A.J. McCoy sitting chilly, followed by ImageOfAKnight and BaskervillesBobby a half-length behind. HotDogsAndBeer is fourth. On the outside, FraziersFury is making a move. Jockey, Carl Lawson, is asking Fury for more speed and getting it. Nordstrom is still in front, then

BaskervillesBobby, and HotDogsAndBeer. ImageOfAKnight has dropped out of it, but look at FraziersFury!"

Countless spectators rose from their seats, their cheers uniting in a cacophony that swarmed the arena.

"On the far outside, FraziersFury is gaining with every stride. There are three furlongs to go. Nordstrom and BaskervillesBobby are battling for the lead. FraziersFury is moving up to challenge. Any one of them can win. Nordstrom has moved past BaskervillesBobby on the inside. FraziersFury is moving right with him, trying to take command on the outside. McCoy gave two taps of the right-hand whip and Nordstrom has responded with a leap to the lead. With steady urging FraziersFury is digging in. They are coming to the wire. It's too close to call!"

Nordstrom might have held on, but Fury was gaining on the outside. A head bob could decide the winner. BaskervillesBobby was third.

"Did Fury catch him, Jeff?" Natalie wasn't sure.

"I don't know," Jeff answered. "It was awfully close. Fury's nose was coming up just as they hit the wire. First or second, he ran a great race. I'm proud of him and Carl."

Jeff jumped over the rail and then turned to help his wife over. Hand in hand, both ran onto the track to wait for Carl to gallop out and bring Fury back.

Natalie eagerly looked up into her husband's sea-colored eyes. "While it would be beyond thrilling if Fury did win in company like this, I will still be delighted with a second place for him," she said.

Santos approached. "Fury caught him, Nat. Fury won."

Is it possible that we have a starter for the Million Dollar Derby? Natalie thought. She wasn't yet ready to ask that question out loud.

The Million Dollar Derby was the first of the Triple Million Race Series for three-year-old horses. It was a group of three races, each with a purse of one million dollars. There was a bonus of two million dollars to the winner of two of the three races, and a bonus of three million dollars to the winner of all three. The only way to race in the Million Dollar Derby was to be one of the top twenty money earners who were interested in entering.

Natalie and Jeff had worked with horses for years. They had a small operation. They weren't rich, but earned enough to pay their expenses and live comfortably. Jeff's interest was in training winning race horses. Natalie was more involved in breeding and genetics that produced longevity and sound horses.

Natalie never tired of studying the pedigrees and following careers. Fury and his younger sister, Flight, weren't Natalie's first home-bred race horses—or even her first stakes winners, but Fury was the first graded stakes winner.

Graded stakes races were determined by the amount of the purse money, and drew the top horses from across the country, even other continents. The competition became more difficult the higher the grade. Fury had won a Grade 3 race, the Rose Stakes. The Celestial Stakes was a Grade 2. All three races in the Triple Million Series would be Grade 1 races. It had been twenty years since a horse had won all three races; winning even one of the three was often the pinnacle of a racing career for a trainer, a breeder, a jockey or an owner.

Followed by Santos, Jeff and Natalie met Carl and Fury in front of the winner's circle. The young grey galloped back easily, seemingly pleased with himself. Natalie was sure Fury knew he had done something special. Fury whinnied, as he lowered his head to greet her, and Natalie rubbed his silky nose.

Somewhat breathless, Carl said, "I think we caught him at the wire. Nordstrom was having one heck of a race, but Fury dug in on his own. He wanted to catch him."

When Natalie and Santos strolled to the tote board, she willed Fury's number to show up on top. What they saw instead was the word "Objection" and Fury's number blinking on the tote board. That meant that the objection was against Fury. That wasn't good news.

"Do you think Fury interfered?" Santos asked her.

"No. I don't think so, but it all happened so fast. I don't have any doubt that Fury was closing faster than Bobby. Carl moved him toward the rail, but there was no contact, and I didn't see Doug check Bobby. I don't think Fury caused Doug to lose first or second place. Fury and Nordstrom were the better horses today."

The voice of the track announcer finally boomed from the public address towers. "Doug Whiteman, riding number five, BaskervillesBobby, who finished third, has lodged a claim of foul against number seven, FraziersFury, ridden by Carl Lawson, for interference in the stretch. Hold all tickets, please."

If they upheld the objection, it wouldn't make any difference if Fury won the race or came in second. The stewards would move Fury behind Bobby, putting him into third place and Bobby into second place.

"No, the stewards won't uphold the claim," Santos said confidently. "Carl moved Fury toward the inside in the last furlong, but Bobby was done after Nordstrom passed him."

Also confident there was no interference, but unsure if the stewards would agree, Natalie said, "There is nothing to do but wait for the decision. The worst-case scenario is that the racing stewards move Fury into third place. If that happens, I'll still be proud of his effort." She refused to allow anything to destroy her enthusiasm about the race her horse had run.

"You're right. It was a great effort and third place in a Grade 2 race isn't bad at all." Santos said. He knew it was the jockey's right to object, and that Doug Whiteman was just taking a chance that the stewards could find in his favor. Still, Santos was furious with Doug, and if the jockey had been standing there, Santos was afraid it would be hard to resist knocking him out cold.

Santos scowled and paced until the loudspeaker crackled. Natalie held her breath.

"After a review of the race," the announcer began, "the stewards have determined that FraziersFury did not interfere with BaskervillesBobby and the order of finish in the Celestial Stakes is official. Nordstrom and FraziersFury finished in a dead heat for first. BaskervillesBobby was third. HotDogsAndBeer was fourth."

With that, Santos jumped three feet in the air. "I knew it. Carl and Fury got there!" He took Natalie's hand and dragged her to the winner's circle, where they reunited with Jeff, Carl and Fury for a picture of their dead heat win in the Grade 2 Celestial Stakes.

2

Photograph taken, Jeff took control of Fury and led him to the test barn where all winners had to be tested for drugs immediately following the race. Santos walked Natalie back to Barn 17 to take care of the other horses, clean the stalls and wait for Jeff to bring Fury back and settle him in for the night.

That Santos planned to spend the night at the barn didn't surprise to Natalie. It wasn't unusual for Santos to stay overnight, sometimes even in the stall with one of the horses, particularly with Fury. The young grey had been sick as a foal and nearly died of septicemia. Natalie and Jeff spent hours with him and his dam back then, but Santos had actually moved into the stall with both horses. Although Santos was an animal whisperer of sorts, his connection to Fury seemed almost a psychic bond.

"Why don't you go grab some dinner," Natalie suggested. Experience told her that Santos would rarely leave the barn for the next 48 hours, to be sure

Fury had suffered no silent injury or illness following the race. “I’ll finish up here. Jeff should be back within half an hour.”

“Want me to help you clean the water buckets first?” Santos asked.

“No, thanks. It will keep me busy while I wait for Jeff. Besides, I’m sure you could use a break. I know you won’t leave the barn for anything until Jeff gets here in the morning. So just go. Go get something to eat.” With a playful shove, Natalie pushed him toward barn door.

“Okay! Okay! You convinced me,” Santos surrendered. “I want to catch up with Carl, then I’ll grab some dinner in the horseman’s kitchen. I’ll be back in an hour or less. Oh, I almost forgot; Sonny called earlier and said he has the pedigree for that filly he told you about last week.”

Sonny Owens was the other member of the Frazier crew. A jack of all trades, Sonny worked for Jeff on a part-time basis. He did anything that Jeff needed done, always cheerfully. A stocky, muscular man, Sonny had years of experience breeding and foaling thoroughbreds, and he was also good with a hammer and nails. He was an excellent horseman, yet never minded hot walking or mucking out stalls if that was the business of the day.

Sonny lived with his wife, Vanessa, and her brother, Charlie, at the Williams horse farm a few miles from Angelina Race Track. Vanessa’s parents and grandparents had raised Quarter Horses on the farm. They spent years expanding it into a successful boarding stable. The three of them had grown up together and were a close-knit bunch. They had moved into the old farmhouse after Vanessa's father passed away. Vanessa's mother was up in years and no longer able to keep up with the business. Sonny split his time between working for Jeff and taking care of the horses with Charlie at the Williams farm, where Charlie worked full time and handled the breeding end of the business.

Since the farm was close to the track, it was sometimes convenient for Jeff to send a horse or two to Charlie for boarding. Sometimes Jeff needed an extra stall in the barn at the track, or he would want to give one of his charges some time off from racing. The Williams farm had several paddocks, and they were always willing to work with the Fraziers. That arrangement also gave Jeff flexibility when he wanted to ship in a horse for a new client, or bring a young horse in to get started in training.

While she went about taking care of the never ending list of chores, Natalie kept up a steady stream of conversation with the horses.

It wasn't long before Jeff got back to the barn, leading the animated FraziersFury. "He looks good and isn't worn out," he informed Natalie after he locked the colt behind the gate. Fury stood calmly and nickered at Flight, who nickered back from the next stall. Chaser, the barn cat, appeared and began rubbing against Jeff's ankle.

Jeff reached down to pet the little grey cat. "Fury looked great today, but sharing first place cost us 20% of the purse money. We'll need to win a Grade 2, or hit the board in a Grade 1 race, for Fury to earn enough in time for an invitation to the Million Dollar Derby."

"Do you think we really have a chance?" Natalie asked.

"It's a long shot," Jeff said in his business voice. "If we get the invitation, which is nowhere close to a sure thing, it will be a tough race for a lot of reasons. The entry fees are expensive, and the costs associated with shipping and travel will use a big portion of any profit we've made from his races so far. The decision would be much simpler if we didn't have to worry about finances."

Jeff's response was a reminder that he wanted his wife to at least consider a partnership arrangement with Fury. A partnership meant sharing the expenses of a high level race campaign, as well as a hefty check upon an agreement. If it was his decision, Jeff would sell a share of Fury, even if it meant giving up the training of the colt. It meant more to him for Natalie to own a champion and collect all the purses that would go with that championship than for him to be the trainer of a colt that might have been.

"Fury has won enough to get us to the next race, including the shipping costs, our transportation and accommodations," she said.

Jeff pursed his lips. "A bigger concern is that Fury has only raced at Angelina. We don't know how he'll run on a different surface, and we have no idea how he'll react to a new environment. We could throw all that money away, if he won't adapt. There are a few Grade 1 races coming up, but we need to look at the dates and figure out the expenses. In the meantime, I'd like to give Fury a few weeks off."

The sparkle dulled in Natalie's eyes. "I don't care if we spend every penny he made. I want to give

Fury a chance, and I don't want to be bound by the wishes of a partner who is in this just for the money."

Jeff shoved his hands into his pockets, as he always did when annoyed. "Okay, I get it. You're the owner. I'm the trainer. All I can do is tell you what I think is best for the horse. You make the final decisions, alright?"

Rather than add another argument to the number they'd had since David Marsico's offer, Natalie proposed, "The Sapphire Stakes is coming up in Laredo. It is a Grade 1. We can enter, see how Fury handles being shipped, and whether he'll be comfortable running on another track."

"The Sapphire might work," Jeff compromised, avoiding another confrontation. "I'm going to the jockeys' room to see Carl. I'll be back in a few minutes."

"Okay, I'm just about finished here. Santos should be back any time now. I'll catch up with you at home."

When Jeff left, Natalie went to Fury's stall. He lowered his head so she could easily reach up to stroke his neck. He nuzzled her shoulder.

"Want to go to Kentucky?" She asked the colt. "First, we'll need to go to Laredo."

3

Near twilight was Angie McCoy's favorite time of day. With the setting sun flaring its last rays before night, it decorated the deep blue sky with sporadic wisps of white, resembling oversized spider webs. Angie was fighting downheartedness, though, as she watched Dreamweaver graze. She just couldn't get over the fact that her two-year-old colt was the image of FraziersFury in almost every way, except talent. It simply wasn't fair.

Angie stood inside the paddock, struggling to control her depression at the unfairness of her situation. She tapped her godfather's cell phone number and, while waiting for Nelson Dickenson to answer his phone, watched her beautiful two-year-old colt canter easily around the outside of the enclosure, his coat glistening in the sun's rays reflected off of the deep grey, as if tiny diamonds were being tossed into the air.

When Nelson answered her call, Angie immediately cajoled the attorney. "I can't wait until you get here. I'm sure you can do something to convince them to sell that colt. I want FraziersFury and I have a stall all ready for him."

Dickenson patiently responded to his best friend's only child, "Angelina, my love, I shall use logic, reason, and my unwavering charm, but unless Jeff and Natalie Frazier are interested in selling, there is nothing that we can do to force a sale. If there is any way I can obtain him for you, you shall have him."

"They don't have a lot of money," Angie pointed out. "You will need to stress the impact that a substantial upfront payment would have with regard to their barn as a whole, and their ability to finance the careers of their other thoroughbreds."

"Of course, I will emphasize that," her godfather replied. "You are forgetting that Fury has acquired a considerable purse or two for his last couple of races. Since Mr. Frazier is the trainer and Mrs. Frazier is the owner, they have earned both the owner's and trainer's share of each purse. I suspect they are planning to enter him in the Angelina Derby. If he moves forward in that race, which I expect would be their goal, that purse should give him the earnings necessary to qualify for a starting spot in the Million Dollar Derby. If that occurs, I imagine they will pull out all the stops to get their young star to Louisville. The question is whether receipt of a hefty sales price and the credit that comes with being the breeder is enough. Are you willing to keep Jeff Frazier on as the trainer, if that becomes an issue?"

Angie hesitated before she replied. "Alright. Jeff can train him through the Triple Million Race Series, if that's what it takes to get a deal. I want that horse, Nelson. I'd love to have him before the Angelina Derby."

"I quite doubt that their plan to enter that race will make any difference when we make the offer. If that colt wins the Angelina Derby, he'll have won enough money to earn a spot in the Million Dollar Derby, and enough to finance the trip," the attorney said. "If they don't want to sell now, but he races and loses the Million Dollar Derby, eliminating the possibility of a Triple Million victory, it might be worth approaching them again, in the event you are still interested in obtaining him."

"Maybe." Angie sighed, frustrated. "But what if Fury wins?"

"If they won't sell him outright under any condition now, they won't sell him outright if he wins. The question becomes whether you are interested in my offering to purchase a share, as a partnership?"

Angie paused. "I never really thought of that. I suppose part of a champion would be better than none of a champion. Yes, if you are absolutely convinced we can't purchase Fury outright, try to negotiate a partnership agreement."

"You might also be able to purchase a share when he is retired from racing. I believe I can convince the Fraziers that your family would be in a much better position to promote Fury's services. His line-breeding shows a history of classic distance runners and that what he should produce. You could breed him to a couple of your mares and expect exemplary results with the pedigree combinations."

"We can talk about that later," Angie replied. Her godfather's suggestion gave her another, more daring, idea.

"With that, my dear, I will be there day after tomorrow." Nelson said, concluding their conversation.

Angie McCoy turned her attention back to her two-year-old Dreamweaver as she pondered what Nelson suggested.

Angie's parents had named her after the Angelina Race Course. Her father, Anthony McCoy, formerly a thoroughbred trainer, was now a successful bloodstock agent, who also bred and trained his own thoroughbreds. Angie's mother, Martha, was an accomplished horsewoman. She'd met Anthony on the day she won an Olympic silver medal in the Equestrian Competition. After the Olympics, Martha competed in a variety of equestrian events, including Show Jumping, both individual and team, as well as Dressage, and she won more often than she lost. Before she was able to walk unassisted, Angie rode her family's thoroughbreds. Without a doubt, thoroughbred horses were in Angie's blood. Her parents were established and quite knowledgeable in the thoroughbred industry, and Angie began absorbing that knowledge as a toddler. She'd grown up around and among horses and racing, spending every spare moment watching them, handicapping races, or studying pedigrees. Her love for horses and the knowledge she possessed helped her save the life of more than one newborn foal. She diagnosed a sick horse's problem as well as almost any veterinarian and knew what treatment they needed. Angie's dream, however, was to own that once in a lifetime champion. She thought her father had found him in Nordstrom until FraziersFury.

She turned her gaze from Dreamweaver slowly walked back to the house, as she replayed Nordstrom's race in her mind. Before the race, she expected the big bay to win. Nordstrom was exceptionally fit. His coat was dappled, he was happy, and working well. He'd earned enough purse money to qualify for the Million Dollar Derby, but Fury needed just one more race to qualify as well. FraziersFury had finished in a dead heat with her father's undefeated champion. That grey colt was the one who might be able to keep Nordstrom from winning the Derby.

Angie's review of the past performances of all the horses entered in the Celestial Stakes had indicated BaskervillesBobby was Nordstrom's main competition, and Fury strode right by him. FraziersFury was a nice horse, above average in talent, had won two races, but both wins were by less than a neck. Nordstrom was undefeated, and had won each of his races by daylight, until today. She wondered if the problem was that Nordstrom couldn't handle an eye to eye challenge; no other horse had ever gotten close enough to challenge him until today. Her father was pointing Nordstrom toward the Angelina Derby. The timing was perfect. It would give the big bay colt one more race before the Million Dollar Derby, and it would likely give him one more win. Unless, of course, FraziersFury was being primed for the same race.

Nordstrom, a regally bred colt, was originally purchased as a weanling for one of her father's clients, Scott Anderson. Unfortunately, Scott became involved in a bitter divorce and was forced to sell Nordstrom six months after the purchase, and asked Angie's dad to manage the sale. When Anthony McCoy met with Scott to get Nordstrom ready for auction, he'd been impressed with the colt's development. The well-muscled, energetic colt was everything that Mr. McCoy wanted in a race horse, and so he bought the young bay himself.

Everything had been going as planned. Nordstrom had been training well and was continuing to improve. Both Angie and her father were convinced the horse was well on his way to becoming the favorite for the prestigious Million Dollar Derby. Then Nordstrom raced against that grey monster, FraziersFury, who finished with Nordstrom in a dead heat for first. Technically, Nordstrom remained undefeated, but a dead heat was too close to second as far as Angie was concerned. Carl hadn't gotten a clean trip and still caught her colt. Had a better jockey been on Fury, Angie was sure Nordstrom would have lost by a length or more.

Jeff and Natalie Frazier were nice enough people, and they treated their horses well, but who would have thought they would manage to be connected to a colt of the caliber of Fury? Under normal circumstances, Angie might have been happy for their success. The problem was that their lightly raced colt was standing in the way of her family's first real shot at a horse of the year championship, not to mention the Million Dollar Derby. After all the years she and her father had been racing toward that goal, it simply wasn't fair.

Angie imagined standing in the winner's circle, accepting the trophy after Nordstrom was first across the finish line in a classic race victory. The thought of owning a Triple Million Race winner actually gave her chills. If there any horse was able stop Nordstrom's rise to fame, Angie would own him or destroy him.

Yawning and alone in the house, Angie crept up the stairs and into her bedroom. She crawled into bed for a brief nap, recalling, once again, the dramatic finish in the Celestial Stakes. "Frazier's *Fury should be mine," she muttered. "He is ridden by a mediocre jockey and is being trained by a local trainer who is in over his head. If Fury's handled correctly, he can win the Million Dollar Triple, and I know how to handle him."*

Angie had a plan. She understood what needed to be done. As she drifted off to sleep, her signature phrase floated through her mind: *the end justifies the means.*

4

Natalie was rarely happier than when she was working in the barn with the horses. It had been three days since the Celestial Stakes. Fury was doing quite well. He was full of energy, eating every bit of his food, and didn't appear to have lost any weight. All indications were that he would soon be ready to race again.

She was filling the last bucket when she heard someone moving behind her. Expecting her husband, and without turning to look up from her inspection, she said, "Hi, honey. This is the last bucket, then I'm ready to go. Santos should be back any minute."

When Natalie turned her head and squinted at the sunlight streaming through the barn's open door, she became flustered and a bit intimidated by the measured approach in the shadow of not her husband, but a suited stranger. It was unusual for a stranger to come into her barn unannounced. She stepped backward toward Fury's stall. Fury snorted and stomped a foot, as if he knew something had scared her.

"Sorry, I thought you were my husband. He'll be back any minute," she warned him. "What can I do for you?"

The man halted, perhaps realizing he had thoughtlessly surprised the woman. He smiled and asked, "Are you Natalie Frazier?"

Natalie nodded. “Yes, I am.”

The tall, well-dressed man had wavy grey hair and spoke with a slight British accent. “Mrs. Frazier, my name is Nelson Dickenson. My apologies if I’ve startled you. First, please accept my sincere congratulations on a most impressive race in the Celestial Stakes.”

“Thank you,” Natalie said, still wary.

“I’m an attorney representing a client who is most interested in purchasing FraziersFury. He is certainly a fine looking thoroughbred, and from the race re-runs I’ve studied, including his effort earlier this week, he has displayed some real talent. I’ve come to discuss an offer to purchase your horse, either wholly or in part. My client is very much interested in acquiring him and I’m sure you will find the offer quite generous.”

Natalie sighed, a bit annoyed. “David Marsico has already made an offer. I’ll tell you the same thing that I told him. I appreciate your interest, but there is nothing to discuss. Fury is not for sale, in whole or in part.”

“Mr. Marsico is not the person I’m representing, and I am glad you didn’t agree to sell Fury to him before I had a chance to speak with you. It has been my experience that everything is for sale, if the price is right,” Dickenson countered. “I don’t know what Mr. Marsico offered, but I will guarantee you that my client will top his offer.”

Natalie arched an eyebrow, not sure whether to be interested or insulted. “Mr. Dickenson, even if Fury was for sale, which he is not, I’m not sure this is the place to discuss the details. Why don’t you give me your card? I'll tell Fury's trainer that you were here, and he can contact you if he feels a meeting is appropriate."

"I understand your hesitance to discuss this now," Dickenson replied, "without the benefit of your husband's input and that of your attorney. Please accept my apology for arriving unannounced at this late hour of the day, but I am only in town until day after tomorrow, and my client has asked that I make a proposal before I leave."

"Not interested," Natalie declined, annoyed by the man's persistence.

"I have reserved a table at Morton's in Anaheim and would be grateful if you and your husband would join me for dinner. The reservation is for tomorrow evening at eight, but I am certain it can be adjusted to suit your schedule if that time is not convenient. I assure you, I can entertain you with stories of racing in England, and I am told that Morton's serves excellent food. I'll outline our offer, and there will be no hard feelings if you reject it. In any case, I'd enjoy the company at dinner, and promise you a pleasant evening. Please consider joining me and allowing me to explain the proposal."

Though Natalie could not imagine a scenario where she would sell Fury, she was flattered that someone came all the way from England to make an offer to buy her colt. Besides that, the gentleman had a charming air about him. Her concern was that by agreeing to meet him for dinner, Jeff would get the idea that she would even consider selling Fury. Maybe it was something she should consider, if not for the monetary benefit, then for the sake of her relationship with her husband. Natalie couldn't remember a time when she and Jeff were so far apart on business matters. He was in total favor of selling at least a share of Fury, if not selling him outright. Natalie, however, was adamantly opposed to any sale or partnership.

Jeff told her a horse like Fury deserved owners that could afford to ship him anywhere in the world where there was a race in which he could be competitive. If Fury was a potential superstar, Jeff believed the horse should be able to race in England and Dubai, and any track across North America. They would need to restructure their entire barn to accommodate the needs of a stallion of that caliber, travel with him, and to handle his future as a sire. Jeff was content with his small band of thoroughbreds. He loved hands-on training and had no desire to become a trainer who didn't interact with his charges daily.

Natalie tried to understand Jeff's reasoning. He was right about the changes that would occur. It would be a different lifestyle, at least for a few years. That didn't alter the fact, however, that Fury was her horse, and while she wanted him to be a success, she was not willing to relinquish control of his future in order for him to accomplish even more.

Everything considered, Natalie decided that there was nothing to lose by hearing the details of Mr. Dickenson's offer, though. Although she doubted it, he might even persuade her to sell a small percentage, to raise additional money for Fury's campaign. or to save her marriage.

"Fine, Mr. Dickenson," she said. "But don't get your hopes up."

He smiled. "Please, call me Nelson. And never say never."

"Okay, Nelson, and you must call me Natalie," she replied. "Jeff and I will meet you at Morton's at eight tomorrow evening."

Nelson Dickenson's smile widened. "Thank you so much, Natalie. I'll look forward to seeing you and your husband then. We shall see if I can change your mind." He offered her a business card and then turned to gaze at Fury before he left the barn.

Natalie looked at the card in her hand. It was cream colored, with gold embossed lettering. His name was printed in an old English script, 'Nelson Dickenson, Esquire' followed by a telephone number and an address in the United Kingdom. There was no law firm listed.

"He is determined to outline his proposal," Natalie murmured to Fury. *"I wonder when he'll tell us the name of his mysterious client?"*

She looked up when Jeff sauntered into the barn.

"Ready, Nat? I'm finished for the day. Shall we stop for a drink on the way home?"

"Jeff, when you crossed the paddock, did you notice a man walking toward the parking lot?"

"Yes. He nodded a greeting when we passed the gate to the backside. Is there a problem? I can probably catch up with him."

"No, no, no," Natalie replied. "It's fine. We're having dinner with him tomorrow evening."

Jeff gave her his 'now what have you done,' look, and asked, "Does this dinner have something to do with Fury?"

Natalie walked three steps toward Jeff and gave him the card. "Yes. Mr. Nelson Dickenson has invited us to dinner to make an offer to purchase Fury."

"What did he say that made you agree to meet with him?" Jeff asked, both eyebrows arched as they did whenever he tried to uncover another small mystery about his wife.

"I told him that Fury isn't for sale, but the guy insisted and I have to admit, I'm curious now. And more than a little flattered that he came all the way from England to make the offer. He said he has a client, not David Marsico, who would like to purchase Fury outright, but is also willing to purchase an interest in him, if we won't agree to an outright sale. I figured that it would be worth a couple of hours to see what he's offering, who his client is, and why he thinks we would sell. I know you want to consider taking on a partner and while I'm not sure if I can come to terms with that, I'm willing to listen one more time."

She paused for a moment, and when Jeff didn't respond, she said, "I hate what this is doing to us. I'm feeling like I need to choose between you and Fury. We never had any issues like this before. Is this what happens when a small outfit has a shot at a big winner? I don't like fighting with you."

Jeff sighed. "I don't like the tension either. It's just that a race campaign like the one he deserves costs more than we can afford, in time or money. While we're worried about how long it will take to ship Fury by trailer, the big outfits are trying to decide which airline equine transport company will be most convenient. Can you imagine for one minute that David Marsico would have any concern about a horse that had only run at one race track? He would have flown Fury anywhere, and everywhere that gave him an opportunity to excel. It's not that I want you to lose control of Fury. I just want you to have a champion, even a Triple Million winner. Natalie, Fury is that good."

"And if you and Fury can accomplish that, I would be thrilled," Natalie said. "But what he has already accomplished is more that I had ever expected of him. If he never wins another race, I'll love him just as much."

"And will you love me just as much?" Impatient for his wife to respond, Jeff explained, "If Fury doesn't reach the potential I see in him, I'll always wonder if it was because I'm just a small time trainer, with a small time budget. I'll lock up here and see you at home in a little while."

Holding back tears, Natalie turned to Fury and rubbed his silken neck. She brushed her cheek across his soft muzzle. Flight whinnied. Natalie reached for her nose and stroking it, assuring her that she too was safe from sale.

5

When Jeff and Natalie arrived at the steakhouse, the maitre de was waiting. "Good evening," he greeted them.

"Good evening," Jeff replied. "We are meeting Nelson Dickenson. Is he here?"

"Yes, Mr. Dickenson is expecting you. Follow me, please."

He escorted them to a table in a private corner of the crowded restaurant where the attorney was already seated. He stood as they approached and extended his hand to Jeff, "I'm Nelson Dickenson. You must be Mr. Frazier."

Jeff met Nelson's hand with a firm grip. "Jeff Frazier," he replied. "Nice to meet you, Mr. Dickenson."

"Nelson, please call me Nelson." He directed his gaze to Natalie. "It is good to see you again, Mrs. Frazier. I appreciate you joining me for dinner on such short notice."

After the trio ordered their meals and small talk was fading, Nelson looked at Jeff and began his pitch. "Your wife has advised me that FraziersFury is not for sale. However, as I'm sure she explained to you, it wasn't easy, but I convinced her that we should meet, and allow me to at least outline my proposal in full."

Jeff shrugged. "If Natalie said Fury isn't for sale, there's nothing I can do. I'm only the trainer."

"I hope that I can convince both the owner and the trainer that it would be of mutual benefit, at the very least, to create a partnership," Dickenson suggested. "My client has some knowledge of the horse business, and an eye for a superior animal. I have represented several clients in equine acquisition and have owned thoroughbreds for most of my life. In my younger days, I was a steeple chase trainer.

My sister and I own a handsome horse that ran second last year in the Queen's Cup. We are planning to have two of our older horses racing this year in Dubai."

"Congratulations on your placement in the Queen's Cup," Natalie said. "That must have been thrilling."

"Thank you. It was exciting. Although he lost by a neck, it was an exciting race."

The attorney sipped his wine, then dabbed his lips with a cloth napkin. "I'm telling you this so that you know I understand the thoroughbred horse business and am not here to parrot information dictated to me. The offer I am about to present will benefit you and my client. If we can come to an agreement, your colt will have every opportunity to compete internationally. From what I've seen, he is quite a racehorse.

As I am sure you are aware, horse racing is not an easy business. The pinnacle of most owners and trainers is that once in a lifetime horse, who can not only run like the wind but do it consistently. Of all the races in the United States, the most coveted trophy seems to be the one given to the winner of Kentucky's Million Dollar Derby."

"Yes, qualifying for the Million Dollar Derby would be quite an accomplishment," Jeff agreed. "Of an estimated forty-thousand thoroughbreds born in a year, there will be twenty who make it to the starting gate for that race. The twenty who get there are seldom the same horses expected to be there when the preparation races began."

Nelson leaned forward. "You're right. Besides having the talent and the earnings, the horse must remain fit and healthy. Even then, to compete with the typically large field of three-year-olds, most of which are going the distance for the very first time, the colt has to get a good trip. It is an exciting race, but can be a harrowing experience, not only for the equine athletes, but for the riders, too. My client and I agree that FraziersFury may have what it takes, not only to contend in that race, but to prevail."

Though thrilled someone had said out loud what she had been dreaming of for Fury, Natalie still had to say, "I appreciate your comments and your encouragement, Nelson. I also believe that if all the stars align, Fury might be that good, but whether he is, or he isn't, I'm not convinced that I want to sell him."

"Please hear me out," their host implored. "Along with having a quality animal, the connections must be financially capable of providing everything necessary to make the trip to Louisville. That means providing the care, the personnel, and the security that should surround a Million Dollar Derby starter. Although the purse is substantial, the investment is also, and I need not remind you, there is only one winner."

"As for the circumstances of the Million Dollar Derby, or any race, nothing you've said comes as a surprise," Jeff interrupted. "If Fury qualifies, we will get him to the race. The Angelina Stakes is just around the corner, and I suspect that race will tell the tale."

"As I said, from what I've seen, it looks like your colt has what it takes. That is also my client's opinion. I have been authorized to agree to any reasonable price you request, in order to purchase the colt outright."

Before Jeff had a chance to respond, Natalie declared, "I will not consider any offer for an outright purchase of Fury."

Nelson smiled even broader. "I am prepared to write you a check this evening, in the amount of $1,200,000.00 for a seventy-five percent share of your colt. If that isn't a consideration, my client will pay you $700,000.00, for a fifty-one percent interest."

Natalie blinked twice and reached for her wineglass. She looked at Jeff before taking a drink. There was no question that she and Jeff could use the money. Besides setting them up financially, a sale like the one Nelson was offering would put them on the radar as successful breeders for future sales. It would be a credit to Jeff that he had trained a home-bred thoroughbred through qualification for the Million Dollar Derby.

She knew Jeff would be ready to jump on an offer like that, but Jeff loved the horses because they were horses. He didn't get attached to them the same way that she did. Natalie loved Fury, but it was because he was Fury, not because he was a winner. She also loved Jeff because he was Jeff, but for the past few weeks he hadn't been her Jeff, and she knew it resulted from her refusal to consider selling Fury.

Besides, if Fury won the next couple of stakes races, and the Million Dollar Derby, they would have almost that much in purse money, and still own the horse. But there would be substantial expenses. Winning three graded stakes in a row was unlikely, and if Fury lost more than one of them, the expenses for the races would put them in more debt than they could easily pay.

"Jeff and I will need time to discuss your offer."

Believing he was making progress with Natalie, Nelson pressed on, "Any sale will, of course, be subject to a specific partnership agreement."

When neither Jeff nor Natalie responded, Nelson focused on Jeff and added, "Fury will remain in your barn, unless otherwise agreed, and you will remain involved with his training, along with a trainer of my client's choice, who will be the primary trainer. The primary trainer will have the final decisions as to his racing career, including the date of his retirement from racing. Determinations as to his career, following his retirement from racing, and the possibility of syndication will be mutually agreed upon. We prefer that Fury remains within the United States, though we will consider offers from outside the USA."

Again, before Jeff could speak, Natalie shook her head. "I appreciate your offer. It is more than fair, but. . ." She glanced at Jeff. The set of his jaw showed that he'd clenched his teeth, and his forehead furrowed as he studied his wineglass.

Nelson held his hand up as if to stop traffic, "Take a day or so to consider my offer. Keep in mind that there will be no major change in your operation or your relationship with the colt. Fury will remain in your barn, and Mr. Frazier will have significant input into his training and career. Except for your receipt of a substantial sum of money, followed by a trainer's fee each month, and sharing costs and future purses, nothing will change for you, until the time of the colt's retirement from racing. It is quite a generous offer, from someone who can well afford the insurmountable costs of thoroughbred ownership. My client only wants to be a part of what we all believe to be an electrifying colt. Please, don't give me your final answer this evening."

Jeff cleared his throat. "We will think about your offer and call you tomorrow or the day after."

"I will wait to hear from you."

They ordered dessert, and Nelson diffused the tension by turning the discussion to the differences between horse racing in United Kingdom and the United States. Both Jeff and Natalie enjoyed Nelson's company, and he enjoyed theirs. The three horsemen agreed that whatever the outcome of the proposed partnership, they would stay in touch.

It was clear to Nelson that it would be quite a hard sell to convince Natalie to give up even a part of her colt. He left the restaurant hoping that Jeff could sway her.

6

"Jeff and Natalie Frazier seem to be a nice young couple," Nelson began. "Mrs. Frazier is determined to keep Fury, though it appears that Mr. Frazier would be willing to negotiate an agreement. Mr. Frazier said he would call within the next two days with a decision, but I doubt it will be in our favor, so don't get your hopes up."

"You didn't tell them I was your client, did you?" Angie asked her godfather.

"No. I told them that I would share all the details if we reached an agreement, but that otherwise my client would remain anonymous. We didn't get into any detailed discussion about the status of the colt, following the end of his racing career. After speaking with the Fraziers, I expect we might get lucky with a breeding rights contract, although it is a little early to broach that subject."

Nelson Dickenson was one of the best attorneys in the thoroughbred racing circuit, and his skills as a negotiator were valued. Angie was convinced that if Nelson couldn't get a purchase agreement, no one could.

"Thanks, Nelson. I'm sure you will have Fury in my barn if it is at all possible."

Angie's mind wandered away from her godfather's less than hopeful report. She thought about Dreamweaver. She had raised him by hand, when his dam died unexpectedly as the result of unusual complications with his delivery. He was a sweet horse, and she'd had high hopes for his future as a race horse. As his training began, however, it became apparent while Dreamweaver was a gorgeous animal who would pay for his keep by winning his share of races, stakes included; it was unlikely the grey colt would be a multiple Grade 1 winner, let alone a classic winner. But. from what she'd seen, FraziersFury had all the ability and the heart to be not only a multiple Grade 1 winner, but a Triple Million winner, and Angie desperately wanted him.

Nelson interrupted his goddaughter's thoughts, "Would you like to join your father and me this evening?" He asked. "I'm planning to leave after tomorrow, and it would be lovely to spend some time catching up before I go."

"Yes," she replied. "Thanks. That would be wonderful. What time should I be ready?"

"Will seven o'clock work? Your father will meet me at the hotel. I will send a car for you." Nelson Dickenson felt protective of Angie as if she were his own child.

"Perfect," she told him. "And, Nelson, thank you for trying to make the deal for me. I know you did your best."

"It is always my pleasure to assist you," he said, "Keep in mind that if we approach them again, it could be helpful if they know who their future partner would be. I understand your desire for secrecy, but that should all change after the Derby. Don't worry, my dear, I'm confident that one day you'll have your champion horse of the year."

Pondering how she could make that happen, Angie turned away from the paddock and walked back toward the house. There was always Plan B.

7

There was no doubt the money would've come in handy. Natalie understood that she had let her heart rule her decision. Watching Fury gallop around the training track, however, she was still not sorry that she had refused Nelson's offer, only that she had decided at dinner. In hindsight, she realized she should have at least let Jeff plead his case before she rejected the whole thing. She had been prepared to apologize, and was even considering a counter offer of a ten percent, or even a fifteen percent partnership, but Jeff had pounced on her as soon as they had gotten home. The tension between them was becoming unbearable.

Three weeks had passed since Nelson had asked Jeff and Natalie if they would consider the sale of Natalie's pride and joy. During those three weeks, the couple had fought bitterly. For the first time since she had fallen in love with him, Natalie told Jeff that she needed some space. She'd reserved a room at a hotel in the next town. She figured that a few days of separation would help them both, though she would see Jeff daily at the barn; so the separation wasn't a total one.

Please, please, please behave yourself on Saturday, she silently pleaded with her horse, confident Fury had the raw talent, but worried his ability had been compromised in previous races, when he was determined to run the way he wanted to run and not the way his jockey wanted him to run.

Jeff just wouldn't stop his badgering. "I hope you made the right choice. As your trainer, I'm telling you that you didn't, but as your husband, I'm trying to come to terms with it."

Natalie was determined not to get into another shouting match. "Oh, Jeff, he is gorgeous. Carl was so excited with the way he has been responding, and he seems to be doing what he's being asked out there today. If he runs well on Saturday, we'll get the money we need to move onto the next race." She spoke without taking her eyes from Fury.

"Yes, if he wins, our share of the purse will cover what we need for now." Jeff said, hurt by her stiffening when he placed his hands on her shoulders. "He's ready for the Angelina Stakes, and I just got word he made the roster." Fury had been entered over a week ago, but with the long list of entries for the race, there was no guarantee he would draw a spot.

"How wonderful! Do you think he'll handle the extra one and a half furlongs?" Natalie was afraid to get her hopes up too high for both Fury and the chances for survival of her marriage.

"Yes, from the way he's been working, it looks like he'll appreciate the extra distance. His condition couldn't be better, and he seems to thrive on racing." Jeff said, removing his hands from his wife's s shoulders and into his pockets. "He got up in time at eight furlongs, and I'm sure he got something out of that race. He's been working well, and he's acting more focused. If he comes out of the Angelina okay on Saturday, I'll make the arrangements to get him to Laredo. It will be a quick turnaround, only three weeks, but that will tell us if we can set our sights on the Sapphire in Laredo."

Jeff's assessment comforted Natalie. She was also encouraged by her husband's awkward attempts to put their differences behind them and deal with the fact that his wife would continue to be hopelessly stubborn about the fate of her colt.

"I'll call Sarah," she said. "She watched the live stream of his last race on her computer, but she said she wanted to be here for the next one."

"Good thinking," her husband agreed. "We can use all the luck we can get. I swear that woman can perform magic."

Sarah Myers and Natalie were close friends since the days they were college roommates, and, with their similar appearance and age, often mistaken for sisters. Though a lawyer, Sarah also owned a small shop where she dealt in artifacts, rocks, gems and fetishes.

Sarah answered on the second ring, "Hey, stranger! How are things in horse country?"

Natalie stepped outside the barn so Jeff wouldn't hear. "Good in horse country, but rocky on the home front," she confided to her friend. "Jeff and I are still fighting. I stayed at the hotel again last night and reserved the room for tonight, too, but I'm not going to stay. Jeff was being horrible again yesterday, and I just needed to get away. He is trying to be civil this morning, though, so maybe we can get through the night together in peace."

Sarah replied, "Sorry to hear about the problems, but a lot of it is frustration on Jeff's part. He wants you to have a champion, but he isn't as sure as you are that he can do everything that's needed. Cancel your reservation and stay home tonight."

"You're right. The good news is that he said Fury is raring to go, and I agree. He's racing in three days, and he has a shot at winning. Carl worked him a few days ago and came back ecstatic. He said Fury rated much better for him and was responding more and fighting less. I just watched them gallop around the training track and they look great. Carl took him for a walk around the backside yesterday. I think he wanted to discuss racing strategy with him. You're still coming, aren't you?"

"I wouldn't miss this race for the world," Sarah assured. Sarah had been with Natalie in Fury's first three races, but, "I had to miss the Rose and Celestial races. I'm not about to miss the Angelina Stakes."

"I'd love for you to see him in the morning," Natalie told her, "before we take him over to the stakes barn. Can you come the night before and stay over?"

"Thanks for the offer, but I've got a meeting that I can't postpone. Besides, it sounds like you two should have some time alone tonight. What time is the race?"

"The race isn't until three, but if you want to see Fury before the race, you need to be here by about ten or ten-thirty."

"Okay, I'll see you Saturday for a pre-race hug from Fury."

"Thanks, Sarah."

"I wouldn't miss it. See you then."

Natalie walked back into the barn where Jeff was tossing around some bales of straw. "I missed you last night," she admitted.

"I missed you too," he replied, "but you were right. We both needed to cool off."

"Let's not discuss money or partnerships anymore until the day after the race," she suggested.

"In the meantime, I'll go on back to the house and cook something wonderful for dinner."

Jeff managed a hint of a smile. "Okay. I'll see you in a couple of hours."

8

Saturday came quickly. Besides Fury, three of Jeff's other charges entered for Sunday's competition. As they did every morning, Jeff and Natalie got to the barn about 5:30 that morning. They walked from stall to stall doing a visual assessment of each horse. Most days, Sonny showed up about six to do the early morning works for the horses scheduled that day. Both Sonny and Santos exercised the horses, but Carl did most of the formally timed works.

Every day, each of the horses got a hands-on check. Even the horses that weren't scheduled to work were taken for a walk around the track. Extra attention was given to the horses scheduled to race the next day, with Jeff looking for anything, however small, that might cause a problem. Like all trainers, Jeff wanted to win races, but, unlike some, a win for Jeff was never worth risking illness or an injury.

"Flight is on the schedule for a half mile gallop this morning," Jeff told Natalie. "Do you want Sonny to ride her after he works Legend, or do you want Santos to take her?" Santos arrived every morning, at about six o'clock, to feed the horses and clean the water buckets. He'd be in and out all day until he did a final check at seven or eight in the evening.

"I think I'd rather have Santos ride Flight. She has gotten so attached to him. She follows him around like a puppy, and she responds to him so well."

Jeff agreed, "That's what I thought, too. Legend is listed for a five-furlong workout this morning. Sonny can take him out, then gallop the three mares afterward. Fury and the other three that are entered tomorrow can walk the shedrow, and that will take care of everybody."

"I'll take Fury out for a walk," Natalie said. "Santos will want to take the others."

As if on cue, Santos walked into the barn. "What others will I want to take?"

In his younger years, Santos spent his days working on his family's ranch, and his nights bare knuckle fighting. Overall, he was a good natured sort, yet trouble seemed to follow him, most often in the form of a barroom brawl, after he'd downed too much tequila. Several of his scuffles earned him arrests: disturbing the peace, aggravated assault, and the last conviction, involuntary manslaughter, after he beat a provoker to death. The groom had mellowed somewhat over the years; though he still didn't always have the discipline to walk away when challenged. His last prison stretch, however, taught him to exert more self-control; that and the fact he valued, more than his pride, was Jeff's trust. He didn't want to do anything to let his friend down.

Jeff and Santos had met soon after Santos finished serving his ten-year prison sentence for the involuntary manslaughter conviction. Jeff was hauling a horse trailer with two mares, both horses on their way to another farm for breeding. A pickup truck sped out of a side road and hit the back corner of the horse trailer, causing Jeff to veer off the road into a three-foot-deep ditch. The pickup truck only sped up and escaped down the road.

His trucks half in the ditch, Jeff had jumped from the cab and raced back into the trailer to check on his passengers. He'd lead the older mare, SundaysSong, out of the trailer first. Calm and sweet-tempered, she appeared unfazed by the unexpected jolt.

Twice Jeff walked SundaysSong slowly up and down the road, studying her for any sign of distress. The black mare walked with her usual long, easy stride as she took in the scenery. Eleven years old, almost 16 hands tall, and her coat dappled and glistening, SundaysSong filled Jeff with pride as he tied her to the hitching bar on the side of the trailer.

But when Jeff climbed back into the trailer to rescue his second mare, Crescendo, he realized she hadn't handled the mishap well. Her nostrils flared and the whites of her eyes bulged, as though Jeff was the grim reaper and she his next victim.

"Easy, lady. It's me. Settle down, you'll be fine," Jeff murmured. He snapped the lead rope onto her halter.

Because of the angle of the trailer and the ditch on the side, Jeff needed to back Crescendo out of the trailer rather than walk her out the side door, but the mare tried to rear up on her hind legs. At six-feet-three-inches and about two-hundred-thirty pounds, Jeff was no lightweight, yet he needed every bit of muscle to keep the spooked animal from connecting with the trailer roof. With a firm hold, Jeff managed to keep her head down.

"Stop this nonsense, Crescendo. You're going to get us both hurt." Jeff spoke to the mare while looking her over as best he could for any appearances of injury. After allowing her to calm down a bit, he'd been able to back her into the empty area behind the trailer stall. He maneuvered around and out of the trailer just as another beat-up pickup pulled up in front of his truck.

"Looks like you could use a little help," the pickup's driver said.

"Sure could," Jeff accepted as the frightened mare reared up again.

It had taken all the strength Jeff could muster to hang onto Crescendo and get her front feet back on the ground. Without saying another word, the pickup driver got out of his truck and walked over with a rope in his hand and a question in his eyes. "Do you want me to snap this on her?"

Jeff nodded quickly.

The other man swiftly, yet gently, grabbed the mare's halter and clipped his rope onto the ring. "Whoa there, pretty girl, you're going to get hurt," he whispered.

"She's a strong little girl, isn't she?" the stranger said. "We can just walk her a bit to settle her down, if you think that would help."

"Thanks, that is just what she needs," Jeff said. "You've handled horses before?"

"I've been handling horses since before I could talk," the man bragged as he moved to face Crescendo and began a soft dialogue. She pricked her ears, and, to Jeff's amazement, relaxed, stood still and even winked at the stranger.

"My name's Santos, Santos Velasquez," the man revealed as he slipped his fingers under the edge of Crescendo's halter and faced her, nose to nose; he kept talking to her in a soothing voice Jeff would soon grow accustomed to hearing.

Shaking his head in amazement, Jeff said, "I've never seen this mare take to a stranger that way." He'd extended his right hand, "I'm Jeff Frazier."

Santos unhooked his rope and then shook Jeff's hand. Jeff walked Crescendo over to Song and tied her next to the older mare.

"I might be able to pull your truck back out of that ditch, if we unhook the trailer," Santos suggested.

Jeff nodded. "I sure would appreciate it."

The two men had used their combined strength to push Jeff's truck back onto the road, then hooked up the trailer and re-loaded the mares.

"I've been looking for some full time work," Santos told Jeff. "I want to tell you up front that I just got out of jail a week ago. The truth is, I've done some stupid things in the past, and I spent some time, in a small cell, thinking about what I needed to do to get on the right track. All I know is horses and fighting, and I'm done fighting. If you know anyone who's hiring, I can exercise horses, hot walk, clean stalls, green break, just about anything. I've delivered a lot of foals and can handle a stallion in the breeding shed. And I'll work cheap."

Although Jeff had been looking for some help with his race horses, and the man's handling of

Crescendo impressed him, he wasn't ready to offer a job to a self-proclaimed brawler and jailbird. However, he felt a bit of an obligation to, at least, put out the word that Santos was looking for work.

"Where can I reach you? I have a few horses at Angelina Race Track, and I know a lot of the trainers there. I'll ask around."

Santos had dashed to his truck, where he tore a page from a small tablet and wrote his name and telephone number.

"This is my cell phone number. My phone is always with me. I was going out to Angelina when I saw your truck. Maybe I can come by your barn in a day or so and I'll show you what I can do. It won't cost you anything. There would be no commitment."

"Now that's an offer I can hardly refuse. After I drop these mares at the Whittingham Farm, I'll be going back home. Come by tomorrow morning and I'll show you around the track. I'm in Barn 17."

Three weeks after the accident, Santos was working full time for Jeff. By then, Jeff was not only Santos's boss, he was his friend.

"Which horses, Boss?"

Santos's loud question snapped Jeff's thoughts back to the present. "Sonny is working Legend, then galloping the mares," he answered. "We thought you'd like to ride Flight, and then walk Tory, Aztec and Musician, since they're entered tomorrow. Natalie is walking Fury."

"That's a plan," Santos agreed. Their day was planned. Everyone went to work.

It was mid-afternoon. All the horses were back in their stalls, which were clean and raked. The hustle-bustle of a typical day on the racetrack's backside was fading into a quiet evening.

Jeff and Natalie finished the barn chores, and were putting the equipment away, when Chaser came dashing into the barn and jumped up onto a bale of straw. Natalie walked over to the little grey cat and petted her.

"You have an exciting evening ahead," she said. "Santos will stay with you tonight." Chaser purred contentedly.

"Sometimes I think these animals really understand what we say," Jeff said.

Natalie cuddled Chaser, "They understand. Fury understands he's happy here and doesn't want to live anywhere but with us." As soon as the words about Fury slipped out of her mouth, Natalie wished she could choke them back.

Jeff's shoved his hands into his pockets. "Can't we have one day that we don't argue about Fury?" He didn't give his wife a chance to respond. "You are being unreasonable by not even considering a very generous offer for a partnership in that colt. With the money we would get, along with the help with future costs, we'd be able to upgrade the fencing at home, buy a couple of new saddles, and put a chunk of money on the mortgage to refinance the house for a shorter term. It isn't like you would lose your colt. He would still be yours."

Natalie stiffened. "He would be part mine, and part someone else's," she rebuked her husband. "I wouldn't have complete control in any decision regarding his welfare or his future. We are making the payments on the house, and I don't plan on moving. If it takes another twenty-five years to pay it off, so be it."

As though upset by the tension, Chaser jumped from Natalie's arms and climbed to the loft, disappearing into her favorite hiding spot between the bales.

Jeff turned his back to Natalie and said, "I'll be in the truck," before he stormed out of the barn.

Sorry that she had scolded her husband, but resolute in her decision, Natalie took a deep breath and promised herself that she would not bring up Fury's sale again, for fear another argument might cause lasting damage.

9

Sonny had gone home early in the afternoon. He planned to meet everyone the next morning to help get the horses ready for the day's racing. After Santos had dinner with his sister, he returned to spend the night at the barn.

Santos stayed overnight at the barn more often than he slept in his own home. He spent those nights up in the hayloft on an army cot he claimed was as comfortable as any bed. For the third night in a row, he'd be staying in the barn because of a dream.

Dreams and premonitions had guided Santos throughout his life. Twice during the past week, he had dreamed Fury ran off and galloped down the highway. In his dream, he chased Fury, caught him, and turned him back toward home. But when they began the walk back to the racetrack, the colt disintegrated, only to reappear back in his stall, where he was waiting when Santos returned to the barn. Santos had no idea what the dream was trying to tell him, but he believed it contained a message, a warning of some sort.

Santos did one last check of the equine athletes before he turned out the lights, climbed the ladder to the loft, and settled onto the cot for the night. Chaser curled up in the bend of his elbow.

The barn cat was purring softly, and Santos sleeping peacefully, until she startled him awake by leaping onto his shoulder, brushing his cheek with her paw. Her purrs were replaced by a sound between a growl and a hiss.

The reflection of a flashlight got Santos's attention when shined off the barn floor. As he sat up to look for the source of the light, there was a rattle from one of the safety chains mounted on each of the stall doors. Flight whinnied, a high-pitched frightened sound, and one of the horses kicked the back of the stall. With his senses on high alert, Santos slid to the floor and moved as quietly as possible toward the edge of the loft. Hidden behind stacked bales of hay, he looked down at the barn below.

Chaser followed him and jumped to the top bale. Also staring down from the loft, she meowed loudly. The flashlight's beam moved upward and focused on the grey and white cat. Santos hoped Chaser's appearance convinced whoever was down there that the cat was responsible for any noise in the loft.

Santos waited until the light dropped back to the stalls, then cautiously moved to the steps. He descended quickly, almost silently, though any sounds he may have made were muted by the stomping and snorting of the horses. The chain rattled again, followed by the click of a latch being opened.

Some son of a bitch is trying to steal one of the horses, Santos thought, fight-mode activated. *After I get finished with you, you won't even be able to steal chickens.*

The main light switch was at the end of the barn, but an overhead light was at the foot of the ladder. When he got to the bottom of the ladder, Santos saw the hammer. He had used it earlier to repair a step and was glad he'd left it on the window ledge. He grabbed it. Not sure whether to turn on the light or go after the horse thief in the dark, he decided to throw caution to the wind. He pulled the overhead light switch and dashed into the center of the barn, yelling, "What the hell are you're doing?"

Standing in the front of the partially opened gate to Fury's stall, a large man held a flashlight in one gloved hand and a rope in the other.

The intruder remained still, his back to Santos.

"Back away from the horse and close that gate," Santos growled. Furious that anyone would dare enter the barn and approach the horses, Santos had no qualms about taking on the burly interloper. In fact, he was eager to do just that. He raised the hammer like a club and stalked toward the burglar.

The man dropped the flashlight into his coat pocket. Still holding the rope, he slowly raised his arms, as if in surrender, but then slammed his hand against the sliding gate, pushing it open the entire way; it banged against the wall. The masked prowler pivoted, and side-stepped Santos. He moved faster than his size should have allowed. Santos managed to grab burglar's gloved hand, but the glove slipped off. The masked man escaped the groom's grasp, but not before Santo saw a dark patch on his wrist.

Fury reared up, eyeing the opening that led out of the barn. Ears pinned back, the colt lowered his head and started out of his stall.

More intent on closing the gate than chasing the intruder, Santos dropped the hammer and moved to block Fury's exit.

"Easy Fury," he whispered as he pushed the gate closed.

Santos reached down and retrieved the hammer. After hitting the light switches to brighten the barn, both inside and out, he ran outside. The would-be horse thief couldn't have gotten far. He had no idea which direction the man took, but the groom stood still and listened. When he heard nothing, he returned to the barn, closing the door behind him.

Fury kicked the back wall with a thud, snorted, and pawed the straw covered floor.

"Easy, Fury," Santos soothed. "You're okay, buddy. Settle down, now. It isn't time to go out yet."

Santos called racetrack security, the local police and Jeff Frazier, in that order. It was 3:45 a.m.

Though he realized the burglar was probably long gone, Santos went outside again. He looked in all directions. There was no sign of the big man, just the night and the silence.

Back inside the barn, he picked up the burglar's glove, briefly examined it, and then tossed it onto the workbench before walking to Fury's stall.

He didn't think that the intruder had time to do anything to hurt the thoroughbred, but he needed to be sure.

Fury was nervous at the disruption, as were all the horses. The colt settled down when Santos hooked a rope to his bridle, and he allowed the groom to lead him from the stall and hook him in the cross ties.

Santos examined him inch by inch, running his hands first over Fury's legs, lifting each foot, stroking every part of the big grey. It was rare that Fury kicked the wall, and, while unlikely the horse had done any damage to his legs, Santos had to see for himself.

When two racetrack security guards arrived, Santos still had Fury in the cross ties.

"Did you get a look at the guy?" Randy, the tallest guard, asked.

"Yes and no," Santos answered. "He was a big guy. I'd say at least six feet, with broad shoulders, about two-hundred pounds. He was wearing a black ski mask, so his face was covered. When I pulled off his glove, I noticed something on the back of his right arm, at the edge of his sleeve. It might have been a tattoo, but could have been a bruise, or even some mud. I don't know. It was a wide, dark mark across his wrist. Everything happened so fast."

"Okay, we'll check identification of anyone who is out tonight, and I'll ask about getting some extra security for a couple of days to do some random identification checks of the backside residents."

"Thanks," Santos said. "I called the police, too. They should be here soon."

"If you don't mind, would you give them my name?" Randy gave Santos a card, "I'd appreciate it if they would give me a call so we can coordinate efforts. It's been quite some time since we've had a horse thief around here."

"Sure," Santos agreed. He unhooked Fury and walked him back to his stall, then got some carrots out of the small refrigerator. He fed the treats to each of the horses to distract them and help settle them down after the chaos in the barn.

Natalie and Jeff arrived seconds before the policeman. Natalie was frantic. Her red-rimmed eyes were in stark contrast to her colorless cheeks. Her voice broke as she asked, "Are the horses okay?"

"Yes, the creep didn't have time to hurt Fury, even if he wanted to. He had a rope in his hand. I think he was going to steal him," Santos reported. "As a matter of fact, it was probably Fury's rope he was holding. It isn't hanging by the gate. He must have taken it with him when he ran out."

A Chino Police Officer, dressed in a freshly pressed, dark blue uniform, arrived at the barn. His badge glistened under the barn lights, the result of its recent assignment to Officer Adams.

"I'm Officer Derek Adams, Chino Police. I got a call about a stolen horse," he announced in a sing-song voice, as he shifted his weight from one foot to the other.

Jeff responded, "It was an attempt to steal a horse. Santos stopped the guy, and he took off."

The officer produced a notebook and a pen and began writing.

"Did you get a good look at him?"

"No. He was wearing a black ski mask. He left this, though." Santos handed the glove to Officer Adams, who dropped the glove inside a small bag that he pulled from his pocket.

"Anything missing?"

"A six-foot lead rope."

"Don't imagine there is much chance in recovering a rope."

Natalie glared at the officer. "The rope that's missing is unique. It has Fury's name woven near the top. The letters don't stand out boldly, but they are woven with a darker fiber. His name is clear if you know it's there, but it would be easy to miss."

The officer's voice dropped to a mumble when he replied, "Maybe it will turn up somewhere." He scribbled more notes on his pad, then took a statement from Santos and promised to coordinate with the track security. "The perp wore gloves, so it's unlikely he left fingerprints, but I'll call it in. One of the forensic guys can try lifting some prints, anyway."

"Track Security said they would keep someone close to the barn for the next few days," Santos told the Fraziers.

By the time the policeman left with the bagged glove, it was close to six o'clock in the morning. "There isn't much sense in anyone trying to get back to sleep," Jeff said. "Shall we go to the diner for breakfast? It's on me."

"That sounds good to me," Santos said. "We need to bring back a special treat for Chaser. If she hadn't awakened me, I might not have heard that guy until it was too late."

"That sweet little cat is certainly a heroine today," Natalie agreed. "Where is she?"

"Last I saw her, she was standing on top of the bales over there, distracting the horse thief, while I was sneaking down the stairs," Santos said. "Now that the commotion is over, she's probably curled up on the cot again."

Jeff locked the barn doors. All three got into Jeff's truck and traveled to the local diner for breakfast. It was going to be a long day.

10

Three and a half hours of driving had passed since Sarah Myers had pulled out of her home in Quartzsite, a small, intimate community that survived on tourism and trading. She pulled over to the brim of the road and called Natalie to let her know she was about twenty minutes away.

"Hi, Sarah." Natalie's voice was just above a whisper. "You will not believe the story I have to tell you."

"Is everything okay?" Sarah interrupted, knowing Natalie and Jeff were at odds about Fury's future, and worried that their problems had escalated.

"Yes, I think things are okay now, but we had some excitement about 3:00 this morning. I'll fill you in when you get here. Jeff left your name at the security gate, and Jay has a pass for you. Go straight to the barn. The guys are there now. Jeff and I came home to shower and change clothes, but we'll be leaving in a few minutes to head back down."

"Okay, see you in a few minutes," Sarah replied. She steered her car back onto the road, daring to accelerate to five miles above the speed limit.

Earlier that year, Natalie Sarah invited to join her and Jeff in the owner's box for Fury's first race as a three-year-old. Before the race, Sarah had given Carl a tiny falcon carved from amber. She told him that the falcon would help Fury fly around the oval track, and that in ancient times, amber had been believed to bring good luck to warriors going into battle.

"Now, before you say this is ridiculous," Sarah had told Carl when she gave him the fetish, "let me explain what I've learned about horse racing. I know that a healthy horse is a necessity. Conditioning of the horse is important, some natural talent required, but the horse's desire to win is imperative. That being said, the racing goddess must also grant you her approval. That approval brings racing luck, and many times it is racing luck that wins the race. The amber falcon is a little extra nudge and an extra nudge can never hurt."

She remembered Carl's chuckle when he thanked her for the falcon. "It's a scientific fact, Carl," she'd said as she winked at him."I believe you," Carl replied. "I know about charms, and the amber falcon will be in my boot every time I ride Fury in a race."

Sarah's fascination with the grey colt began with his first race, a maiden special weight. She had driven out to the track to see Natalie. Fury had come out of the gate in a clean jump and raced about mid-pack until the horses moved out of the turn at the head of the stretch. The young grey perked his soft velvety ears, focused on the leader, extended that long neck, and just sailed around

the other horses to win by half a length with energy to spare. Sarah had gone with Natalie, Jeff, Sonny and Santos into the winner's circle, where the track photographer snapped their picture as they stood alongside the winning horse and jockey. Sarah framed that picture and hung in her shop, so she could point to it and explain to everyone who came in that her friend's very special colt was with her in that photograph, and gush her belief he would be a champion. She was crazy about Fury, and not only because they shared the same birthdate, though forty years between.
"We're Capricorns," she'd say. "That means Fury is a workaholic, just like me." But, as she drove the last few miles to the racetrack, her business sense nagged at her. Sarah's opinion was that Natalie needed to reconsider the offer of a partnership purchase, and Sarah planned to talk to her about it after the race.
Sarah was trackside again, when Fury finished second, by a nose, in his next race. And when Jeff entered him in a graded stakes race, Sarah had been beside herself with excitement. In that race, however, instead a quick jump, Fury strolled out of the gate, content to follow all the other horses for three quarters of a mile. By the time Carl convinced him to kick it up a notch and start moving, they had to go to the far outside. The colt gave a super effort, but too late. He ran second again, yet only half a length from the winner. And he'd run the last two furlongs in an outstanding time, finishing two lengths ahead of the third place, and why Jeff had declared it to be an outstanding race. To Sarah, the effort was as good as a win. She loved that colt almost as much as Natalie, though Flight was her favorite.

The Angelina Derby was an important race. A Grade One race, it carried a purse of seven-hundred-fifty-thousand dollars. After expenses, the winner's share would be close to three-hundred-thousand dollars. If Fury could run first or second today, there would be just one more race, the Sapphire, which would determine whether Jeff would enter FraziersFury in the Million Dollar Derby.

Fury winning the Million Dollar Derby was a long shot, and his entry into that race was far from certain, but it was Natalie's dream, and so it had become Sarah's dream, too.

11

Sarah found a parking spot in the vast lot of the Angelina Race Track, picked up her guest pass for the day, and made her way to Barn 17. She saw Natalie and Jeff walking just a few yards ahead of her and called out to them, "Hey, Fraziers!"

Jeff turned, looked at his watch. "When you say 10:30, you mean 10:30."

Sarah waved as she ran to catch up to them. "So what in the world happened this morning?"

Natalie hugged her dearest friend. "The short version is that Santos slept in the barn last night. Chaser heard something and woke him, and Santos saw a man going into Fury's stall. Santos went after him and the guy took off."

"Oh, no. Is Fury okay?"

"He seems fine. It irritated him that he was rousted at 3:00 a.m., but he calmed down within a few minutes. We had the vet look at him, as an extra precaution." Jeff said. "I don't know if the intruder wanted to steal the horse, or turn him loose, or do something to hurt him, but it's a good thing that Santos was there."

"Wow, what luck that he stayed," Sarah agreed.

"I'm not sure how much luck it was," Natalie replied. "He said he had been having a recurring dream about Fury. He said that the dream seemed to be warning him of something, and he didn't know what, but he had a strong urge to stay in the barn last night and the night before."

"We're going to start locking the barn doors at night," Jeff said. "I never liked to do that, in case of a fire, but after this morning's break-in, I think it's necessary. We were also thinking of hiring nighttime security, at least until we figure out what's going on."

Sarah asked, "Were any other barns bothered?"

Jeff shrugged. "Not that we've heard of. Sonny and Santos may have heard something by now, though."

Sarah frowned. "Perhaps someone is trying to stop Fury from racing?"

"That didn't occur to me." Natalie said. "I agreed with Santos that someone was trying to steal him."

"Maybe Fury is winning too many races," Sarah said. "If he's scratched, somebody's horse would have a better chance, right?"

Natalie nodded. "I suppose that's possible. I'm not sure which is more frightening, a flat out horse thief or a disgruntled competitor."

"No, I can't imagine someone would do that," Jeff disagreed, "At least not any of the trainers around here."

"Does it need to be a trainer?" Sarah asked. Law school had taught her to look at all angles. "It could be an owner, a jockey, a backside worker, or even a race fan, someone who wants to place a bet on a particular horse for better odds, or a bookie trying to fix the race."

"The whole situation is nerve-wracking. I've never worried about anyone trying to hurt any of the horses, but who knows? A few weeks ago, an attorney who was representing a potential buyer for Fury approached us. He said he wasn't at liberty to reveal the identity of the interested party, unless we agreed to his proposal. We didn't reach any agreement. Now I'm more interested than ever in just who sent attorney Nelson Dickenson to make the offer."

"Did you tell the police about Dickenson?" Sarah asked, intrigued by the angle someone might try to steal a horse that they couldn't buy.

"It really makes little sense for someone to steal a horse if they wanted to race it," Jeff countered.

Doubtful herself, but tired of the prolonged disagreement she'd been having with her husband, Natalie leaped at an opportunity to agree with him on something. "Jeff's right. Not only have thousands of people seen Fury, but he's tattooed, and any racetrack would recognize his number. I think it was a random attempt to steal a horse. Someone wanted a horse,

wandered into our barn and saw Fury. Many people are drawn to grey horses, and he is a striking colt."
They entered the barn where Sonny and Santos were busy doing the morning's chores. Carl was there, too. He had stopped by to make sure Fury was healthy and ready to race, and Santos explained what happened the night before.

"Fury's fine, though," Santos said. "Jeff got here within a few minutes and we both checked him over. He's okay."

"Of all the times for an interruption to his routine, this is one of the worst," Carl said shaking his head. "I appreciate the opportunity to ride Fury. Jeff has such confidence in me, I don't want to disappoint him, but I'm worried that a disruption like this could have stressed Fury."

"With some other horses, I'd agree," Sonny said. "But Fury is intelligent, and he's professional. Santos got the situation under control before any real harm was done. Don't let it shake you up, Carl. Fury is ready to race. Just go out there and ride."

"Keep that falcon in your boot and make sure you don't fall off," Santos teased.

Natalie said, "Go get something to eat and relax for a while, Carl. You're riding Magical Musician in the fourth race, aren't you?"

"Yes, that race will give me a good feel for the track today. Then I can study the form until the tenth."

"As if you don't have all the entries for the tenth race etched into your brain already," Santos cracked.

On his way out of the barn, Carl greeted Sarah with a hug and whispered in her ear, "The amber falcon is riding with us, and despite this morning's chaos, Fury told me he's ready to run."

"I'll be sending all the positive thoughts I can muster," Sarah whispered back. "Good luck today, Carl. I have a great feeling about this race."

"Fury is in with some tough competitors today," Santos said, "but he is as good as any of them. He'll run a good race and Carl will see that he comes home safe."

"You can count on it," Carl said.

Sarah continued through the barn to where Fury was nickering and pawing.

"You're hoping for a peppermint," Sarah muttered, as she stroked his nose and told him what a gorgeous boy he was. "No peppermints for you until after the race," she said. "Then, win or lose, we'll celebrate."

Fury bobbed his head, and everyone laughed.

"It's almost like he understands what you've said to him," Jeff said.

Santos bragged for Fury, "He does."

"I ran over to the tack shop and picked up the new saddle pad you ordered," Sonny told Jeff.

"I'd like you to come along to walk Fury over to the stakes barn, Sonny," Jeff said. "We need to be there in half an hour, so we have a little time, but I don't want to leave the barn unattended at all today, unless we lock it up tight."

"I'll walk Fury over, Boss," Santos offered. "Sonny wants to walk the mares today, so he'll be here for the first few races."

"I would like to watch Musician and Fury run," Sonny said.

"Okay," Jeff said. "Come on, Santos. We'll take Fury, then grab some sandwiches and come back and have lunch here with Sonny. Why don't you ladies go to the clubhouse and relax for a couple of hours? You can have lunch and catch up. We'll see you in the paddock a little later."

"Sounds perfect to me," Sarah said, turning her attention to Flight. "Because Fury can't have peppermints before the race, none for you either. I'll be back later with peppermints for everyone," she promised the filly. "And because I like you best, you'll get two, but don't tell the others."

Flight nickered.

12

There was a crowd at the clubhouse, but Natalie and Sarah claimed a small table in the corner overlooking the racetrack.

"If we can finish this race in the top three, with a decent effort, we might really have a Triple Million contender." Natalie said, talking to herself as much as to her companion.

"I don't want to rain on your parade," Sarah began, "but that break-in this morning is frightening." Natalie sighed. "One of the security officers wondered if it could have been theft for ransom attempt. He said that he'd worked on a case like that at one of the bigger tracks in the east."

"Well, I'm sure that Santos will spend more nights at the barn. It's a pain to have the barn doors chained and locked, but that will give you added security." Sarah leaned closer. "How difficult would it be to padlock the individual stall gates? You could get a master key for all of them, or use a combination lock. It wouldn't stop someone who had bolt cutters, but it should deter a casual thief."

"I like the idea of individual padlocks," Natalie said, "except that in an emergency, a fire for instance, it would make it almost impossible to get all the stalls open and the horses out if the person responding didn't have a key or bolt cutters on hand. I'll ask Jeff about hiring someone for 24-hour coverage, at least for a while. Santos will stay at the barn tonight. He usually stays after a race, and he's furious about what happened, but I can't ask him to live there. To hire security will be expensive, but I'm thinking about it, at least for the short term."

"If I know Santos, he'll end up spending a lot more nights there, whether you ask him to or not." Sarah patted her friend's hand and changed the subject, "How are things between you and Jeff?"

"I'm not sure," Natalie replied. "He has this idea that I'm choosing Fury over him."

"Are you?"

"No, it isn't a matter of choosing, it's a matter of what decision is best for the horse."

"The best decision for the horse, or the best decision for you?"

Natalie was slow to respond, "I suppose I am deciding what's best for me. We don't need to sell any part of that colt, and I don't want to sell any part of him. Jeff is looking at the money, and I don't care about the money."

"I understand how you feel, Nat, but stop and reason a minute. If you had the money that they offered you for a share in Fury, would there be any problem hiring twenty-four-hour security, no matter whether Santos was in the barn?"

"How can you take his side in this, Sarah?"

"I'm not taking his side. I'm offering you a different perspective. You and Jeff have been incredibly successful for all the years I've known you. Your horses are healthy, they are happy, and you win your share of purses. You've carved out a decent living doing something that you both love. Now you've got a chance to move from the local circuit to the national circuit, make a pot full of money, enhance your reputation and your clientele. That doesn't even consider Fury's value as a sire, if a stud farm managed him."

"I understand your aversion to dealing with Marsico, but I want you to know that I would never want your loyalty to me to stop you from making a business decision that would as lucrative as what he can offer. He is a rat, but he's quite a successful one. That having been said, you have to agree—"

"I don't have to agree with a thing," Natalie snapped. "David Marsico couldn't offer me enough money to buy a share of Fury, even if Fury was for sale. It has nothing to do with loyalty to you. It is a simple matter of morals. After Marsico did what he did to you, I'd never trust him to care about my horse. You can forget any discussion about that creep's offer."

"What I was about to say was that David's offer was an absolute complement, but that Attorney Dickenson's offer is outstanding."

"I'll think about it tomorrow, after this race," Natalie said.

Sarah knew her friend well enough to bet she wouldn't give it another thought at all.

13

Angie checked the entries for the race. So far, there were no scratches, and the Angelina Stakes was only three hours away. The grey thoroughbred had run a dead heat with Nordstrom in the Celestial Stakes at 8 furlongs. No one had expected that. Under most circumstances, Angie would have been a fan of the talented three-year-old, but not today. Today she was riding Nordstrom in a race that carried her name.

The Angelina Stakes race was 9 1/2 furlongs. Indications were that the extra distance would benefit Natalie's colt, and Fury's odds were four to one. Nordstrom was still the morning line favorite, at odds of five to two. Angie always bet Nordstrom and at those odds, when Nordstrom won, she would get seven hundred dollars for a two-hundred-dollar bet. It was an easy way to make five-hundred dollars.

As she was comparing past performances of the other entries, the office door opened.

"I've been waiting for you," she said.

One of the guys was having some trouble finishing up a load of hay, so I gave him a hand."

"Always helpful, aren't you?"

"I try."

There was a knock on the door.

"Who's there," she called through the door, as she motioned her visitor toward the powder room.

"Derek."

At the sound of his familiar voice, Angie said, "One minute."

She waited until the man in her office disappeared behind her and then opened the door where a grinning police officer held a leather glove in front of his face.

"I've got a present for you."

Angie snatched the glove with her left hand and caressed his cheek with her right. She whispered, "I'll pay you later," then closed the door and locked it.

"You doing him, too?" her visitor asked as he came out of the powder room.

"At least he can deliver," Angie snapped, tossing the glove at him.

The man had been more worried about losing that glove than failing in his mission to abduct the colt. He folded the glove and shoved it in his jacket pocket.

"Talk around the track is that Santos surprised a horse thief in Frazier's barn. The rumor is that someone planned to hold their colt for ransom, so that's good news for us." he told Angie.

"The good news is that you escaped a felony theft charge by the skin of your teeth," she said.

Angie's short, white skirt hugged the curves of her rock-hard backside and accented the tan of her long legs. Though it had been several years, the big man remembered those legs wrapped around his waist. He had loved to run his hands over the powerful muscles that allowed five-feet tall woman to pilot a half-ton horse. He brushed that image from his mind and concentrated on the present.

"Here's a souvenir." He offered her a braided rope. It was well made with a brass snap on one end and a leather loop on the other.

"I didn't realize I was still holding this until I was almost back to the truck. I didn't want to drop it just in case someone would remember me being parked there. Can't be too careful."

"Thanks, but I wanted a grey colt attached to it." She took the rope from him and shoved it into her duffle bag.

"That grey sure is one handsome colt, and he acts like he's got some intelligence to go with those looks. Jeff Frazier has him well-conditioned. He's beautifully structured, with good angulation, great looking feet and a ton of attitude. If he passes on some of those traits, he might be an outstanding sire. There are many people who would pay a lot of money for a thoroughbred of that caliber. You should consider breeding your filly to him."

"If you'd have gotten him for me, I'd have been able to breed him to all the girls." the woman pouted. "Now we won't get a second chance. They're being more cautious since Santos saw you. Tell me what happened."

"I got into the barn with no problem, grabbed the rope and was opening Fury's stall, when I heard rustling in the loft. When I looked up, I saw a cat sitting on top of a bale of straw and figured she'd made the noise, so I opened Fury's gate. I had no idea Santos was sleeping in the loft until a light came on and he came at me with a hammer. He must have heard the horses carrying on. I knew Santos was a tough guy, but I didn't know how tough. That groom isn't much more than half my size and he had every intention of burying that hammer in the side of my head. I rushed him and twisted away. It's a blessing that all he got was my glove."

A former amateur heavyweight boxer, the man stayed in shape. It had been years since his last fight, but he continued to work out, refusing to allow his body to become soft. His strength was an advantage in handling the horses he dealt with daily, yet he had not given a moment's thought to taking on the furious groom.

"Are you sure he didn't recognize you?"

"I was wearing a ski mask, and the light wasn't good. Besides, if he even suspected it was me, the police would have questioned me by now."

The former boxer's attention strayed from recollecting the bungled burglary to the woman standing in front of him. Angie's golden skin was a stark contrast to her hip-length blond hair, bleached almost white by the California sun. He remembered perfectly her manicured fingers stroking his body, and the touch of her exquisite, skilled mouth.

For the past three years, he had been immune to her, but at that moment, raw sex appeal emanated from the woman and he reacted. In one swift motion, reached a well-muscled arm behind her back, pulled her onto his lap where he held her like a baby.

"I've missed you," he whispered, determined to summon the passion she had once poured over him. He covered her mouth with his.

She raised her hands to his chest as if to push herself away, but her arms betrayed her and she pulled him toward her instead. The man cupped her face in his beefy hands.

"Do you remember how it was? We can have that again."

She didn't want to remember. He still had the ability to drive her wild. He had been the most desirable and experienced lover she had ever known, and she had known quite a few. When he held her, jolts of electricity hit all of her pleasure zones. He sensed what she wanted and how to provide it. With him, she lost all control, and that was why she'd had to end their relationship.

"That's over," she replied, with just enough hesitation to prove that it wasn't.

He lifted her chin and said, "You're wrong."

When he moved his lips to her throat, she pulled him closer. He knew her body better than his own. Their time apart had not dulled his memory. Biceps bulging, he lifted her without effort, and his mouth did something magical, while his tongue explored her ears, her neck, all the familiar territories.

He kicked the chair out from under them and unfolded her onto the desk. His mouth still covering hers, he unbuttoned her blouse.

Trembling, she whispered, "Just once more."

She tugged at his belt and unsnapped his jeans as he lifted her from the chair and laid her on the desk. As they scrambled out of their clothes, memories of all the nights they'd spent together came flooding back to Angie, and she hated herself for allowing him to make her remember.

Standing in front of the desk, the man grabbed her hips, pulled her to the edge of the wide oak surface, and slowly entered her.

Angie clamped her legs around his waist, hating him for what he could do to her, yet loving what he was doing.

"Just one more time," she whispered.

"We'll see," he replied.

14

The ninth race had finished, and there was a call for the horses entered in the tenth, the Angelina Stakes. Sarah and Natalie went to the paddock to wait for the guys to bring Fury to the fifth stall.

Jeff and Santos walked into the paddock with the animated colt, but Sonny wasn't with them.

"Did you forget Sonny?" Natalie asked.

"No, he said he would watch the race on the computer," Santos replied. "He didn't want to leave the barn unattended. I told him we had planned to lock it up, but after what happened this morning, with all eyes on the race, Sonny figured it would be the perfect opportunity for someone to cause some problems. Can't say that I disagree with him, but I'm sorry he won't be here to see the race first hand like he wanted."

Nine horses were entered in the Angelina Stakes, and Fury's post position, number five, put him in the center coming out of the gate. Jeff had no complaints about the draw. The center spot would allow Fury to avoid traffic and go to the rail, to move out in front, or to tuck in just off the pace, depending on how the field broke.

The competition included three of the horses Fury had raced against in the Celestial Stakes. Nordstrom, HotDogsAndBeer, and ImageOfAKnight, along with two horses that had finished in front of Fury in a prior race, one who Fury had beaten in the Special Weight, and two horses Fury had not yet faced on the track. Nordstrom, Hotdog and Image were definitely threats on the oval course, but the one colt that Jeff was most concerned about was Ivory Prince, the three-year-old, who shipped in from Ireland.

Prince was undefeated in six races, two of which were graded stakes. The question was whether Prince would take to the Angelina dirt track. Based on the colt's workout, however, Jeff believed that the handsome Irish-bred colt would take to the track's surface with no problem.

Fury was behaving like a perfect gentleman. Santos had no trouble keeping him under control as they walked in slow circles around the paddock. Jeff took that opportunity to talk to Carl about the way he expected the race to unfold.

"I expect Image-Of-A-Knight to go for the front with Hotdog. They will battle for the lead, and may very well knock each other out with a fast pace. Nordstrom will want to be sitting about three lengths back and Prince will trail the field for the first three furlongs. In the best-case scenario, Fury should be just off the pace and in front of Nordstrom. Today you can't allow him to battle for the lead. Image is a speedster. I think nine furlongs will be too much for him, but he'll be out there moving and trying to steal the race on the front end. Hotdog can run all day, but I'm not sure how he'll handle a head-to-head battle, and without a doubt, Image will give him a battle."

"I agree," Carl told the trainer. "I don't expect it to be a problem to keep Fury close, before I let him go at the top of the stretch. In a head-to-head confrontation, he'll demand the lead. I can't see him being out-gamed."

Santos brought Fury back to the stall and Natalie gave him a kiss on the nose. Sarah ran her fingers through his forelock, but resisted the urge to throw her arms around his long, soft neck and give him a giant hug.

The announcer called, "Riders up."

"Do your best," Jeff said, as he gave Carl a leg up, then walked with Santos, Natalie, and Sarah to their seats in the owner's box to watch the race.

"Fury is more relaxed today," Jeff said, watching the colt warm up on the track.

Santos agreed. "He was a perfect gentleman in the paddock too. There's no doubt that he knows why he's here."

"He is such a gorgeous animal," Sarah added.

Natalie was quiet, never taking her eyes from the beautiful colt while he moved effortlessly over the track. As he looked at the crowd, it seemed like Fury understood that he was the center of their attention. Natalie never tired of watching him.

Carl pointed Fury toward the starting gate. Fury stood still as a statue, waiting for his invitation to join the other horses, and when his turn came, he walked into the small enclosure without hesitation.

"The horses are in the starting gate," the announcer called, "and they are off in the thirty-second running of the Angelina Stakes."

"Nice, clean start, Carl," Natalie whispered. "Now, pay attention, Fury. You can run with this group."

Carl and Fury broke third out of the gate, inside of the first two. Carl angled the colt toward the rail and gave the lead to ImageOfAKnight.

"ImageOfAKnight is in the lead, with FraziersFury back a length and a half," the announcer bellowed. "After a slow start, HotDogsAndBeer has moved up even with FraziersFury, then it's three lengths back to Nordstrom on the rail, followed by the rest of the field, with IvoryPrince trailing."

"With a slow break from Hotdog, Image hasn't gotten the early pressure I would have expected," Jeff commented. "I hope Carl can keep Fury relaxed and out of a head-to-head battle just yet."

Whatever else Jeff said was drowned-out by the announcer, "With half a mile to go, HotDogsAndBeer is on the outside challenging ImageOfAKnight for the lead. FraziersFury seems content to stay just off the pace, but has moved up to within a length of the leaders. Here comes Ivory

Prince. He's coming up the rail, moving like a locomotive, but will the rail stay clear? They are at the head of the stretch. Nordstrom is making a move. Jockey A.J. McCoy is urging him on and the big bay is responding. HotDogsAndBeer has taken over the lead. After a brutal pace, ImageOfAKnight is tiring. Carl Lawson is second and has yet to ask FraziersFury for a run. IvoryPrince is gaining ground on the inside. Nordstrom has gone to the outside of ImageOfAKnight and has overtaken FraziersFury. He needs half a length to catch HotDogsAndBeer."

"It's time, Carl," Jeff said, as if the jockey could hear him.

"Come on, Carl," Sarah yelled, "you can get there first."

Natalie stood motionless, willing her colt to move forward, yet almost afraid that he would. If Fury got past both Nordstrom and Ivory Prince, Jeff would be more determined than ever to push her toward an agreement to sell him, at least in part, before the next race. She was torn between wanting that grey beauty to hit the wire first, and wanting him to place second, or even third. If he didn't win the race, she would have less of a battle with Jeff. She wanted a winner, but she wanted Fury more.

The announcer's voice rose in excitement. "Jockey Carl Lawson is asking his mount to pick up the pace, and FraziersFury is responding with apparent ease. IvoryPrince is gaining ground with every stride, staying on the inside, now neck and neck with FraziersFury, who has angled out to open the rail. Nordstrom has the lead by a nose, but HotDogsAndBeer isn't giving up. FraziersFury and

IvoryPrince refuse to let the leaders get away as they race toward the finish line."

Santos was beside himself as he and Natalie shouted encouragement to Fury and his jockey. "Come on, Carl. Dig in Fury. Get up there."

"Ivory Prince is on the inside and FraziersFury is matching him stride for stride. They have moved up within a length of the leaders. It's a four horse race as they head for the wire. Nordstrom is still in front, then half a length to HotDogsAndBeer. IvoryPrince and FraziersFury are another half-length behind and running side by side. Then, it's three lengths to ImageOfAKnight, followed by the rest of the field."

"We aren't out of this yet," Jeff said, "Come on Carl, give him a push."

"Nordstrom is still in front, HotDogsAndBeer is dropping back. IvoryPrince is on the inside, with FraziersFury alongside. They are racing stride for stride and are gaining on the leader. It's Nordstrom, Ivory Prince, and FraziersFury battling in the final furlong. IvoryPrince is on the rail, FraziersFury has moved to the outside has taken the lead. They are at the wire, it is FraziersFury, IvoryPrince and Nordstrom hanging on for third. HotDogsAndBeer is fourth, followed by ImageofAKnight."

"What a race!" Santos shouted.

Sarah whooped and hollered, hugging Natalie and then Santos.

"Fury just won the Angelina Stakes," Natalie whispered, almost in disbelief, as Jeff picked her up with a bear hug and did a pirouette. "I'll see you all in the winner's circle."

Jeff dashed down to stairs to the track to meet Carl and Fury as they came back. Natalie, Sarah and Santos followed not far behind.

Jeff and Carl led Fury to the winner's circle for their third picture in a row. Still full of energy, Fury bobbed his head and pawed the dirt. Once again, he seemed to know he had done something good.

Jeff draped his arm around his wife's shoulders, and whispered, "We're on our way."

Natalie resisted the urge to say, *and now we can easily afford it*. She would save that conversation for a later date. She knew Jeff would want to discuss it again.

Carl winked at Sarah, "I think we had a bit of help from a little amber falcon, about three strides before we hit the wire."

Sarah winked back. "There is not a doubt in my mind."

"I don't know where he got that last surge," Carl said, sliding his arm around Sarah's waist, "but Fury was determined to get his head out in front."

15

Three days later, Fury's biggest fans were still jubilant. The Million Dollar Derby was their goal, and Fury's earnings were enough to guarantee him a starting spot in the first leg of the Triple Million Series.

Santos had taken Flight out for some exercise when Sonny came into the barn. "Morning, Jeff," he called to the trainer.

"Hey, Sonny," Jeff greeted back.

Sonny sat on a stool. "Are you and Nat talking about the Sapphire Stakes next?"

"Yes. Since he's never raced anywhere but here at Angelina, Natalie got it in her head that she'd like to see him shipped up to Laredo. I was thinking that the Emerald might be a better race for him, though. The Sapphire is just three weeks away; the Emerald is here, and it's five weeks out. I wouldn't mind letting him rest a couple of extra weeks before the next race, but we're probably going to Laredo."

Sonny paused a minute before saying, "She may have a point, Jeff. The competition at Laredo usually isn't as tough, yet the purses are pretty substantial now that they've gotten hooked up with that new casino. As long as he keeps his weight, I don't think you'll have a problem."

"Well, do me a favor, and don't tell Natalie that you agree with her just yet!" Jeff protested. "If she hears that, the decision will be made for me."

Grinning, Sonny said, "I hear you. My lips are sealed."

"Your lips are sealed, why?" Natalie asked as she came strolling down the shed row.

"I can't get away with a thing," Jeff said, rolling his eyes.

"I don't know why you try." Looking at Sonny, Natalie asked, "So, have you gentlemen been talking about my young stallion?"

Sonny bowed his head. "I know nothing."

"We were just tossing a couple of ideas around," Jeff crisply told his wife. "One of them was to race Fury in the Sapphire, but forget the Emerald.

The races are only two weeks apart, so it is highly unlikely that we would actually race in both, though I have considered it. We need to see how he's working and make the decision as to which of the two looks better when we get closer to the race dates. If it looks like this race took a lot out of him, we'll find out soon enough."

Natalie folded her arms and coolly said, "Have I mentioned that if the decision were mine alone, I'd really prefer we ship Fury to Laredo? I'd really like to see him at a different racetrack and see how he handles the confusion of shipping. If we take him to any one of the Triple Million races, it will be pretty expensive and I'd rather know in advance that he'll handle the trip."

"That's the reason so many top horses are owned in partnership, unless the owners have plenty of money," Jeff replied.

Natalie only turned and silently walked away.

16

Sarah had a Greek salad in the fridge and a prime rib roast in the oven. A bottle of Bordeaux was waiting to be poured. Carl had called her a couple of days after the Angelina Stakes and asked if he could take her to dinner. She had refused and asked him to join her at her place instead.

"I enjoy cooking, and it isn't nearly as much fun to cook just for me," she'd told him. "Besides, it's a long drive to get here, and if we stay in, you can kick off your boots and relax."

Carl lived just west of Desert Center, California. Halfway between Sarah's home in Quartzsite and Angelina Race Track, it was about a ninety-minute drive.

She had asked him what kinds of food he liked, since most jockeys had to be careful about their diets. Carl had, however, assured her that there wasn't much he didn't eat, and that he even drank a little wine. Blessed with a high metabolism, he loved exercise. When he wasn't racing or working at the barn, he enjoyed jogging, shadow boxing, and Tai Chi. He had no trouble meeting the weight limits.

Both friends of Jeff and Natalie, Sarah and Carl had met two years prior. Recently, however, because of her involvement with Fury, Sarah had spent more time at the barn and saw Carl more frequently. She'd been impressed by his work ethic and his interaction with the horses, which prompted her to give him the little falcon, carved from amber.

Sarah believed in the power of positive thinking, especially when coupled with lucky charms, fetishes, or magic spells, even though a lot of people considered anything mystical or magical ridiculous. Her interest in Carl peaked when he said he would carry the fetish with him each time he rode Fury. What a coincidence that Carl was a student of the ancient belief in the power of stones and crystals. She wondered how much more they had in common?

It was not a coincidence that the carving Sarah had given Carl had been made from amber. Those who believed in the power of stones understood that amber encouraged clear thinking along with the removal of negativity. Most importantly, amber could summon protective energy, and if anyone could use protective energy, it was a race horse and his jockey.

At five-foot-three-inches tall, Carl was slightly shorter than Sarah, although thick dark hair added a bit extra to his height. Wavy bangs hovered above eyebrows that arched over deep brown eyes and the muscles of his California tanned arms bulged above hands that were as strong as vice grips. An all-around nice guy, with a sense of humor that could make her laugh every day, Carl had gotten Sarah's interest, and she hoped to get to know more about Fury's jockey.

Expecting Carl any minute, Sarah was surprised at her jitters, when the crunch of gravel told her Carl had arrived. She ran down the stairs, nearly tripping in her rush to meet him at the door.

She took a few seconds to compose herself before she opened the front door. "Hi!" she called to him, "How was the trip?"

"Not a bad drive at all," he said. He smiled broadly as he approached the door. "It took just over an hour to get here."

Once inside, Carl glanced quickly around the shop. "You've got quite a collection. Can I look around?"

"Of course. I'll give you the grand tour."

Sarah lived on the second floor of the two story building she had purchased several years before.

She had turned the first floor of the building into a retail shop, where she sold art work and artifacts, as well as jewelry, featuring crystals from around the world, along with a book section and a small coffee bar. A licensed and occasionally practicing attorney, Sarah spent most of her time managing her shop. The hours were irregular, which was not uncommon for many establishments in Quartzsite, known as a town that catered to travelers.

"About five years ago, after I sold my partnership in a Boston law firm, I bought this place. Although I enjoyed practicing law, I love working with crystals and the freedom of not having a schedule. I came to Quartzsite because I'd read so much about it. After a crisis in my personal life, I needed to escape for a while. When I got here, I stayed. Now I do some travelling to find unique stones, crystals, fetishes and some jewelry, but most often I'm here, either hanging out with the locals, or meeting the never-ending parade of people who find their way to the desert."

"This is a great shop," Carl said. "I might need to spend some time wandering around. You have some beautiful displays." He nodded toward a spotless, stainless steel coffee machine. "Do you make the coffee, too?"

"Oh, yes. I'm my only employee. There's always boiling water, and I make the coffee to order. I considered hiring some help, but this place is such a part of me that I'd rather keep shorter hours and handle it myself."

"I don't blame you. When the time comes for me to retire from racing, I wouldn't mind having a business like this. If that day comes, it's likely I'll handle it the same way you do. When I'm here, it's open and when I'm not it's closed."

Sarah pointed to her picture of Fury in the winner's circle after his first race. Carl sat in the saddle with Sarah, Jeff, Natalie, Santos and Sonny gathered around him.

"You'll notice your picture is on the wall," she said.

"I noticed." Carl chuckled. "That makes me feel special."

"Come on upstairs. There's a roast in the oven, and a bottle of wine waiting. Dinner will be ready in about twenty minutes. Are you hungry?"

"I'm a jockey," Carl said. "Jockeys are always hungry."

Dinner was such a success that before Sarah realized it, almost five hours had passed since Carl's arrival.

"It's about time for me to head back down the road," Carl told her.

"I didn't realize that it had gotten so late," Sarah said. "Can I fix you a cup of coffee for the road?"

"No. Thanks for the offer, but I'm a night owl. Won't have any trouble staying awake." He stood. "Thank you for dinner and a wonderful evening."

Sarah smiled. "You are more than welcome for dinner, and yes, it was a nice evening."

Carl reached for her hand and their fingers entwined. They walked across the room to the stairs, and down to the shop together.

"Have you ever been to Laredo?" Carl asked.

"No, I haven't. I talked to Natalie yesterday, and she said it would make sense for me to stay with her and Jeff the night before the race. That way I can ride to the track with them in the morning."

"Yes, that would be better than driving yourself," Carl agreed. "It's a pretty lonely stretch of highway from here to Laredo."

He leaned close and brushed her lips with his. "I'll call you in a day or two."

"I'll look forward to it," she told him.

17

"Fury is training well, and seems full of himself," Jeff told his wife while they sipped cappuccino after their dinner at the Winner's Circle restaurant.

"Carl said he was a handful this morning," Natalie said, trying to be cheerful, but failing. She couldn't stand Jeff's indecision any longer. "Are we going to Laredo? I'll need to cancel our reservations if you scratch him."

Jeff nodded, "Yes. He's going to the Sapphire. It worried me that it might be too soon after that last race, but he's ready to run again. That crazy colt seems to thrive on aggressive training. He has come back from the races in great shape. He hasn't missed a bite of food and even gained a few pounds since the Celestial. Besides that, you're right. It's a good idea to enter him in a race away from his home track and see what happens."

"Thank you." As if to reinforce her husband's surrender, perhaps to drown out her feelings of guilt in victory, Natalie repeated, "I really believe it will be the better race. We need to find out if he can handle the competition in an unfamiliar place."

"I'm considering shipping him up a few days early, even tomorrow," Jeff suggested. "It's tough to decide between getting him there early and acclimated to Laredo and keeping him home in comfortable surroundings for as long as possible. What do you think?"

"It might make more sense to send him early. If he goes there tomorrow, he could work on Wednesday and get familiar with a fresh track and the unfamiliar environment."

"That's how I see it, too."

"Maybe I should go along, just to keep him company."

"Santos will be there, and no doubt be living in the stall with him. I know you'll worry about him, but I'm planning to be there most of the time, too. It might be better if you stayed here and held down the fort."

"I guess you're right. Sarah is coming to stay with us the night before the race, so we can leave early in the morning."

Jeff tilted his cup and stared at the inside. "If you agree with the plan, I'll drive with Santos to Laredo early tomorrow morning. I called the race track manager this morning to see what the barn situation is, and they can have a stall ready for us tomorrow. I just need to tell them if we'll be there in the morning. Santos said it's no trouble for him to stay at Laredo through Sunday. I haven't talked to Sonny, but if he can help us with a few extra hours, you won't need to kill yourself taking care of things while we're gone."

"You won't stay there until race day then?"

"I can, but I'd rather drive back here after his gallop on Wednesday, then go back up early Friday and watch him in the morning. Carl is racing here on Friday afternoon, but will drive down to Laredo early Saturday. You and Sarah can ride to the track with Carl."

"That will work. Sarah will like that, too. So," she raised an eyebrow, "has Carl said anything to you about Sarah?"

Jeff looked up from his cup. "Do you think for one minute that Carl would kiss and tell?"

"How do you know he kissed her?"

Jeff shrugged. "It was a figure of speech."

"Sarah really seems interested in Carl," Natalie gossiped. "I would be thrilled if she began seeing someone. She's been alone a long time now."

"Some things take a long time to get over," Jeff said, almost to himself. "I will say that Carl seems infatuated."

18

The next morning, Santos was at the barn before Jeff and Natalie arrived. As usual, he had things under control, ready with fresh straw for the trailer and a bucket of water for the trailer stall.

"Good morning," Santos called.

Jeff waved as he backed the trailer into the doorway of the barn.

When Jeff got out of the truck, he and Santos began tossing the straw onto the floor of the trailer. Natalie climbed up to the loft and tossed a bale of hay down. The horses realized the trailer meant somebody was going for a ride, so they watched with interest.

After Jeff wrapped Fury's legs, Natalie led the horse into the trailer where fresh hay filled the trough. Santos carried in a fresh bucket of water and all the grooming tools he'd need for the next several days.

With Fury loaded and settled for the four-hour drive, Santos turned to Natalie. "Don't worry, I will stay close to Fury. Nothing will happen to him at Laredo." He turned away to toss a bag of carrots into the cab of the truck.

Natalie smiled at her friend, "I know you'll take care of him, Santos. Have a safe trip."

Jeff put his arms around his wife. "I'll be back in time for lunch on Wednesday. Sonny will pick up some of the slack. He said things are slow at the farm, and it won't cause him any problem to spend an extra hour or two here for the next few days. Make sure you keep your phone charged." He kissed her forehead. "And keep the house locked up tight, while I'm gone."

"My phone is in my pocket. I charged it last night," she told him. "I'll be here for a couple hours, at least until Sonny gets here. Is Carl coming tomorrow to ride Flight and the mares?"

"Yes, I forgot to tell you," Jeff replied. "Carl said he'd gallop whoever needed the exercise, and he's scheduled to work Musician on Thursday morning."

Natalie nodded, "Okay. I guess everything is under control. Call me when you get there and settle Fury in."

"Will do," he kissed her forehead again, then stepped up into the truck and started the engine.

Natalie watched the truck pull away and turn toward the highway that would take them to Laredo. She was always a little sad when Jeff was away, and after the recent incident with Fury, she was also more than a little nervous about being alone.

The barn seemed empty without Fury, but the days following his shipment to Laredo passed quickly. Jeff drove back home on Wednesday, reporting that Fury had settled in well and galloped easily over the Laredo dirt track that morning.

Jeff stayed in telephone contact with Santos, who told both Jeff and Natalie that he and Fury were sharing a bachelor pad in the barn at the track. Although Jeff had arranged for a motel room a few miles away, Santos said that he preferred to stay in the barn. He assured Natalie that he was fine in his sleeping bag on the folding cot he had taken along. He told her that he appreciated having the motel room because the motel was within easy walking distance from the track, and the room allowed Santos to go back and forth to shower, change clothes, take advantage of their continental breakfast and fill his thermos with coffee.

"Santos is so easy to please," Natalie told her husband while he packed to drive back to Laredo on

Friday morning. "Sometimes I worry that he doesn't take as care of himself as well as he does the horses."

Jeff agreed, "You're right. Santos credits them with giving him a purpose, and he feels that he owes his life to them. He thanked me again just yesterday for giving him a job when he needed one most. That was eight years ago."

"It's hard to believe it's been that long, but I know I would trust him with my life," Natalie said.

Jeff nodded in agreement. "And so would I. Is Sarah coming here tonight or tomorrow morning?"

"She called earlier and said that since we weren't leaving until tomorrow, she would meet Carl and me at the barn about 7:30," Natalie reported. "Fury's race is at 5:00. Carl said we could leave at eight in the morning. We could check on Fury, have plenty of time for lunch at the track, and watch a few races before the Sapphire. Then, she'll stay overnight after the race and ride back with us on Sunday."

"Did you ask her to stay at our place on Sunday night?" Jeff asked. "It will be a grueling trip to ride four hours to Angelina, then another three hours back to Quartzsite."

"I did, and she said she would stay if she could take us to dinner. I told her that would work if she invited Carl, too."

Jeff muffled a laugh. "I guess things are under control here, so I'll hit the road to Laredo."

"Okay." His wife raised her arms around his neck. "We'll see you around lunchtime tomorrow." She gave Jeff a hug, and he kissed her. Sorry to see him leave, Natalie was sorrier that he didn't seem to mind leaving.

19

Sarah parked in the familiar lot, threw her backpack over her shoulder and trotted to the security desk. Natalie had arranged for a pass to allow Sarah access to the barns on the backside of the track. She signed the register, picked up her pass, and jogged to Barn 17. It surprised her to find the barn door locked, and she glanced at her watch. It was seven-fifteen. Natalie was never late.

Sarah knew that Santos and Jeff were already at Laredo, and Sonny wouldn't get to the barn until a little later. So where was Natalie?

Sarah was about to call Natalie when Carl walked around the corner, singing some country tune. He stopped mid-lyric when he saw Sarah standing outside the barn door.

"Is Natalie on her way?" He asked. "I hope so," Sarah answered. "I was supposed to meet her at seven o'clock."

"Maybe she ran over to the tack shop for something she needed at the last minute."

"If she did, she locked the barn when she left. Do you have keys?"

With a flourish, Carl produced a set of keys. "I do." He unlocked the door, turned on the lights and asked, "How was your drive?"

"Good," Sarah replied. "There's no traffic at 4:00 a.m."

Carl opened the barn door and Chaser rushed over and began rubbing against his legs. It was a clear sign that she hadn't been fed.

"I'll call her," they said at the same time.

Sarah's phone was in her hand, her speed dial tracking Natalie down, as Carl reached into his pocket for his. Natalie's number rang once, twice, then voice mail repeated Natalie's familiar message:

"Hi, you found me. Leave a message or text me. I'll get back to you. If I don't call back soon, it's because I forgot to charge my battery . . . again (laughter)."

"Nat, it's me. Carl and I are at the barn. Where are you? Call me."

Carl looked concerned, but not panicked. "It is not at all like Natalie to be late getting here."

Sarah's eyes surveyed the barn in vain for some sign Natalie had been there.

"Okay," Carl told her, going into calm-take-control-mode. "You stay here; in case she shows up. She sometimes takes the side road and circles around the park, rather than driving right in on West Huntington. She always forgets to charge her phone. She might have gotten a flat tire or something. I'll take a quick trip around the track, head out the main entrance and back track to their house to see if she broke down somewhere on the way. There's not much traffic out there this time of day. If she had car trouble, she might be walking home. I'll probably find her trudging up the hill."

Sonny strolled into the barn. "Find who? Did one of the mares get out?"

Carl approached Sonny. "Natalie was supposed to meet us this morning. She said she'd come in early and feed the cat and top off the water buckets, but we got here a few minutes ago and it's clear she hasn't been here all morning. She's not answering her cell, so I'm going to take a ride and see if she got stuck somewhere between home and the barn."

"I'll walk over and check the tack shop and the café." Sonny offered. "If she isn't there, someone might have seen her."

"Excellent idea," Carl agreed. "Sarah, will you be okay waiting here in case she shows up?"

"Of course," Sarah said. Although Natalie was only a few minutes late, Sarah sensed her best friend was in some kind of trouble. She hoped it was something as simple as a flat tire. Natalie could change a tire as fast as Jeff and knew her way around the truck's engine, too. If it was a breakdown she couldn't fix, and her phone was dead, she'd jog back home and called for help. Carl could be right, but Carl's expression said he was more concerned that he admitted.

By seven-forty-five, Sonny had circled the grounds on the backside of the racetrack and made his way through the general parking area, toward the road, with no sign of Natalie. He stopped a couple of grooms and a trainer and asked them to keep an eye out for her.

Driving the six miles to Jeff and Natalie's home, Carl fought a feeling of impending doom. Determined to be optimistic, he asked and answered silent questions. Why hadn't she called? She forgot to charge her phone again. Why haven't I seen her? She's either right around the bend or she hitched a ride. Where is her truck? She took a different route than usual.

And then he murmured, "Who am I kidding?"

Something was very wrong. Two more miles and Carl got to the house, with no sign of Natalie or the truck. He called Sarah.

"Tell me you found her," Sarah pleaded when she answered.

"I didn't. Did Sonny get back yet?"

"No. He said he'd call if he found her."

"I'll alert security, in case Sonny hasn't already done that," Carl advised. "Wait there until I get back."

20

Having found no sign of Natalie at the Frazier home, Carl returned to his truck and sat inside with his legs dangling outside. He stared below the open door at the asphalt of the driveway, trying to think with a mind that seemed to have gone blank. He reached to the truck's console for his cell phone, defeated, and tapped Sarah's number.

"I think it's time to call Jeff and let him know what's going on here," Carl said when Sarah answered.

It was 8:30; almost an hour past the time Natalie was to meet Sarah. "Yes," Sarah agreed. "I'll stay here at the barn and wait for some word about Natalie, but I'm going to go see if Sonny's heard anything."

"Okay." Carl tapped Jeff's number.

"Hey, Carl!" Jeff answered. "Are you guys on the road?"

"Not yet," Carl said hesitantly. "We have a problem."

"Santos and I just finished breakfast and are about to go back to check on Fury," Jeff said. "Hang on a second," Carl could hear him talking to Santos, then a rustling sound when Jeff repressed his phone to his ear. "Okay, Carl. I'm good. What's going on?"

"Sarah got to the barn a few minutes before I did." Carl paused, dreading telling Jeff, "Natalie wasn't there, Jeff. Sarah called her, but there was no answer, so she left a message on Natalie's cell phone, then tried the house. There was no answer there, either. We figured Natalie might have run over to the horseman's kitchen and locked up before she left. When I unlocked the barn, though, it was clear that she hadn't been there this morning. I took a ride out to your place to see if she had broken down somewhere along the way, and Sarah explained to security that she was supposed to have met Natalie, and she wasn't here. The guard said he'd alert the other security staff and have a look around the track. He checked back with Sarah a few minutes ago and said that so far they'd had no luck. There's no sign of her, and she hasn't returned Sarah's call."

"You said you went to the house. Was the red truck there?"

"I'm still outside your house," Carl informed. "The truck is gone. I checked the house doors and they were locked. I even walked around and checked the windows. As far as I could see, nothing seemed out of place."

"She always forgets to charge her darn phone," Jeff grumbled. "Still, she wouldn't be late getting to the barn, particularly today. What time was she planning to meet you and Sarah?"

"I told her I'd be there by eight. Sarah was planning to meet her at 7:30. She got to the barn at 7:15. I was there shortly after that." Carl said.

The telephone line went silent. Carl waited.

"Did you call the police?" Jeff asked.

"No," the jockey replied. "We wanted to talk to you before we called the police. We were hoping that you might have spoken to her, or had an idea where she could have gone."

"I'll call the police," Jeff said. "I'll tell Santos what's going on, and then I'm driving back home. I'm leaving here as soon as I can. Tell Sarah I'll meet her at the track, and take her back to the house to wait."

"Do you want me to drive to Laredo to ride Fury?" Carl hated to ask under such worrying circumstances, but he needed an answer. "Or should I stay here and keep searching for Natalie?"

"You come on down to Laredo and plan to ride. If I scratch that colt, Natalie will have my head. Santos will be able to get Fury to the paddock and get him saddled. We know enough people down here that I can find somebody to help Santos. I'd appreciate it if you can get to the paddock a little early in case they need another pair of hands. Natalie is usually there to keep him settled. If she doesn't make it to the paddock, it will probably be helpful for you to be there in her place. He responds well to you."

"No problem," Carl said. "Do you want me to see if Sonny can shake loose and ride along? It would make it easier if we had him with us, before the race. He was going to stay here and take care of the horses, but if you're coming back, Sonny might be of more help in Laredo."

"Good idea," Jeff agreed. "Talk to Sonny, or have him call me. If he can ride up with you, it will solve our paddock problem. Fury is raring to go. Ride him like you did in the Angelina, and you have a good chance to cross the wire in front. Can you stay overnight and follow Santos and Fury home tomorrow?"

"Sure, Jeff," Carl told his friend. "Not a problem. I'll take care of it for you. Just let me know if there's anything else I can do."

"Thanks, Carl. Are you driving your truck?" Jeff asked.

"Yes," Carl responded. "I'll put a trailer hitch on it, so I'm good to tow Fury back tomorrow."

"That would be great." Jeff said. "I'd rather not leave him there any longer than necessary. I brought the small trailer, so it shouldn't be a problem for you."

Carl closed his door and started the engine, "We won't have any problems, don't worry. Besides, Santos will be with me, and maybe Sonny as well."

"Alright. I'll talk to Santos and be on the road in a few minutes." Jeff said. "I'll watch for your truck on the highway."

"I'll fill Sonny and Sarah in, and one of us will call and let you know if Sonny will be along with me." Carl promised. "Either way, Sarah said she's going to wait at the barn until we know something, so you can meet her here when you get back."

"Thanks, Carl," Jeff's voice quavered, slightly. "I'll talk to you soon."

When Carl finally arrived back, Sarah and Sonny were quietly talking outside of the barn.

"Jeff is on his way back from Laredo now," he shouted as he stepped out of his truck. "I'll need your help, Sonny. I've got to attach a trailer hitch to my truck. We're racing Fury."

Sonny looked surprised, but Sarah looked relieved. "I was hoping Jeff wouldn't scratch him," she said. "No matter what, Natalie would want Fury to run this afternoon."

"True," Carl said. "Sonny, Jeff wanted me to ask if you could go to Laredo with me. Santos will be by himself, and even with me in the paddock before the race, we sure could use your help."

Sonny nodded. "Absolutely. I'll help you with the hitch, but I'll need about twenty minutes to go home and throw some clothes together."

"No problem. I'll follow you and we can leave from your place." Carl turned to Sarah. "I'm sorry you won't be coming along with us."

"I think it will be better that I wait here," Sarah said, smiling nervously at the jockey. "The race is being live streamed, so I can watch the race with Jeff on my computer when he gets home. Maybe Natalie will be back by then to watch with us."

While Carl and Sonny struggled with the hitch, Sarah escaped into the barn to hide her tears. Flight whinnied, so Sarah stroked filly's face. "Where could she have gone, Flight?" Flight snorted and shook her head, as if to say she had no idea, either.

21

Natalie woke to a pounding on the inside of her skull, like a sledgehammer was trying to batter its way out of her brain. The excruciating pain, combined with her very queasy stomach, made her afraid of even trying to get out of bed.

Today of all days, she thought, *I can't be sick.*

Head throbbing, Natalie braced herself for the shock of daylight rushing into her eyes as she slowly opened them just enough to see the clock on the nightstand. The light was momentarily blinding, but worse was the hammering of her heart when she realized she wasn't home.

Natalie tried to sit up, only to become more confused when she couldn't move her hands. Her vision blurred against walls moving in a circle around her. She collapsed back into a bed of what, alarmingly, was thick straw.

She took a couple of deep breaths, which only caused the nausea to threaten to overtake her. She didn't know where she was, or if she was alone. Lying perfectly still, she concentrated on breathing evenly, only then realizing that someone had bound her hands and feet. *Okay, Natalie, calm down*, she thought, closing her eyes to think. *What is the last thing you remember*?

She remembered packing her clothes for the trip to Laredo. She had poured herself a glass of wine and was reviewing Saturday's racing program. It hadn't been late, probably around nine-thirty. She'd finished her wine and gone to bed.

When her headache lessened somewhat, Natalie dared reopen her eyes, but the nausea continued to plague her. Still, she struggled to remember.

She'd wakened, as usual, before the alarm sounded, slid out of bed and into the shower. She had been planning to meet Sarah and Carl at the barn to drive to Laredo for the Sapphire Stakes. She remembered getting dressed, grabbing her duffle bag, and hurrying to the truck to drive to the track and meet her friends. She'd left her house at about six, so she could get the horses taken care of and have coffee ready when Sarah got there at 7:30. It was all coming back now.

A phone call, on the way to the barn, from Leo, the veterinarian, she hadn't immediately recognized his hoarse and husky voice. He told her he had a terrible head cold that had been going around, that Sonny had called him and told him something was wrong with Flight. He said the filly was standing on three legs, with the weight off her right front leg. Leo had said his truck had a blown tire, and he needed Natalie to pick him up near the entrance of Bonita Park.

Natalie remembered speeding down the road, past the track entrance and spotting what she thought was Leo's dark blue truck off the side of the road near the entrance of the park. When she had pulled over, her passenger door opened—except the guy who climbed into her truck was wearing a black mask, definitely not Leo. The masked man had reached behind her neck, pulled her forward, and covered her mouth and nose with something that smelled like antifreeze.

Natalie's confusion faded into fear. *The man kidnapped me.*

She stiffened, closed her eyes again and listened, but heard nothing. She raised her eyelids just enough to squint at her surroundings. She was in a stall in what looked to be a barn. Lying on her back, she couldn't move her fingers or her feet. When she lifted her arms, she saw that someone had wrapped duct tape around her hands from the tips of her fingers to beyond both wrists, pressing her palms together, as if in prayer.

Deciding prayer was an excellent idea, Natalie closed her eyes and pleaded with God for strength and the means to escape.

Natalie cautiously bent her legs, sat up and rose onto her knees, relieved to discover that while someone had taped her ankles together, her feet were free. She wondered how long she'd been in the strange barn. The bright sun peeked through the cracks in the barn siding, leading her to suspect it was afternoon, but what day?

Was it only this morning that they took me? She asked herself. *Was it yesterday? What happened to Flight? Was Fury in Laredo?*

Despite the few rays of sun penetrating it, most of the barn was dark, smelling of fresh straw mixed with moldy hay. The gate of the stall Natalie kneeled in was closed. She didn't hear any barn noises—no whirl of a fan, no animal sounds or voices. Natalie knew that she should be frightened—and she was, but her anger was stronger than her fear.

Natalie considered calling out for help, then thought better of it. If there was someone who could hear her and provide any help, her abductors wouldn't have left her alone. If there were guards outside the barn, there was no sense alerting them that she was awake. Better to concentrate on getting her hands free and then work on getting out of wherever they had stashed her.

The sound of a sputtering engine, the slam of the vehicle's door, then voices; terrified, she laid back down to feign unconsciousness, concentrating on keeping her breathing slow and even. As the voices gained volume, their words were becoming clearer, just outside the barn.

"No, she'll be out for a while yet. She was moaning a couple of hours ago, so I gave her another dose of ether," a baritone was talking, the masked man.

"For God's sake, don't kill her," a second, oddly familiar, high-pitched voice responded.

Baritone replied, "Don't worry, brother. It won't kill her. She'll have a nasty headache, no worse than a hangover, but she'll live. You want him out, don't you?"

"Yeah, but I didn't sign on to do any actual damage to the woman," high-pitch said. "I'll check on her now, then we can get the hell out of here."

"Wait, put this mask on, in case she's coming around. I'll stay out here."

Natalie heard the barn door slide open. Footsteps approached. She concentrated on breathing slowly and evenly, praying that they couldn't hear her pounding heart. She wanted the men to believe she remained unconscious.

The gate to the stall rattled, followed by a pounding on the front wall of the enclosure. Natalie didn't move. She continued to breathe slowly and evenly, now waiting for the footsteps to retreat and the door to slide closed again.

"Hey, there," the high-pitched voice called. "Wake up."

Natalie stayed motionless, trying desperately to recall face to fit his voice. She heard something land on the hay beside her and the footsteps walking away. When the barn door closed, she heard the man say, "She's still out."

The baritone ordered, "Lock the barn and let's get the hell out of here."

Relief flooded through her body, yet Natalie remained still. She heard the slam of the vehicle doors and the start of its engine. Alone again, even while she listened to the sound of the engine fading, she didn't move until she could no longer hear any trace of it.

Wondering what time it was, Natalie looked at her wrist. A lump on her left arm told her it was still there, but covered with tape. She couldn't tell whether her cell phone was in her pocket, but thought she'd probably left it on the truck seat after she had spoken with Leo, or whoever had invaded her truck.

The words of the baritone echoed in Natalie's mind: *you want him out, don't you*? She wondered who the 'him' was, either Jeff or Fury? Could her kidnapping be tied to the attempted theft of Fury? It had to be. If so, did baritone's question mean that they wanted 'him' out of the barn, out of a race, or even dead? Why would someone abduct her, unless it would be to put pressure on Jeff? She almost laughed. She and Jeff sure didn't have enough money to make her a worthwhile ransom target. This had to be about Fury.

Trying to act logically, Natalie decided she'd be wise to check the status of her body. She started with her shoulders, first tensing, and then relaxing them. She moved her limbs slowly, one at a time, relieved to discover nothing seemed broken. Except for her headache, she didn't have any pain.

The next priority was to get out of the barn and find a telephone. She raised her hands to her mouth and furiously chewed at the duct tape that bound her wrists. She tried not to move her head too quickly, because every snap of her neck felt like anvils smashing against her temples. It was an exhausting struggle. Her nausea subsided, but her thirst was becoming unbearable.

While she continued to gnaw at the tape, Natalie found it strange they had left her alone in the barn, but had not taped her mouth. Was that a sign her kidnappers weren't concerned someone might hear her calling for help? The tape tasted disgusting and was making her mouth as dry as a desert. She almost cried when she spied a bottle of water in the corner by her feet. She wondered if they had left it there intentionally and, if they did, whether it was safe to drink.

Natalie had freed her fingertips enough to forklift the neck of the bottle, but not free enough to twist its cap off—she had to use her teeth and gently rotate the bottle in the vise of her pressed together forearms. Just when she felt herself go faint from the effort, the cap tumbled into her mouth and she spit it out. Holding the bottle steady between her arms, she took small sips at first, and then gulps until she downed half of it. The water was cool, and it occurred to her the bottle was what she'd heard fall besides her minutes before. Her captor must have tossed it to her before he left, which might have meant he didn't want her to be any more miserable than necessary.

Unable to recap the bottle, but not knowing when or if she'd be able to find more, she maneuvered the container into the straw at her left side and prayed the bedding would keep it propped.

Jeff will be out of his mind with worry, Natalie thought. Sarah would be beside herself, knowing that she would never intentionally stand her up. She bit at the tape, ripped out a tiny strip, spit it out, and bit again. *Is Fury okay? Did he race in the Sapphire? God, where am I? Is anyone looking for me?*

Natalie froze, listening. She briefly heard what sounded like a car engine or maybe a tractor. Then everything quieted again. She continued to work at the tape for what seemed like hours until her aching teeth pulled a nice chuck from the thick layers binding her hands.

The bottom layer of the sticky fabric ripped down the middle, promising her freedom soon. She took one more bite of the tape, and a strip of the broad band slipped like dental floss between her aching teeth. With all the strength she could muster, Natalie twisted and pulled until the tape could not withstand the final hard jerk that freed her hands at last.

After tugging the tape away from her watch, Natalie squinted at the timepiece. Time of day eleven-ten, the calendar showed the date as the twenty-fourth. Five hours ago, she'd been on her way to the barn. It was still Saturday, which meant Fury had yet to race in the Sapphire Stakes. She needed to contact Jeff. He couldn't scratch that colt.

After the battle she'd gone through freeing her hands, ripping the duct tape from her ankles was easy. Back on her knees, she crouched below the open window and crawled to the door of the stall, supporting herself with her right hand while clasping the water bottle in her left.

Corrosion on the sliding door of Natalie's temporary prison, made it difficult to move, and noisy as the wooden gate jerked across the runner. Natalie eased the barrier open far enough to squeeze through. She stood and, staying close to the wooden framework, stepped out onto the shedrow, grateful to whoever had dumped her in fresh straw, because the runway was anything but fresh.

As quietly as she could manage, Natalie stayed close to the wall, as she crept along the edge of the structure to the front of the barn where the immense sliding door to the outside was closed.

I can either try to open the door or go out through a window, she thought. She momentarily considered climbing the ladder to the upper window, then jumping down from the loft, but decided to at least try to escape through the oversized sliding door, instead.

Natalie grabbed the wooden handhold and pulled it to her left. The enormous door wouldn't budge. She couldn't tell if it was from lack of use, or locked from the outside. She had been certain the door was the one her recent visitor had used. Then again, in her terror, she could have easily have confused his pathway.

Too weak to fight with the door any longer, yet beginning to feel confident she wasn't being watched, or at least she wasn't being seen, Natalie remained close to the wall. She took a few more swallows of the water.

Though some bright sunshine filtered into the barn, light within the bulk of the building was dim. Squinting more to keep any floating particulates from drifting into her eyes, she made her way back along the edge of the shedrow to the other end of the barn where there was another, smaller door. It was also a sliding door, though newer looking two-by-fours had replaced the cross bars on both its top and the bottom panels.

Natalie tucked the water bottle under her arm, and, using both hands, tugged evenly on the sliding door. She felt her heart race when the door moved and opened it just enough of a gap for her to slip through to the outside. She closed the door behind her in case her captors came back. At least they wouldn't be immediately alerted to her escape,

Her back pressed against the exterior of the barn, Natalie surveyed her surroundings. The barn sat in the middle of a field. About three-hundred yards to the right, there was an old, and, from the look of it, much neglected farmhouse. Remnants of a split-rail fence surrounded the property, and some orange and lemon trees stood near the farthest side of the house. A small cemetery was off to the left, surrounded by a rusted wrought-iron fence, and Natalie could see grass and weeds towering above weatherworn headstones.

Natalie stayed close to the barn as she made her way around the side, hoping to locate a road or neighboring home she could seek rescue in. Rounding the corner, she gasped at the sight of her truck parked behind the barn on a dirt, but cratered and rock-strewn driveway—only twenty yards away.

Like she had just awakened from a nightmare, Natalie crept toward her truck, keeping a careful eye on her surroundings. It surprised her to find that her was truck unlocked. She set the bottle of water in the beverage holder of the console and eagerly climbed in and locked the doors.

The keys were not in the ignition. Momentarily heartsick, Natalie recovered when she spied her cell phone on the passenger seat, only to discover the battery was dead. Desperate, she opened the glove box, pulled out her charger and plugged it into the DC outlet. A sigh of relief escaped when the little charger's arrow lit up. A speed dial to Jeff and she'd be in good shape. But her hope crashed to frustration when the service bars didn't appear. There was no service.

The time and date on her cell phone's screen confirmed the accuracy of her watch. It was eleven-forty-five on the day of the Sapphire Stakes. Someone had kidnapped her that morning. That meant she couldn't be more than five hours from home, maybe not more than three or four hours; at the most she was two-hundred miles from where they had grabbed her. Her truck had double fuel tanks, each with about a three-hundred-mile range. She had filled those tanks two days before, so there was at least three-quarters of a tank of gas between them. If she could start her truck, the gas gauge would tell her how they had taken her.

"Okay, Nat," she murmured. "How difficult can it be to hot-wire this truck?" Years ago, her father had an old clunker he'd used around his farm. He'd routinely started it by touching the wires that hung below the steering column. She could figure it out.

Abruptly, she thought about her house keys, a key for Jeff's truck, and the keys to the barn and the horse trailer—all attached to her key ring. The kidnappers had access to Jeff's truck, her home and the barn. She had to get word to Jeff, but first she needed to get away from wherever she was.

Natalie checked again to be sure she locked the truck doors before she moved the seat back to more easily access the steering column. Ready to hunt for wires she could cross to spur the ignition into action, her foot slid over a lump in the floor mat.

It couldn't be, could it? She dared hope.

Natalie's left hand trembled as she lifted the mat, uncovering her key ring. She grabbed the keys and rammed the truck's ignition key into the starter. The truck started.

The gas gauge was halfway between empty and a quarter of a tank. Natalie calculated she had about two gallons left in the first tank, but the second tank should be full; enough to get her back to civilization.

Natalie turned on the GPS, pushed the "home" key, and had faith the GPS would guide her to safety. Unfortunately, instead of the comforting sound of the robotic voice telling her that it was searching for the best route, she heard the four beeps that alerted it could find no satellite signal.

No problem, she thought, still feeling the temporary euphoria of having escaped the barn and locating her truck keys. *I'll drive until there is a signal.*

Out of the barn and ready to get on her way home, Natalie put her truck in gear, and then steered toward the farmhouse and ultimately onto the road. She would have much preferred to floor the accelerator and drive out of there as fast as the truck would go, but rocks covered the uneven driveway, and potentially damaging holes and craters. Even in her panic, she realized what a disaster a flat tire, or a broken axel would become. Slowly, her truck advanced toward the road.

22

"Santos, I'm so sorry to dump this on you at the last minute." Jeff said to his groom.

Santos assured, "I can handle Fury. You need to worry about finding Natalie. Let me worry about saddling Fury, and Carl can worry about winning the race."

"Carl said he'd check with Sonny to see if he could ride along and help you with Fury," Jeff told Santos.

"If Sonny comes, I'll appreciate the help, but if he can't make it, I'll have no trouble finding someone to assist in the paddock. I'll be able to handle whatever needs done. Don't worry about anything here. Call me as soon as you know something about Natalie."

The two men shook hands.

When Jeff hopped up into his truck, he phoned the California State Police and asked for Officer Ray Savage, who had been Jeff's friend since third grade. Although their lives had taken unique paths, and they seldom got together since Jeff's wedding, they had a bond of friendship that time and distance could never erode.

After a minute of waiting, Jeff heard Ray's familiar voice, "Trooper Savage."

"Ray, it's Jeff Frazier. I'm so glad you're there."

"Jeff, how the hell are you? What a surprise," his old friend said. "It's been way too long, man."

"Too long," Jeff agreed. "Unfortunately, the reason I'm calling is that I've got some trouble, and I'm hoping you can help me out."

"Sure, Jeff. If there's anything I can do, I will. You know that. What do you need?"

"It's Natalie. We can't find her. Her truck is missing, too. She left the house and never got to the barn to check on the horses. A friend drove the road from the track to our place, and it looks like she isn't broke-down anywhere. We notified the track's security personnel and they are on the lookout. I'm leaving Laredo now, heading back to Angelina. Natalie has been missing for about four or five hours. That might be too soon for a missing person report, but something is wrong, Ray."

"Is there any possibility that she needed to get away for a day or so?" the trooper had to ask.

"Absolutely not," Jeff denied. "She planned to meet a friend of ours this morning, but never showed up. They were planning to drive down to Laredo to see her colt race. She would never stand her friend Sarah up, and she would never miss Fury's race."

"I might not be able to get a missing person report filed, but I can get an unofficial 'be on the lookout' circulated. Have you contacted your local police?"

"Yes. They said they would keep an eye out for her truck, but won't file a report for forty-eight-hours. There's something else. Two weeks ago, our groom surprised someone in our barn, at three o'clock in the morning. He was likely trying to steal Natalie's horse. I can't help but believe that it's all somehow related."

"Okay. I've got a friend in Chino," Ray said. "I'll see if he can get some word out locally. What is she driving?"

"It's a red Ford pickup. The license plate is FRZRFURY."

"Okay, I'm on it, but call me back if you hear from her."

"Thanks, Ray. I can't tell you how much I appreciate this. I owe you."

"You don't owe me a thing." Ray replied. "After we find Natalie, I'll be interested in hearing more about that break-in. In the meantime, I'll keep a close watch on things and see if we can give it a priority status. We aren't exactly backed-up with investigations for a change."

"Thanks again, Ray. This means a lot."

The trip back from Laredo was uneventful. When Jeff arrived at his barn, he found Sarah inside feeding carrots to the horses.

Without uttering a sound, Sarah moved toward Jeff and into a hug. "Nothing yet," she told him. It was 1:00 p.m. Natalie had been missing for about six, maybe seven hours. "Security people have come by three or four times so far this morning, and one of Anthony McCoy's stable workers, Marty Adams, was here a couple of hours ago. Marty told me that Mr. McCoy heard about Natalie and knew you were shorthanded, with everyone down in Laredo. He said that Mr. McCoy had sent him over to help. He wasn't very pleasant, but he insisted on cleaning the stalls and filling the water buckets. He told me to tell you that Mr. McCoy knows that the last thing you need to worry about right now is dirty stalls or thirsty horses. You're supposed to call Marty, if you want him to come back later to feed. The number is on the desk, and I put it in my phone, too."

Anthony's offer didn't surprise Jeff. A horseman his entire life, Anthony McCoy was usually the first to offer support, or a helping hand, when someone needed it.

"He probably heard about everything from Angie," Jeff said. "I imagine the word spread pretty quickly between the track security guards and Sonny looking around this morning. The McCoys are going to Laredo today, too, but it's just like Anthony to think about how he can help. I am a little surprised he sent Marty though."

Sarah sat on an overturned crate. "Well, he acted sullen, and I heard him muttering to himself, while he was filling the buckets, but he was nice enough to me. Was I wrong to allow him to help?"

"No, not at all," Jeff assured her. "It's just that sometimes, well most of the time, Marty drinks too much. He can be volatile on the morning after, which is most mornings; even most afternoons. He is very loyal to Anthony, but Anthony usually keeps a close eye on him."

"Marty said to be sure and call if there was anything else he can do. He told me he would be at the farm for a few hours, then he was coming back to the track, and would be at McCoy's barn until dinnertime."

"Thanks, Sarah. I'll just check on all the tenants here, then we might as well go back to the house and wait. I'll give Anthony a call and let him know I'm back."

Jeff reached up for a couple of bales of hay, pulled off a few flakes and began filling the bins that were low. He almost wished the stalls were a mess, so he would have something that needed done, besides waiting. Not knowing what had happened to Natalie was tormenting him, and he didn't know what to do with himself. He had never been good at sitting still.

23

Her truck crept along the driveway. Natalie estimated another fifty yards to the road, yet it seemed to take forever to travel the distance. When she finally made it to the road, Natalie discovered the roadway was narrow, uneven, and marred with ruts. Although disappointed with the condition of the dirt throughway, she was grateful that it was in better condition than the driveway she had bounced over. She looked around in all directions. There were no houses or other structures within sight. She knew she was facing east, which meant the road in front of her was running north and south. In her head, she tossed a coin. *Heads turn left and go north, tails turn right and go south.*

Natalie turned left. The damaged thoroughfare wouldn't allow her to dare drive much over fifteen miles an hour, eager though she was to press the accelerator to the floor. She did not have a clue where she was, but she knew that wherever she was, she was on her way home.

Natalie continued along the road with one eye on her cell phone, hoping for a signal. *At least the battery is charging,* she thought.

Her headache had settled into a dull, but endurable throb. Grateful the nausea had passed, she reached for the water bottle and drank until the container was empty; then, wishing for more and not daring to take her eyes off the bumpy road, set the empty container back in the cup holder. Still, she was in one piece, adrenaline had kicked in, and, though physically exhausted, she was alert. She'd driven about twenty miles before, at last, a cell phone signal. She called Jeff.

24

Jeff had been in the barn with Sarah for less than fifteen minutes when his phone's ringtone trumpeted. He almost couldn't believe the sight of Natalie's number. "Natalie, where are you? Are you okay? What happened? We've been worried to death. The police are looking for you. Sarah is beside herself. Are you okay? Where are you?"

"Jeff, thank God, you're there. I'm okay. Is Flight okay? What about Fury?"

"Flight is fine. I'm here with her now. Fury is in Laredo with Santos, and he's ready to race." A flash of anger swept across Jeff's face. "We've been going crazy here. Where have you been?"

"I was on my way to the barn, early this morning, when I got a call from a man who said he was Leo. He told me that Sonny had called him and that Flight was hurt. He said his truck broke down on his way to the barn. He said he was near the entrance to Bonita Park and asked if I could pick him up and go with him to look at Flight. So I high-tailed it to

Bonita Park. There was a black truck off to the side, which I figured was Leo's. When I stopped, a man wearing a ski mask got in and covered my nose and mouth with a towel with some kind of chemical that knocked me out."

Hearing herself remember what had happened mildly revived the fear she'd experience back at that strange barn. Natalie applied more pressure on the accelerator.

"When I woke up, I was in a barn with my hands and feet taped. I finally got the duct tape off, and when I got out of the barn, I found my truck. They'd left me a bottle of water, and the straw was clean, but there was no cell service. I've been driving for about half an hour, but I'm on a dirt road, full of ruts."

"Tell me what you're seeing," her husband directed. "Are there road signs or buildings? I'll drive to meet you."

"I'm on a dirt road. I'm heading north or northwest. I've been driving for about twenty miles. It's desert country. There's no traffic since I got away from the farmhouse. I would think that my GPS should kick in soon. I can't be more than a couple of hundred miles away. It's a road I don't recall ever being on before. Wait, there's an intersection coming up–finally. Hang on, there's a sign on the other side of the road. I need to back up and see what it says."

"Don't get out of the truck," Jeff pleaded.

"It's an old wooden sign that says: 'Yuma–7 *mill.'* It's hand painted, but I imagine it's accurate. Okay, so I'm on a road heading west about seven miles from Yuma, if the sign is telling me the truth.

That means I must be near Route 8. I hope I'm not in Mexico."

Jeff also hoped she wasn't in Mexico. "How much gas is in the truck?"

"The first tank is almost empty, but the second tank should be full," she replied. "I'll get gas as soon as I can find a gas station. I had money in my back pocket, and it's still there. Jeff, this entire thing is crazy. I heard two men talking. One of them said that *they wanted him out*. I'm sure that he was referring to Fury."

"I don't know what the heck's going on," Jeff said, "but I intend to find out. In the meantime, you just keep driving west. Sarah can call you back. Talk to her while I call Ray Savage. I'll let him know where you are and see if he can intercept you. In the meantime, I'll get to Route 8 and start driving towards you. Stay on the phone with me until I get to you. Keep your doors locked and don't stop for anything, including gas. If you run out of gas, pull over and wait for me or the police."

Jeff disconnected with Natalie and motioned to Sarah to use hers to reconnect.

"Natalie," Sarah cried out, unable to remain calm, "are you alright?"

"I need a shower and I have the back end of what was a brutal headache, but otherwise I'm okay," Natalie told her friend.

Satisfied Sarah would keep Natalie on the phone, Jeff turned his attention to dialing for help. Since the kidnapping happened locally, it was technically the Chino Police who had jurisdiction, but he also had confidence that Ray would add help from the California State Police. He was certain Ray Savage would send someone out immediately to intercept his wife. He dialed Ray's number first.

"Trooper Savage," Ray answered.

"Ray, it's Jeff. Natalie called. Somebody kidnapped her. They grabbed her this morning and left her at a deserted barn. She got out and is driving west about seven miles outside of Yuma. Her GPS doesn't have a signal yet, but I imagine it will kick in any time now. Do you have anybody that could meet her out there?"

"Give me her cell number and we'll try to locate her," Ray told Jeff. "I'll see if we have anybody in that general vicinity."

Natalie heaved a sigh of relief when she heard the mechanical voice say, *Your GPS signal has been recovered*, and it began to dictate the route home.

Sarah heard the voice, too. She waved her arm at Jeff. "Her GPS is working."

Jeff relayed that news to Ray.

"I can have a car intercept her within the next twenty miles," Ray said. "Tell her to stay north on Route 8."

"I don't know how to thank you," Jeff said. "I'm on my way to meet her. I'll call you later. Thanks again, Ray." He spoke with the trooper a minute more, and then motioned Sarah to hand over her phone.

"Natalie, Jeff wants to talk to you. We'll see you soon." She gave Jeff her phone.

"I talked to Ray. He's sending a trooper to meet you and escort you to the state police barracks," Jeff instructed his wife. "He's about twenty miles from you. Sarah and I are driving to the barracks to pick you up, but we're closer to a hundred and ten miles away. Ray said they will probably want to take your truck back to their garage to see if they can find any evidence. They'll also want a statement, but you can give it right there at the barracks. By the time that's taken care of, we should be there to take you home. Do not open the door or roll down the window until you see uniformed police with ID," he warned his wife.

"What about Fury?" Natalie needed to know.

"Fury is fine. Carl should be in Laredo by now. Sonny went along with him to help Santos in the paddock. They are all staying overnight and bringing Fury back in the morning," Jeff said. "With a little luck, you might even make it home in time to watch the race."

Jeff detected the relief in Natalie's voice as she praised, "I'm so glad you didn't scratch him. I'll figure out a way to watch the race. Maybe I can get it on my phone."

"Leave it to you," Jeff said, trying to keep his wife calm, even though he wasn't. "Kidnapped, lost and terrified, but the first thing you think about is watching a horse race."

His wife laughed. "I escaped, the cavalry is on the way and I'm no longer lost. Besides that, the race is not an ordinary horse race; it's Fury's horse race!"

Jeff and Natalie continued to converse while Jeff sped his truck in his wife's direction. Sometimes Sarah took over the phone to chat. But Natalie was speaking with her husband again when she announced, "There's a police car. I see the lights flashing. He passed me going the other direction. He's turning around. He's right behind me, now. I'm pulling over."

"Ask for ID," Jeff said.

Natalie told Jeff to hold on. She put her phone on speaker so he could hear the exchange. She lowered her window an inch and said, "Thank you so much for finding me out here. Could you show me your ID? I'm a little paranoid right now."

"I understand, Mrs. Frazier. I am very glad to see you're safe." The trooper pressed a photo ID card against the window. "I'm Trooper Paul Myers. Please get out of your truck and into my car. We need to keep your truck for a few days to go over it for evidence. A tow truck is on the way to move it to our garage."

Satisfied with the officer's ID, Natalie grabbed her cell phone and shifted to get out of her truck. "Thank you so much. You can't imagine how glad I am to see you! My husband is on his way and should meet us at your barracks before long. I think he's probably a little over an hour away."

"Are you injured?" Trooper Myers asked. "I can have a paramedic unit here shortly if you need medical attention, and get you to the hospital, in Santa Reales if need be."

"The statement I can give you now, but no hospital. My headache is all but gone, and aside from being very thirsty, I'm fine." Natalie told him.

Trooper Myers reached behind the seat of his car and brought out a bottle of water. He offered it to Natalie, and she accepted with a smile of gratitude.

In the police car, Natalie told the officer the basics of what had occurred. "I just want to go home," she said.

After the tow truck arrived, Trooper Myers pulled his patrol car back onto the road and sped toward his barracks.

"What makes me feel dumb is that I fell for that story about Flight being hurt," Natalie told her rescuer. "I never called Jeff, because the man impersonating Leo said he had already called him. Whoever did this either knows us, or has a connection to somebody who knows our schedules."

"We'll do all we can to find out who's behind this," Trooper Myers replied without taking his eyes off the road.

"What's really bizarre is whoever did this didn't take my watch, my money, or my truck," Natalie said. "They left the truck parked close to the barn, with the keys under the mat. My cell phone was even there on the seat. I think whoever did this wanted me to get out of that barn and back home."

In the side mirror, Natalie could see the tow truck traveling about a quarter mile behind.

"When will I get my truck back?" she asked.

"Shouldn't be too long. Probably just a few days." Trooper Myers steered his patrol car into the lot of his barracks.

Jeff and Sarah arrived at the barracks about an hour later.

"Thank you so much for finding my wife," Jeff said, shaking Officer Myers's hand. Natalie came out of the restroom and threw her arms around her husband's neck, kissing him.

"It is always a good feeling to finish the day with a happy ending, and this is most definitely a happy ending," Trooper Myers said. "Do you want me to follow you back to Chino, to make sure you don't run into any problems?"

"Thanks for the offer, but I'm familiar with the road, and I don't expect any more trouble," Jeff said. "Sarah is riding shotgun, and we'll keep Natalie sandwiched safely between the two of us."

Natalie turned from her husband to hug her best friend. She and Sarah began talking at the same time. Sarah started crying, and that got Natalie's tears started, yet within a few seconds they were laughing, both happy that they were together again and Natalie unharmed.

The women got into the truck, but Jeff spoke to Trooper Myers for another minute or two before climbing behind the driver's wheel.

Looking at his watch, Jeff said, "Well, ladies, we've got about two hours before we get home, and about two-and-a-half hours before the race. We might be able to get there in time to see Fury in the paddock."

Natalie touched his shoulder. "Can you call Santos?"

"It's already done. Sarah texted Carl and Santos that you were on your way home, so they know you're safe. Fury is doing fine, and Santos said he is ready to run. Carl will call after the race, and I'm sure you'll be on the phone with the three of them half the night."

Successfully finding the Laredo Race Track live stream on her cell phone, Natalie said, "Fury is the third choice at odds of nine to two. Nordstrom is three to one. Wow, IvoryPrince is the favorite; he's nine to five!"

25

Despite her desire for a shower and change of clothes after her ordeal, Natalie insisted the trio drive to the racetrack, instead of going home. She said they could watch the race in the simulcast area. There was time to get a sandwich and something to drink before Fury's race.

"I'm sure I look like a wrecked ship, but a racetrack meatball sandwich is just what I need," Natalie said. They found a table near the television screen that was showing the Laredo races.

"I think you look beautiful," Jeff said. He ordered their sandwiches, which they quickly devoured.

It was time for the race.

"Good boy," Jeff whispered to the big television when Fury walked alertly into the starting gate.

"He looks confident," Natalie added. "Carl seems relaxed, too."

The announcer declared, "The horses are in the gate," Then after a brief pause, "And they're off, with a clean start for all."

Jeff began speaking to Carl, as though Carl could hear him, "Nice job, Carl. Don't chase Angie. Move to the rail and let Fury settle in."

"Nordstrom has taken the lead," the track announcer called, "with A.J. McCoy moving him easily to the rail. BaskervillesBobby, with first time blinkers, has moved up quickly and jockey Doug Whiteman is content to stay a length behind the leader. FraziersFury is next, racing along the rail with a head in front of Flashing. Then, it's a length and a half back to Ivory Prince, with Runaway and Candyland bringing up the rear. Nordstrom is relaxed in front, completing the half in 51 seconds, with nobody interested in challenging him."

"It's time to make a move, Carl," Natalie murmured.

"He's got nowhere to go," Jeff said. "Bobby's got him stuck on the rail, and Nordstorm is slowing a bit. They should spread out at the top of the stretch. Carl will ask him to run as soon as there's a hole."

"The horses are at the top of the stretch, and the field is turning for home," the announcer bellowed. "Ivory Prince is moving like a freight train on the outside, chewing up the distance with every stride. BaskervillesBobby has gotten up even with Nordstrom and is challenging for the lead, with a length and a half back to Carl Lawson and FraziersFury. BaskervillesBobby has a head in front. Carl Lawson hasn't asked FraziersFury for anything, but the grey colt has begun to move. Nordstrom is coming off the rail, opening it up for FraziersFury. IvoryPrince is racing to the outside of FraziersFury and still gaining on the leaders. If FraziersFury has a chance, he's got to get through on the rail, and there he goes. Nordstrom is fighting back and has a nose in front of BaskervillesBobby, IvoryPrince is on the outside. FraziersFury is racing third, with BaskervillesBobby dropping to fourth. Now it's IvoryPrince in front, but Nordstrom is fighting back trying to hold off FraziersFury, who is racing strongly on the inside."

"Come on, Carl," Sarah pleaded. "Come on, Fury."

"Keep your eyes on the wire, Carl," Jeff advised, though he knew the jockey was doing just that.

Natalie bit her lip, willing her colt to find one last surge that would propel him ahead of Nordstrom.

The announcer continued, "With a furlong to go, FraziersFury is gaining on the front runner. Back two lengths BaskervillesBobby is racing fourth, followed by Wildandfree and Runaway. Nordstrom has pulled ahead of Ivory Prince, but not for long. IvoryPrince is back in the lead. They are approaching the wire. FraziersFury surging on the inside, getting a nose in front. . ."

A seeming unanimous gasp by the spectators overwhelmed the announcer's voice when Nordstorm lugged in toward the rail, bumping Fury hard and sending Natalie's horse into the rail a stride before the wire. Carl somehow managed to stay in the saddle. A.J. was thrown off balance, but also stayed seated, and Ivory Prince, who had been striding evenly with Nordstrom, was checked, losing what would likely have been second place.

"It looked like Nordstrom crossed the finish line in front, by a nose, with FraziersFury second. IvoryPrince finished third with Runaway fourth, but the stewards have posted an inquiry," the announcer alerted.

"Oh, no," Sarah cried out at the same time that Natalie exclaimed, "Fury!"

"Pull him up, Carl," Jeff yelled.

Carl slowed Fury and got him stopped a few yards past the finish line, immediately jumping out of the saddle to check on the colt who was tossing his head and pawing the ground. Blood was running from a gash in Fury's left front leg. The horse ambulance was moving from trackside toward Carl and his injured mount.

"Maybe he just banged his leg when Nordstrom cut into him," Jeff said, trying to calm his wife, yet not taking his eyes off the television. "The bleeding could look worse than it really is."

Jeff didn't believe what he had just said. The injury looked serious to him. He watched both Sonny and Santos running across the track to where Carl and Fury were standing. He dialed Santos.

"Jeff," Santos answered, panting. "I'm on the track now. Hang on." He dropped to his knees in front of Fury and carefully ran his fingers along the back and sides of the horse's leg.

Jeff's view of Fury and crew ended when the camera cut to a view of the horses for the following race. Over the phone, he heard Santos say, "Tell Jeff I can't feel anything out of place in the knee or down to the fetlock. There's a cut on the front of the left front pastern and a chunk off the front of the hoof."

Jeff well knew the drill coming after. Carl would go to weigh in and lodge an objection. Although the stewards' inquiry would probably yield the same result, Carl would want it to be clear that, whether Nordstrom's collision with Fury was unintended or not, Fury had been in front and would have beaten Nordstrom at the finish line. Jeff was aware, as was Carl and most of the racing community, that Angie, Nordstrom's jockey, had been penalized more than once for inappropriate actions in a race; that she was a tough competitor, but sometimes she played dangerously rough.

The television went to a split screen between the start of the next race and the ambulance pulling alongside of the injured colt. The track vet approached Fury with an inflatable cast and wrapped the brace around Fury's leg. Fury appeared calm, even curious of all the activity.

Natalie waited anxiously for a follow-up report on Fury, along with the official results. She knew that the track stewards would not make a decision until they had spoken to both jockeys involved.

Jeff told Sonny over the phone, "Tell Santos I want Fury taken off the track by ambulance, and authorize the vet to do whatever is necessary to stabilize that leg. I want x-rays of both front legs and an MRI if the vet thinks it would be of benefit. How badly is he cut?"

"There's a fair amount of blood, so I'd expect the leg will need stitches," Sonny said. "Here's Santos."

"Hey, Jeff. What a scare," Santos said. "Carl is okay. He's lodging an objection. He said Nordstrom came right into them. Fury banged into the rail, but he never stopped running. Carl said he's not sure if they crossed the wire first or second, but he said they were clearly ahead of Nordstrom when he lugged in."

Natalie twirled a finger at her right ear to signal her husband to put his cellphone on speaker so she could hear Santo's report, too.

"Fury's got a good-sized slice across the pastern," Santos continued. "His shoe came off, and the hoof will need a patch. Sonny is riding in the van and will stay with Fury until the vet goes over him. Carl is getting the process figured out with the stewards. We're still waiting for the official results. I think Nordstrom will be taken down. How's Natalie?"

"Natalie is fine," Natalie answered, "or will be if Fury's okay."

Cheers erupted from several horsemen when the results unfolded on the right side of the television screen. The stewards had decided. Though Fury finished second, they had placed him first, with Nordstrom finishing first, but placed third and Ivory Prince, who had been gaining on Nordstrom, moved up to second.

"The van is taking Fury to the receiving barn," Santos advised, "I can make the arrangements to transport him to the equine clinic here, or we can head back home now and get him to the clinic near Angelina."

"If the track vet can stitch up the leg and doesn't see any obvious damage other than that, I'd rather have him back here with Leo," Jeff decided.

"Okay. Let me see what the track vet tells me, and I'll call you back." Santos replied. "I'll get the trailer hooked up and ask Carl to get the truck packed and ready to go, so we can leave immediately if we're given the go ahead."

"I'll call Leo and put him on notice that we might need him tonight," Jeff advised.

"Just make sure he's the real Leo," Natalie said.

26

Sonny rode with Fury to the barn in the back of the horse ambulance. The injury to the colt's leg looked nasty, but, as long as there were no fractures, it wasn't life threatening. He truly liked the horse, even hoped to make some arrangement with Jeff to breed one of his own mares with Fury sometime in the future. He had mentioned it to Charlie a couple of weeks ago.

The ambulance slowed as it approached the receiving barn, where the Laredo Race Track Veterinarian would examine him. Sonny's cell phone vibrated. He slipped the phone from his pants pocket, saw his brother-in-law's number and tapped the talk icon. Sunny sent a quick text message to Angie: *Hope Nordstrom came back okay. Not sure of Fury's status. Will advise. See you soon.*

He pressed the send key

"Sonny," Charlie bellowed. "I was watching the races and saw you on my screen. Why didn't you tell me you were coming to Laredo? How's the horse?"

"His leg is sliced, but I think he'll be fine," Sonny assured his brother-in-law. "Jeff Frazier had some trouble earlier and was needed at home. It left him shorthanded for the race, so I rode up with Carl."

"Do you have time to join me for dinner?"

"No, not tonight, but thanks, anyway," Sonny declined. "I'm in the van now, getting ready to unload Fury, then I expect we'll be tied up most of the evening."

"If there's anything I can do to help, let me know." Charlie offered.

"I'll do that. I've got to run." Sonny tapped his phone's screen to end Charlie's call.

Sonny waited until the ambulance doors opened before unhooking the cross ties and backing the injured Fury out. He led the colt to the clean stall and then settled in to wait for Santos and the vet. He gave Jeff a quick call.

"Hey, Jeff. I just wanted to let you know that Fury is putting weight on all four legs. He doesn't seem to be in any distress. We just got to the stall, and he's interested in his hay. We're waiting for the doc now, and one of us will call as soon as we know anything."

"Thanks, Sonny. I appreciate what you guys are doing down there. Natalie, Sarah and I are on the road, going back home," Jeff told him. "If the vet thinks Fury is okay to travel, Santos will haul him back tonight rather than tomorrow. It makes a long day for you, but if I can get him back here, I'd prefer that Leo take care of him."

Sonny's stomach did a flip. He thought they'd be leaving in the morning and had been looking forward to spending the night elsewhere. It hadn't occurred to him that they could go home today.

Though his mind was saying, *"no way am I coming home this evening,"* he told Jeff, "Whatever is best for Fury."

"How is he?" Carl appeared so abruptly, Sonny dropped his cell phone.

Still a bit startled, Sonny rescued his phone, said, "Goodbye," to Jeff and tapped off the call.

"We just got here and I'm waiting for the vet now," Sonny replied, as Santos and a man Sonny recognized to be veterinarian Dr. Daniel Evans approached them.

They made quick introductions before Dr. Evans began talking quietly to Fury, gently opening the door to the stall, Santos trailing him. Santos hooked a lead rope to Fury's halter. The vet removed the inflated split and winced at the sight of the slash above the colt's foot. "I think the best thing to do is transport him to the clinic and get some x-rays, the sooner the better," he said. "I'd like to get that cut stitched up, too. If the x-rays come back negative, you'll want to get the farrier to trim the hoof, maybe put a patch on it."

"Would it be possible to ship Fury back home this evening?" Santos asked for Jeff.

The doctor released a soft whistle. "Possible, yes, but practical, no. Judging from the way this colt stands and his demeanor, there's an excellent chance there is no fracture, but there's still a chance that there is. I wouldn't want to have him shipped any distance until we know."

"Okay," Santos agreed. "Can you help us arrange his transport to the clinic?"

"Sure can." The vet stood. "I'm on call there tonight anyway, so I'll go along with him and follow up on the x-rays."

"Can I go along and stay with him?" Santos requested.

"I can't see why not," Dr. Evans replied.

"Sonny, you and Carl might as well go get some dinner," Santos suggested. "I'll stay with Fury and call as soon as we know his status."

Happy he'd be staying in Laredo for the night, after all, Sonny cheerfully said, "I'll get everything ready so we can leave as soon as Fury's able. Maybe the x-rays will be good and he'll be okay to leave first thing in the morning."

"I'll keep everybody posted," Santos promised. "If you don't have any plans, Carl, I'll need a ride back to the hotel later."

Carl chuckled. "My only plans are waiting to hear about Fury and then getting you back tonight to help me get the trailer ready to roll."

Carl and Sonny went back to the motel with minimal conversation, each lost in his own thoughts about the day's happenings.

When they got to the lobby, Carl broke the silence. "Something is awfully strange about this complete mess."

Sonny nodded. "I know what you're saying. Why would anyone go after Natalie like that?"

"I don't just mean snatching Natalie," Carl explained. "I mean the entire thing. First some lug tries to take Fury in the early morning hours of a race day. The horse thief sounds like somebody familiar with the barn, based on what Santos said. Then,

Natalie disappears on her way to meet me again on a race day, because of a ruse by someone, who not only knew when she was on her way to the barn but also who her vet is and the model truck he drives."

"None of that information is secret," Sonny said. "Anybody who spent a little time around Angelina could have gotten that information."

"You're right, but there's more Sonny. Look at the complete picture. Jeff told me that Anthony McCoy sent Marty over to the barn this morning to help. How the heck would Mr. McCoy know about what happened quickly enough to know that all of Jeff's help was out of town or on the road? I know Anthony is always one of the first to help out, and I don't mean to detract from that, but my question is, how did he know so quickly? Then today, when Nordstrom cut over and banged into Fury, it was almost like Angie cut in on purpose. I've ridden against her many times. Angie is a good jockey, but think about it. Nordstrom is her father's horse. Angelina Jane McCoy has more than a professional interest in knocking Fury out of the competition. I'm seeing a pattern. Now, maybe it's just coincidence, but I don't like it."

Sonny's palms began to sweat, and he felt his pulse speed up. He had been the one who indirectly got the information to Anthony McCoy. "I was all over the backside of the track, asking about Natalie and telling people to let me know if they saw her," he confessed to Carl. "I'm sure I must have talked to Marty, and he likely told Mr. McCoy. As for the barn being short on staff, everyone at Angelina knew that Fury was going to Laredo."

"You might be right." Carl conceded. "But something just doesn't feel right."

The men paid for their meals and tipped their waitress. Outside, Carl told Sonny, "A bunch of the horseman are staying at the hotel tonight and said they'll be getting together at Sprinter's Bar. I'm going to meet them there and wait to hear from Santos. Are you coming along?"

"No," Sonny quickly answered. "I'm pretty well shot. I think I'll head upstairs and watch a little television and go to bed early."

Carl shrugged. "Okay. I figure we can get together for breakfast around 6:00 and then get on the road, if the vet clears Fury to travel."

"Works for me," Sonny told him. "See you in the morning."

Carl went to his truck, opened the door and climbed in. Sonny impatiently waited the couple of more minutes it took Carl to slam the truck's door closed and start its engine and finally drive away into the night.

Sonny went to his room and immediately keyed Angie's number.

"Hey, Baby," she answered.

"What room are you in?" he asked.

"Room 721. I'll prop the door open for you."

"I can be there in about ten minutes, unless you'd rather I shower here first," he said.

Angie giggled. "I'll meet you in my shower in ten minutes. Don't be late." She ended the call.

The thought of Angelina, waiting for him in a steaming hot shower, went straight to Sonny's groin.

He was certain neither he nor she would get much sleep tonight.

Sonny took a quick shower, anyway. While he shaved, he couldn't help thinking about Carl's suspicions, wondering if Carl knew more than he'd let on. Though it wasn't a secret that Natalie had been missing, he wouldn't want anybody to know he and Angie McCoy had spoken that morning. Actually, they had done more than speak.

When Jeff asked if Sonny could help him in Laredo, Sonny had jumped at the chance. He knew Angie would be in Laredo and it would give them an unplanned night together. Sonny had called Angie before he'd called his wife.

Sonny pulled on a clean shirt and hurried out of his hotel room, on his way to paradise.

27

Angie McCoy was delighted when Sonny called her earlier that morning to tell her that he could spend the night in Laredo. She would find a lot to keep him occupied when they had an entire night together. She wondered how many Frazier secrets she could pump out of Sonny before sunrise.

She was sorry Fury hurt his leg, particularly because what she did penalized her father's horse from first to third place. Anthony McCoy didn't need the income, but she could see a Horse-of-the-Year award slipping away.

But when Fury hit the rail, it created a need for him to go to the clinic. That allowed Sonny to get away early, so overall, the colt's injury was to her benefit. Besides, Fury was likely out of commission for a while, no threat in the race next month. Nordstrom would win and become the top money earner. The Million Dollar Derby would be hers.

Though others might consider some of her racetrack tactics inappropriate, even illegal, Angie felt no guilt over using them. Her way of thinking was that the end justified the means. Collateral damage didn't matter. With a knack for turning on an apologetic, wide-eyed, innocent demeanor, she had overcome a variety of objections against her over the years. It wasn't often that her act failed. It was unfortunate that today could be one of those times. She hoped that she didn't get slapped with a fine and suspension.

Angie undressed and slipped into the fluffy terry robe that hung on the bathroom door. She called room service and ordered a bottle of champagne, two glasses, and a fruit and cheese tray. They told her that they would deliver the order in about forty-five minutes.

She unlocked her hotel room's door and braced it open with the safety bar. Then she scooted to the bathroom, slipped out of her robe and was just stepping into the shower when she heard a knock on the door.

"Angie?" The splashes of water spraying from the oversized showerhead muffled his voice.

"In the shower," she called.

"Your door was wide open," he said and locked the door before walking to the bathroom

"As I promised." She called. "You must have missed me, sweetheart. You said ten minutes, and it hasn't even been two. Make sure you shut that door. We can start this party in the shower before we move it to the bedroom."

Angie turned to pose for her guest, expecting to see Sonny. She froze when she saw who was standing there.

"What are you doing here?" she demanded.

"It's time for us to have a talk. He—and I know who he is—will have to wait outside."

The man glanced at his watch. "It won't take long to say everything I came here to tell you."

"Get out," she ordered.

Angie shut the water off and grabbed a towel. "You failed me twice now and made everything worse. Now get out or I'll scream rape."

She wrapped the towel around her body and stepped onto the wet tiled floor. As she reached for her robe, she lost her balance and fell sideways. Her head hit the edge of the shower door's frame. She heard the thud before being blinded by a white flash. Pain exploded under her temple and the room went black.

Tonight he had intended to tell Angie that he was finished with her nonsense. She was becoming less and less cautious. Her mischiefs had ballooned into criminal behavior. Blackmail became her preferred means of getting him to do what she wanted, and he was done with it.

If jail looked like a good bet for her, and eventually it would, she'd be fingering all her accomplices, including him, to save her own skin. He planned to get away from her before that happened.

He thought about the number of times he had caressed the exquisite body lying at his feet. The water glistened on her smooth, firm muscles and the tension that distorted her face only a minute ago had disappeared. She looked like a sleeping angel, but looks were deceiving. Angie was no angel.

She knew how to use her flawless body to get what she wanted, and had rewarded him more than once with one of her sensual exhibitions.

As he gazed at the unconscious body at his feet, he realized he had finally come to hate her, almost as much as he hated himself, after what he had done for her.

Angie's antics in that afternoon's race weren't the first that had risked injury to an animal or a person to achieve a goal. Though Angelina Jane McCoy was a top-notch jockey, her career was not without scandal.

Last year officials questioned her about a small amount of tranquilizer found in a rival horse, one that she had been alone with, just before the race. While nothing came of the episode, competing trainers watched her more closely for a few months after that. Although she was involved in more objections than the average jockey, the racing stewards suspended her only twice for racetrack fouls. Angie had a way of pleading innocence that allowed her to win most of the objections called against her.

Most trainers would have shied away from a jockey with her character, yet they didn't. She was a winner, her father known for his outstanding horsemanship and impeccable character and her mother, an equestrian icon. Unlike her father, who believed in hard work and fair play, Angie was out to win no matter what the cost. If not for Anthony McCoy's stellar reputation and vast influence, Angie's career might have ended long ago.

Though she was a beautiful woman, a talented horseman and a fierce competitor, Angie was also a ruthless, arduous and spoiled brat who let nothing and no one stand in the way of what she wanted. He knew that if it was to her benefit, she would even twist the facts to pin some of her crimes on him.

That was Angie. In their past escapades, none that he was proud of, he had taken all the risk. She called the shots, but was always far removed from the acts, with an unimpeachable alibi. Sometimes she paid her henchmen in cash, sometimes in sex. If they balked or strayed too far, she blackmailed them.

Yes, that was Angie. She was dangerous. Throughout the years he'd known her, he'd witnessed the path of destruction she always left behind. She had destroyed more than one man. She would destroy him, too. It was time to end it.

A.J. McCoy would no longer control him. He used to be one of the good guys. That was before Angie. For a few seconds longer, he stared down at the beautiful jockey, and then decided.

He pulled the vial from his pocket: Butazolidin, an anti-inflammatory drug he used routinely around the racetrack, and periodically for his own pain management. He always had the drug with him when on the road. This trip was no exception.

Filling a syringe with enough of the liquid to overdose a horse, he injected the drug into her thigh. An overdose of Butazolidin would drop her blood pressure and ultimately stop her heart. He wanted to be sure her heart stopped forever.

The man wrapped the syringe in tissues and, using a washcloth to avoid leaving fingerprints, depressed the handle, and dropped the syringe down into the swirling toilet bowl. He slipped the vial back in his pocket. He didn't notice the ugly black bruise that was developing at the injection site.

Though she wouldn't have agreed with what he'd done, only because she was the victim this time, he was confident Angie would have understood why he did it. *The end justifies the means;* he'd heard her say it so often.

He left the shower running, and then wrapped the television's remote in the washcloth, before he pressed the power button to turn the television on and raise the volume. After he walked out of the hotel room, he wiped both ends of the doorknob, pulled the door closed behind him, and put the washcloth in his pocket.

He was sure no one had seen him go into Angie's room, and a quick scan of the hallway convinced him there was nobody to see him now. The hotel had no security cameras in the hallway, so the man felt confident in his escape.

He was walking toward the exit that lead to the stairway when a young housekeeper came around the corner with an armful of towels. He smiled and said, "Good evening," hoping the delivery wasn't for Angie. The man breathed a sigh of relief when the housekeeper continued down the hall past room 721.

28

Sonny opened the door of his hotel room and looked out into the hall. No one was there. He eased his door closed and hurried toward the stairs.

"Hey, Sonny, how's your horse doing?"

"Damn," Sonny muttered under his breath when he recognized Doug Whiteman's voice. *Doug, one of the older jockey's, had ridden BaskervillesBobby that day.* "Hi Doug. Fury is at the clinic now and I'm waiting for a call from Santos."

"Man, I don't know how Carl stayed on that colt," Doug said. "I thought he would fly right over Fury's head. Does Doc think there's a fracture?"

"There's a nasty gash on the front pastern, but no obvious fractures. Jeff wants x-rays and an MRI. We're hoping to get an all clear to ship him back home tomorrow, but we won't know until they run all the tests." Sonny started to turn away, but Doug casually placed a friendly hand on his shoulder.

"Glad to hear you're expecting good news," the jockey said. Though Sonny wanted to get away from Doug as soon as he could, he felt obligated to continue the conversation.

"I appreciate that," Sonny replied. "Bobby ran a good race today. He flew through that first mile."

"Thanks," Bobby's jockey said. "He's a nice colt, but I think a mile is his limit. He always gives everything, but he got beat fair and square today. Fury sure is looking like a monster. I hope there's no permanent damage. Did you talk to A.J. after the race? I don't know what the hell she was thinking with that right-handed whip."

"No, I was planning on looking her up later. I guess she'll be down in the bar. I have to go."

"I just saw your brother-in-law a few minutes ago. I'm heading down to join him and some of the other guys at the bar. Can I buy you a drink?" Doug offered.

"Thanks," Sonny said, "but I've got a few more calls to make, then I might need to go back to the clinic and get Santos. He stayed there with Fury."

"I understand," Doug told him, "but if you change your mind, come on down."

Sonny patted Doug's arm. "Thanks again, Doug. If I don't see you later tonight, we'll catch up back at Angelina."

When Doug strolled toward the elevator, Sonny turned back and ambled toward his hotel room. He fumbled with his key and was opening the door to his room, then heard the chime of the elevator. He listened for the elevator doors to close, and when they did, he pulled his door shut and bolted down the hall to the stairway. He raced up the four flights to room 721.

Breathless, but not from running up the stairs, Sonny was anticipating an exquisite night of erotic games with his gorgeous playmate. He buttoned his shirt as he hurried from the 7th floor exit door to Angie's room, but was surprised to find the door locked.

Sonny checked the number on the door. He was at the right place. He knocked. There was no response.

She must be in the shower, he thought, cursing Doug Whiteman for delaying him. He knocked again and placed his ear to the door. He heard the television.

Thinking that the television might be too loud for her to hear his knocking, Sonny dialed Angie's cell phone. He heard it ring from inside her hotel room, but the call went to voice mail. He dialed the number again with the same result. Desperate, he left a voice message, "Hey, Baby, I'm at the door. Open up."

Again, he knocked on the door. He was sure Angie wouldn't have forgotten to leave it open. Maybe a hotel employee had noticed the door was ajar and closed it, thinking that she had accidentally left it open.

"Heaven save us from good Samaritans," he murmured.

Sonny dialed Angie's cell phone number again. She still didn't answer. Frustrated, he ran to the exit door and back down the stairs to his room, where he picked up the hotel telephone and dialed Angie's room number. When the recording asked him to leave a message, he pleaded, "What's going on? Call me. I'm going crazy here."

Sonny expected a call back momentarily. Surely she had heard her cell phone and then her room phone ringing. Angie had a bit of a temper, but even if she was annoyed that he was late, she would understand when she realized that her locked door added to the problem. He wished he hadn't taken time to shower, but body odor and Angie didn't mix. It didn't matter that they would be in the shower together moments after he arrived. Grinning in anticipation, Sonny opened the mini refrigerator, found a light beer, and popped the top. He sat down and waited for his lovely mistress to call.

It didn't take Sonny long to finish the can of beer, still waiting for the call that didn't come. Twenty minutes had passed. He dialed her room again, but hung up when the call went to the hotel answering service. Angie surely would be out of the shower by now. When they spoke earlier, she sounded eager enough to see him. So far, their affair comprised slow, lingering kisses and fast, electrifying sex, with some heavy teasing now and then. Tonight they would have hours of uninterrupted time to fill in any way they chose. He was sure she was looking forward to it as much as he was.

But the woman was as moody as she was seductive. Maybe she was punishing him for being late. This wouldn't be the first time Angie changed her mind, or changed the rules to make a point.

His cell phone rang. Expecting to see Angie's number, but it was Santos calling.

Santos sounded tired. "Doc says the x-rays show a condylar fracture, but it's not displaced. He says Fury should recover completely, but it will take a little time. He'll be off the racetrack for six to eight weeks, and then, if his leg looks good, he can start working slowly to get back into shape. There's no way he'll be healthy in time to race in Kentucky."

Sonny felt like he'd been double-kicked. "Does Jeff know yet?"

"Yes," Santos said. "I just got off the phone with him. He's probably breaking it to Natalie now. Is Carl with you?"

"No. Carl went to hang out downstairs. I wasn't feeling well and came up to my room, planning to try to get some sleep. Are you coming back to the hotel tonight, or staying at the clinic?"

"I'm coming back if Carl picks me up," Santos replied. "Fury is doing okay, and they agreed to keep him here overnight. That will be easier on him than vanning him back to Laredo for the night. We can get him early in the morning and drive back to Angelina from the clinic."

"Okay," Sonny said. "Do you want me to go see if I can find Carl?"

"No need. I'll call him. Do you want to meet for breakfast?"

Sonny would rather have spent every minute with Angie, but knew it would raise some eyebrows if he refused. It looked like he was spending the night alone, anyway. "Carl and I are planning to meet in the morning about six o'clock in the café downstairs. Will that work for you?"

"That's good," Santos agreed. "See you then."

Sonny opened another beer and thought about that cold-hearted, hot-blooded, sexy, blonde jockey. She was a lot of fun, and Sonny enjoyed their time together. On the other hand, she was self-centered and demanding. Angie felt that she had the right to do anything that she wanted to do anytime she wanted to do it, and the end justified the means. Today, however, her means to an end by hurting Fury was just plain wicked.

The more he thought about Angie standing him up, the more Sonny figured that maybe it was for the best. He decided Angie was only a distraction, albeit a sexy distraction, but she was never worth destroying his marriage for. He loved Vanessa, but if he kept playing games with Angie, it was only a matter of time before word of their affair got out. Now was as good a time as any to put an end to the affair. He finished his beer and decided to get some sleep.

29

Throughout the short drive home, Jeff, Natalie and Sarah tried to be hopeful as they all struggled to come down from the emotional roller coaster ride the day had delivered.

"I would rather have had Fury run last than have him injured today," Jeff said. "His tenacity in that race was remarkable. If A.J. hadn't cut in toward the rail, Fury would've surged past Nordstrom and won the race by three-quarters of a length."

"I was thinking the same thing," Natalie said, "He is a very special colt."

"What will happen to him now?" Sarah asked. "Will you keep him at the barn with the other horses or turn him out?"

Jeff's tone turned grim. "I'll keep him in the barn for a week or two and walk him every day. If his leg heals the way the vet expects, we might turn him out for a few weeks; let him be a lazy pet for a while. Then, we can decide whether we want to continue to race him."

"Do you think he'll be the same after he heals?" Sarah asked.

"I hope so. A condylar fracture is a common injury. Although it is serious, in Fury's case it's more like a crack than a two-piece break. It could have easily gone unnoticed but for the x-rays. The bone should mend and has an excellent chance to be as strong as before. We just need to be sure it has the time to heal. The way Fury hit that rail, I was afraid that he would have suffered a career-ending injury. I'm thankful that it wasn't worse." Jeff pulled into the Frazier driveway.

Natalie rested her right hand on Sarah's left. "Maybe that amber falcon protected him. As long as there are no complications, Fury should be ready to get back into training in a few months."

"I'm so sorry that he'll miss the big race," Sarah said.

"There's always next year," Jeff replied. "Flight looks outstanding these days, and if she's got her brother's heart, she just might prove to be a competitor herself. And just because Fury might not be able to run in the Million Dollar Derby doesn't mean he won't be able to run in the second or third leg of the Triple Million Series. As long as he heals the way he should, he will. Fury's racing career isn't over."

"I hope you are planning to stay tonight, Sarah," Natalie offered.

"Yes, thanks," Sarah accepted. "I'm drained, but I wouldn't mind seeing Fury before I leave tomorrow, if the guys get back early enough."

"And Carl?" Natalie teased.

"And Carl," Sarah admitted with a tired smile.

As the three walked toward the house, Jeff looked at his wife. "Much as I hate to take my eyes off of you, I'd feel a lot better going back to the barn to check on the horses and make sure it's locked up tight. Will you be okay with Sarah for half an hour?"

"I'll make sure we lock the house up tight, before we turn in," Sarah promised. "We'll be fine."

Natalie rubbed her husband's lower back. "I'm exhausted. I'll probably be asleep before you get back." She predicted. Yet her exhaustion wasn't enough to mute the memory of her long-deceased grandmother's oft-said foreboding of unwelcome news always coming in threes.

30

The gigantic window, with its eastern exposure, allowed the morning to invade the guest room at Natalie's house. When Sarah opened her eyes, she was pleased to see the cloudless blue sky. The view reminded her why so many people loved California.

Although it seemed like she had just gone to bed, Sarah slid out of the bed alert and full of energy. The house was quiet, so she presumed Jeff and Natalie were at the barn. She was looking forward to some coffee and an hour with the horses before she made the trip back home.

After a quick shower, Sarah dressed and, with her hair still wet, hurried to the kitchen. It didn't surprise her to find a pot of coffee waiting in a thermal carafe and a note from Natalie:

Sarah, morning person who you are not, I just couldn't wake you before we left. Jeff and I will grab some breakfast, then take care of the horses, and wait for the guys and Fury. We expect them about 11:30. There are muffins on the counter. Call when you get up, or just come to the barn. Love you, Nat.

Sarah smiled, poured a cup of coffee and snatched a blueberry muffin from those grouped on a plate beside the carafe. She reached for her phone.

"Good morning, Sarah," Natalie responded.

"Good morning, Nat. Can you guys use an extra hand at the barn?"

"Always." Natalie said. "I didn't want to wake you, so you missed breakfast. Are you coming out?"

"I think I will. I want to go back home this afternoon, but I'd like to see all my two and four-legged friends before I take off." Sarah replied.

"Santos called," Natalie said. "They got Fury loaded in the trailer, with the vet's blessing. Carl is driving, Sonny is navigating and Santos is worrying about Fury. They expect to get here about 11:00 or 11:30."

Sarah chuckled. "With Carl's lead foot, I'd bet on them arriving closer to 10:30 or 11:00. See you in about 15 minutes."

Sarah got her things together, refilled her coffee cup, locked the door on the way out and climbed into her car. Relieved yesterday's disaster was behind her, Sarah sensed more problems might still lurk. Something didn't feel right. She couldn't explain what or why; she felt like another shoe was about to drop.

The drive to the track took less than ten minutes. The guard motioned her through to the backside lot. Sarah waved her thanks, noticing that there didn't seem to be a lot of activity for that time of the morning. The morning workouts were complete and there were no races scheduled.

Sarah spotted Natalie halfway between the parking lot and the barn strolling toward her. Natalie gave her friend a hug and a broad smile. "Well, Sleeping Beauty, are you ready to see the starlet of Barn Seventeen? She's waiting for you."

"I'm most definitely ready to see the starlet of Barn Seventeen," Sarah said, reaching into her purse. "I promised her peppermints and have enough for the whole barn."

The two friends walked into the barn. Flight stood with her head over the stall gate, ears up, neck arched. She nickered expectantly. Jeff passed a couple of carrots to Sarah, who carefully broke them into smaller pieces and gave them, one at a time, to the gentle filly, followed by peppermints for dessert.

"Have you heard anything from the police?" she asked Jeff warily.

"Yes," Jeff replied. "Ray called this morning and said they'd finished going over the truck and found a couple of prints. One was behind the rear-view mirror and another on the seat belt snap. One is a good clear print and the other a partial. The rest of the truck appears to have been wiped almost clean. They don't know whose prints they've found, but they have our fingerprints from the racing licensing office, so they'll be able to eliminate Natalie and me. We can pick the truck up tomorrow."

"That's a positive report. I'm surprised they could check over the truck that quickly." Sarah said. "What about the farmhouse and the barn? Did they locate it?"

"They did." Jeff told her. "It is an abandoned farm, near Andrade, east of Yuma and just off the reservation. An older man, Sam Benjamin, owns the property. He used to have horses and some cattle, but he moved away some years ago. The State Police are trying to locate him now. According to the local Sheriff, no one has lived there for the last twelve years that he knows of, but he pays the taxes."

"They're canvassing the area now," Jeff continued. "The barn on the Benjamin property had fresh straw in one of the stalls, along with some pieces of duct tape, proving Natalie was telling the truth and was in there. Savage said he'd keep us in the loop, but emphasized that it's still early in the investigation."

Sarah clasped Natalie's hands. "Do you think you're going to have problems being alone after what happened to you? It would probably be natural for you to feel uneasy."

Natalie stepped away to pet Flight's neck. "I don't think I'll have a problem. If I hadn't been so trusting and focused on Fury's race, they wouldn't have been able to get to me. As it was, whoever is responsible knows enough about me that they could put a convincing story together. I won't take anything at face value anymore. This has taught me to be more cautious, and much less trusting."

Natalie reached into her pocket and pulled out a fresh battery pack. "Before Jeff would get me anything to eat this morning, he made me plug my phone into the charger and swear that I would never let the battery run down again. Then he left here early enough so he could be at the electronics store when it opened at 9:00. He bought two battery packs and said he would be sure he charged one every night, so all I had to do was pick it up on my way out the door. I had to promise not only to keep my phone charged, but to always have an extra battery with me anytime I'm away from home."

Sarah folded her arms and narrowed her eyes in her familiar manner when mocking her friend's carelessness. "You realize that now you'll never have an excuse not to answer your phone again—ever!"

31

"We should be home within half an hour," Carl said as they passed the road sign that alerted the exit to Angelina Race Track was twenty miles away.

"Fury has probably handled this whole debacle better than any of us," Santos bragged. "Between the stitches on his leg and the stall changes, I expected to see some signs of stress. But he hasn't quit eating and his leg doesn't seem to bother him at all."

"Those trailer trips around the grounds were worth the aggravation," Sonny said. "When we got him this morning, he didn't act any differently than when we loaded him up at Angelina."

Santos needed more assurances. "Since Fury got hurt in his first race away from his home track, do you think he'll remember and spook at races away from Angelina?"

"I'm not sure if Fury will associate the injury with the racetrack," Sonny replied. "He doesn't seem to think it has anything to do with the trailer, and he was fine when they put him in the van to take him off the track. All we can do is get him healed up and fit and try it again."

"Sonny, how much experience do you have with horses who have suffered a condylar fracture like Fury's?" Carl asked.

"A fair amount," Sonny said. "If it is a displaced fracture, the recovery time is longer, but even then a full recovery is typical. In Fury's case, the fracture is non-displaced, and the colt is sensible, not a crazy horse who you'd expect to aggravate the injury. I'm confident that Fury will recover completely within 90 days."

"I've seen a couple of fractures like that one. I don't have nearly as much experience, but from what I have seen, I agree with Sonny," Santos added.

Carl's cell phone rang. He recognized Doug Whiteman's number and answered, "Hey, Doug, what's up?"

"Carl, I wanted to let you know that they took A.J. to the hospital by ambulance a few hours ago," Doug told him. "Her father expected her to meet him this morning, and when she didn't show up, he became concerned. Long story short, he got approval for the hotel security people to go into her room. They found her unresponsive on the bathroom floor, with the shower running. It sounds like she fractured her skull."

"Oh, wow. Is she going to be okay?" Carl asked.

"I don't know," Doug said. "From what I've heard, it doesn't look good. The police have been talking to a few horsemen at the hotel, but most everyone was on the road earlier this morning. It's pretty clear that they have an investigation going on. The police just got done questioning me, and they asked if I knew where to find a couple of trainers and the jockeys who rode against her in the races yesterday. That's why I'm calling. I just wanted to give you a heads up."

"Are you telling me that the police think someone attacked her?" Carl stammered.

Doug said, "I'm not positive, but from what they were asking me, I think that's something they are considering. They asked about the race and had questions about the steward's inquiry and your objection. Then they wanted to know where I was yesterday after the last race and where I was early this morning."

Carl steered the truck onto the exit to Angelina Race Track.

"The last I saw A.J. was in the lobby at the hotel," Doug continued. "That was about 6:00 yesterday evening. In fact, I saw Sonny in the hall not too long after that, so they might look for him to verify the time that we talked."

Carl was grateful to his friend for the information. "I imagine my objection in the Sapphire will send the cops my way soon."

"I'm hearing backside chatter that a lot of the horsemen think that Angie cut Fury off intentionally." Doug said. "How's he doing?"

"It's a condylar fracture, non-displaced. We expect him to be back in training in a couple of months," Carl told him.

"Thank goodness it isn't a career ending injury. He's a nice colt. I'll see you back at Angelina."

"Thanks, Doug. We're about thirty minutes away from the barn, maybe a little less. Are you on the road yet?"

"Yes, I'm riding with Jerry. We're taking a couple of days off and heading for the beach," Doug replied.

Jerry was an apprentice jockey Doug had been mentoring, Carl remembered. "The beach sounds great! Have a splendid time, and don't get Jerry in any trouble," Carl joked. "Thanks again for the heads up."

Since they had heard only Carl's side of the conversation, Sonny and Santos were both looking at him expectantly. When Carl had mentioned the objection, Sonny had a feeling of dread, and that the "her" who someone attacked was Angie.

"What's going on, Carl?" Sonny implored.

Carl slid his phone into his shirt pocket. "That was Doug. Angie didn't meet her dad for breakfast and when he called her, she didn't answer her phone, Anthony got the hotel security staff to let him into her room. They found her on the floor of the bathroom. The shower was on, so, I guess, she must have been getting ready to go to breakfast and fell. They took her to the hospital. Nobody knows how she is, though."

Santos was first to respond. "Damn lucky thing her father was there to get some help. Who knows how long she could have been laying there."

"According to Doug, the police are talking to everybody they can find who had any contact with her yesterday or this morning," Carl revealed. "Doug said they want to talk to all the jockeys and the trainers, among others."

"If she fell in the bathroom and the shower was on, why do the police think it wasn't an accident?" Sonny demanded.

"I don't know," Carl said, shaking his head. "I think it's strange that they would talk to all these people, unless they have a reason to think she had some help to get knocked out. Oh, and Sonny, Doug said he saw you in the hall a little while after he'd seen Angie in the lobby. He said to let you know the police would probably call you, too."

"Okay, thanks." Sonny answered, thinking, *if I hadn't run into Doug, I wonder if I could have prevented what happened–accident or not? Could she have been lying there all night?*

Santos looked blankly at his thick fingers. "I think there's more to this than we're hearing."

"If the police think it wasn't an accident, they must have some reason," Sonny murmured. *Like my voice, and probably my room number, when I left messages for her last night,* he thought. Suddenly light-headed, he fought against the nausea that came quickly after.

Sonny knew a lot of race people who didn't think much of Angie, even despised her. But he couldn't think of a single person who would physically do her harm. His fingerprints had to be on her door. Absent evidence that pointed to someone else, Sonny was afraid he could soon become a suspect in her assault.

Sonny's cellphone vibrated. It was his brother-in-law. "Yeah, Charlie, what's up?"

Without greeting, Charlie demanded, "Did you or Santos spend any time with Angie after the race yesterday?"

The nausea Sonny was fighting morphed into something like an iron fist trying to push its way through his abdomen. "No. We were busy getting things arranged for Fury," he replied, then followed with a tentative, "why?"

"Her father found her this morning, when she didn't show up for breakfast. They called an ambulance and took her to Laredo General. The police are questioning everyone who knew her." Charlie paused. "There's no simple way to say this, Sonny. Angie's dead."

Sonny only then realized he had been holding his breath. "What? How?"

"All I know is that they found her this morning. The word is that she fell and hit her head on the edge of the shower stall. They took her to the hospital, and they pronounced her dead on arrival. They don't know the cause of death, but her father agreed to an autopsy, so I guess we'll find out soon enough."

Tears filled Sonny's eyes. He wasn't sure if they were for Angie or for himself. "Yeah, I guess we will," he stammered. "Let me know if you hear any more details."

Santos had watched the color drain from Sonny's face. The tears alarmed him more. "Are you alright, pal?"

Sonny nodded quickly. Santos didn't press him. Carl kept his eyes on the road and his mouth shut.

A minute or two passed before Sonny could say, "That was my brother-in-law. He called to tell me Angie is dead."

32

When Carl pulled up with the horse trailer, Natalie was the first one out the barn door, with Sarah right behind her and Jeff bringing up the rear. As soon as Carl had the truck parked and the ignition turned off, Natalie hurried to the back of the trailer and unlocked the latch.

Santos jumped out of the truck and scurried to help Natalie and Jeff unload Fury.

Carl strutted toward Sarah and, without saying a word, lowered her face to his and kissed her with a passion that truly shocked her. She returned his kiss, giving as much as he gave, sensing more in his uncharacteristic display of emotion than his kisses could tell her.

Natalie was oblivious to everything and everyone except Fury. She opened the door to the trailer and jumped inside before Santos had time to pull the ramp down. She whispered to the grey colt, and Fury dropped his head and began nuzzling her.

Grinning, Jeff shook his head and said, “She isn’t even that happy to see me after a week away.”

Santos smiled, but his eyes reflected sadness.

Jeff hopped into the trailer and unhooked the cross ties, so that he could back Fury out of the trailer. While he had confidence in the vets at the clinic in Laredo, he was eager to examine Fury’s foot himself, and also to get the x-rays to Leo for a second opinion.

When Fury stepped onto the ground, he pricked his ears at the sounds from inside the barn of Flight’s whinnying and pawing at the ground of her stall. He nickered his sister back and would have bolted for the barn had Jeff not had a good hold on his halter.

Santos hooked the lead rope, and said, "I'll take him in a couple of circles. See what you think."

Jeff nodded, watching the colt walk. He could see a very slight hitch in the front, but was pleased Fury was using his leg without an obvious limp. "Thanks, Santos. His stall is ready. Would you take him in for me?"

"Sure," Santos replied. He walked Fury through the barn to his stall and locked the latch. When he realized Sonny hadn't followed, he went back to the truck and found Sonny was still sitting in the cab, his head in his hands. There were rumors on the backside that Sonny and Angie had something going, and his friend's reaction confirmed them.

"Hey, Sonny," Santos asked quietly, "Would it help to talk?"

Sonny shook his head and said, "I just can't believe she's gone."

"Angie was a hell of a jockey," Santos replied, "and I know from experience, she was one tough lady. Horse racing was her life. We will miss her."

Sonny slid over to the door and shifted out of the truck. "I guess I better head on home."

Santos nodded again. "I'll fill Jeff in. I'm planning to stay at the barn overnight. If you decide not to ride in the morning, just call me. I'll cover it."

"Thanks, Santos. I'll be okay in the morning."

Santos watched Sonny walk away. The groom had thought it was strange last night when Carl went to pick him up at the clinic and Sonny wasn't with him, even though Carl had explained that Sonny said he was tired and was going to bed early. That sure wasn't typical behavior for their party loving friend.

Santos couldn't help wondering if his friend knew more about A.J. McCoy than he was saying. He hoped Sonny really had spent the night in his own hotel room, but his gut sensed something different.

Jeff came around the back of the truck, but Santos gestured for him to stop. Jeff looked questioningly at Santos.

"We were on the way home when Sonny's brother-in-law called and told him that there was an accident at the hotel this morning," Santos explained. "They found Angie McCoy on the floor in her hotel room. Her father had security open the door when she didn't show up for breakfast. Apparently, she fell and hit her head. They took her to the hospital, but, on the way here, Charlie said she was DOA. The news hit Sonny kind of hard."

"How terrible," Jeff exclaimed. "No wonder he's upset. Their families have been friends for generations."

Santos nodded quickly. "I told him I could take care of things in the morning if he isn't up to coming in. Since I'm planning on spending the night here, it won't be any problem for me to gallop a couple of extra horses in the morning. I didn't think you'd mind. Sonny's pretty shaken up."

"You were right to make the offer, and I appreciate it," Jeff told his groom. "Meanwhile, I'm sure there will be more news coming, along with rumors, gossip and conjecture. On the heels of Natalie's kidnapping, it could raise a lot of questions, not only about whether the recent events, but about the overall safety of the horsemen. I guess we'd better break the news to the girls."

The two men trudged back to the barn where Carl and Sarah stood holding hands next to Natalie; all three watching Fury attacking his food bucket.

"I hate to put a damper on this party, but there's something you need to know," Jeff began. "Angie McCoy had an accident at the hotel in Laredo early this morning."

When Natalie saw the grimness all over her husband's face, she wanted to recoil from hearing what would be more grim news. Sarah looked at Carl; saw the pain in his eyes.

"Apparently she fell and hit her head. They couldn't save her."

Natalie's eyes filled with tears. Though she and Angie were not close, Natalie and Jeff had known the McCoy family for over twenty years. They had watched Angie grow up and become an accomplished, though sometimes controversial, thoroughbred jockey. Stunned, Sarah quickly realized why Angie's death had apparently hit Carl hard. Although they were in competition, sometimes fiercely, the horsemen were a close-knit group. An accident like this affected everyone.

"I can't even imagine what her parents are going through," Natalie said. "Martha must be devastated. Jeff, you need to offer any help they need with the horses. I'll see what I can do to put things in motion and organize a memorial race for Angie. I think that would mean a lot to the McCoys." Angie was Anthony and Martha McCoy's only child, and Natalie knew Martha lived for her daughter.

"I've got to get on the road, if I want to make it back before dark," Sarah said, wanting to just escape all the troubles of the last few days, blaring oldies from her dashboard's radio all the way home.

Carl said, "I'm going home, too. Why don't you follow me? That will give you some company halfway home."

"Thanks, I will," Sarah agreed.

"On second thought, come to my place," Carl suggested. "I'll cook dinner, and I'll throw in breakfast for no extra charge. I have two bedrooms, a housekeeper who keeps the place spotless, and I promise to be a perfect gentleman. You can leave early tomorrow, and that way you won't be driving alone in the dark tonight."

Tilting her head to the side, a slow grin spread over Sarah's face. "Breakfast might be nice," she said.

They shared hugs all around, and then everyone went their separate ways to deal with the tragic news of that day in their own way.

33

While following Carl's truck, Sarah could not stop thinking of the events of the past few days: the kidnapping of Natalie Frazier, Fury injured — likely intentionally by a jockey now dead.

Even more confusing was what to do about Carl. She was actually wary of spending the night in his home. He told her that he had an extra bedroom, but she wondered if she wanted to use it.

She thought back to the last time she had been romantically involved with a man. She had sworn after that it would be the last time. Three years ago, she'd been engaged to David Marsico, the man who had tried to purchase Fury; her former fiancé. She remembered the evening she had gone to a local steakhouse, a favorite of hers and David's.

As she'd followed the maître de to her table, anticipating a quiet dinner alone, she heard a strikingly familiar male voice and glanced to the other side of the restaurant where her fiancé was eating dinner and in deep conversation with a laughing woman. David told her he would be at a board of directors meeting, yet there he sat, in their favorite restaurant, with a woman Sarah recognized to be Angelina McCoy.

That evening Angie McCoy wore an elegant black silk dress, with a neckline that dropped to reveal an emerald necklace that looked almost identical to the one that David gave Sarah for Christmas the year before. Angie was holding a martini, vodka no doubt, in her perfectly manicured left hand, the edge of the sparkling crystal glass not quite touching her lip.

The two caret diamond ring, which appeared to float above the fingers of her left hand, demanded even more of Sarah's attention, as it flashed and danced in the candlelight of the dimly lit room. Angie McCoy sat with her right arm draped across the small corner table, her fingers affectionately covered by the masculine hand Sarah knew so well, the same hand that stroked her body the night before, the fingers that he entwined in her hair while his other hand pressed her hips against his.

Sarah could hear David's infectious laugh as he gazed at the jockey, whose eyes never left his face. Angie leaned closer to David, and without hesitation he met her lips with his own.

David and Sarah's romance had been a whirlwind. He was charming, attentive, attractive, and quite a successful thoroughbred trainer. David Marsico swept her off her feet.

Sarah had wished she could have believed whatever even barely amounted to a rational explanation David might have concocted to explain why he was holding hands with another woman, even kissing her. She had craved the ability to accept any excuse he wanted to tell her that night, but she knew herself well enough to know she could not.

Earlier, David called her to let her know his flight had arrived safely in Boston, and that he was on his way to his meeting. The LeMont Steakhouse, however, where Sarah stood watching him fawn over Angie McCoy, was in Philadelphia, not Boston. David had lied to her, his reason clear.

Frozen in place, hands shaking ever so slightly, Sarah had fought the urge to pick up a chair and bludgeon both David and the giggling jockey where they sat.

The maitre de asked Sarah if there was a problem. He probably hadn't heard her stammer that she was not feeling well before she'd pivoted and tearfully left the restaurant.

The morning after, Sarah called Natalie first. Next she called a locksmith who arrived in record time and changed the locks of her apartment. She called the minister, the reception hall, the caterer and the flower shop. Finally, she called her mother, who agreed to send out notices to all the invited guests to announce the cancellation of the wedding they had scheduled the following month.

Though they had separate residences, David had kept many of his personal items in her apartment, which she packed and set outside on the walkway along with her engagement ring, the keys to his apartment, and a letter she'd taped to the box. She remembered every word she'd written: *I trusted you. I believed in you. I loved you. Last night I saw you. I'll never forgive you. I have cancelled the wedding. Give my regards to Angie.* Several months later, she sold her share of a successful law firm to her two partners and moved to Quartzsite.

Over the following two days, David called Sarah a dozen times. She changed her phone number. That was two years ago. Since then, she'd seen him a few times, but hadn't spoken to him since the night she found him with Angie. She hadn't even been on a date since then until Carl. Carl drove down a long driveway and parked in front of his new-looking two-story home. He jumped out of his truck and opened her door. She scooted out while he retrieved her suitcase from the car's trunk.

"Home sweet home," he said. "Come on in."

"What a lovely house and a beautiful location," Sarah gushed.

Padded chairs and rockers and a swing lined the large front porch, where Sarah imagined Carl spent many sunrises and sunsets. She adored the sound of the water cascading over the rocks lining the tall fountain that fed a large pond beside the house.

There were trees all around, providing some shade from the California desert sun.

"Do you keep any fish in that pond?" She asked.

"Yes," Carl said. "It's my little oasis, even equipped with a cooler so the fish don't get too hot. There is a family of lizards that comes by pretty often to get a drink. We see quite a few jack rabbits and occasionally some snakes. In the evenings, it isn't unheard of to see a coyote or two wander in."

"It sounds heavenly." Sarah smiled and followed Carl inside.

"I'll carry your suitcase upstairs. Come on up," he prodded her. "I'll even let you have your choice of the guest rooms."

"I'll probably stay up all night hoping to see a coyote stop by for a drink," she joked.

Carl nodded, "I've done that, and a couple of times I was even rewarded with a visitor." He put her suitcase on the bed. "There's a powder room here in the corner. It just has a small shower, but there's a full bath just down the hall, if you'd prefer a tub."

"A shower is perfect," Sarah replied. "This is a beautiful home. Did you design it?"

A twinge of pain crossed Carl's face. He shook his head. "No. My wife designed the house. She wanted a lot of room. She said it was so we could have lots of guests until we had dozens of kids. Maria died five years ago, shortly after we completed the house. She was an adventure lover. She loved the heat of the desert, adored the snow in the mountains, and had a passion for skiing."

Sarah was stunned that in all the time she'd known Carl, neither he nor anybody else had mentioned he was a widower.

Carl continued, "She and a girlfriend went to Colorado to spend a couple of days on the slopes. Maria had been driving a rented car. The police said that she hit a patch of black ice and careened off the road, through the guide rail and over a fifteen-foot bluff. The coroner said that she probably died instantly. At first I thought I couldn't live here without her, but I couldn't leave, either. It used to be our home, but over the years, I've made many changes, and it has become more mine than what she'd have wanted."

"How sad," Sarah said.

"Maria loved the tracks in New York, Kentucky and Florida, and I only occasionally took a mount at Angelina or Laredo. After she died, I quit riding for almost a year. I quit everything, I guess. That's when I met Jeff. I started exercising for him and a few other trainers. Jeff and I hit it off and became friends, and the rest is history."

Carl's face suddenly lit up. "Are you ready to try the Carl Lawson grilled salmon special?"

Grateful for the change in tone, Sarah replied, "I am. What can I do to help?"

"You can choose a bottle of wine and then keep me company while I create a mouthwatering masterpiece."

After dinner, they poured another glass of wine and went outside to sit on the porch swing. Carl draped his arm around her shoulders and Sarah snuggled up against him.

"So, what are the chances a coyote will visit us?" Sarah asked.

"Slim to none, if you keep talking." Carl chuckled.

Sarah sighed, "Quiet is kind of nice."

They sat quietly together for a while longer until Sarah yawned. Carl stood and reached for her hand. He walked her to the bedroom door, kissed her goodnight, then turned and went down the hall to his room.

The next morning, the smell of coffee drifted up the staircase and woke Sarah. She took a long, hot shower, but didn't bother drying her hair. She dressed and bounded down the stairs, where a cup of hot coffee and Carl were waiting.

"Good morning," he said. He filled his own mug. "Did you sleep well?"

"Good morning," she replied, gratefully sipping her coffee. "I slept wonderfully, thank you."

Carl smiled at her. "I make a mean plate of scrambled eggs, if you're interested."

She smiled back. "I'm interested."

"I'm off today, and was thinking it would be fun to take you exploring, if you don't need to get back home early. There's an old mining town about an hour from here. I don't know a lot about stones, but you said you've found some great rocks in similar places. Maybe we'll find a treasure." He looked into her eyes expectantly.

When she drove out to meet Natalie and Carl, Sarah had planned to be back home in less than twenty-four hours. She had been away over two days now, although she really had nothing scheduled that she couldn't postpone.

"I'd love to accompany you on a rock hunt," she said.

After breakfast, Sarah was rinsing the dishes for Carl to put in the dishwasher when his cell phone rang.

"Carl Lawson," he answered, not recognizing the number displayed.

"Mr. Lawson, this is Detective Sergeant Michaels, Laredo Police Department, Homicide Division. I have a few questions to ask you. Is now a convenient time?"

"Questions relating to what?" Carl murmured.

"I'm investigating the death of Angelina Jane McCoy. I understand you and Ms. McCoy disagreed over an incident on the race track several hours before her death."

"Your understanding is wrong, Detective Michaels," Carl responded flatly. "We were in complete agreement about what happened."

The detective said. "I'm contacting people who might be able to help us reconstruct her activities in Laredo."

"I'll be happy to answer your questions," Carl said. "If you have no objection, I will put you on a speaker. I'm with a friend, Sarah Myers. She's an attorney."

"That's fine," Detective Michaels said."

"Good morning," Sarah said. "Is Mr. Lawson a suspect?"

"No, Mr. Lawson is not a suspect. As I explained to him, I'm calling to ask some questions in connection with an ongoing homicide investigation into the death of Angelina Jane McCoy. It's my understanding Mr. Lawson that you and Ms. McCoy had a disagreement as the result of a race in which you both competed several hours before her death."

"There was no disagreement," Carl repeated. "Angie's horse cut mine off. As a result, there was a steward's inquiry, and I filed a jockey's objection. We both spoke with the stewards and, while Angie denied any intent to move her horse to the rail, she agreed with the fact that it had occurred. Because of the objection, the racing stewards moved Angie's horse from first place to third place, and changed my horse's position from second place to first. It's not at all unusual for a jockey to file objection when something happens that causes a disadvantage to a horse as the result of actions of another horse, Detective."

"So because of your objection and a conversation among the stewards, Ms. McCoy and yourself, your horse earned more money." Sergeant Michaels prodded. "Is that correct?"

"Yes," Carl said. "That's correct. My horse finished second, but the stewards determined that he would have finished first, if Angie's horse hadn't suddenly cut in front of him. In addition, they found that Angie's horse also impeded the horse that finished third. They moved that horse to second, and Angie's horse to third."

"Where did you go after the race?"

"I went to the receiving barn to check on Fury, then to the Laredo Hotel."

"Were you alone?"

"No. I was with two other men, Santos Velasquez and Sonny Owens, until Santos left to go to the clinic with the colt. Then Sonny and I drove to the hotel together."

"Did you spend the evening with Sonny Owens?"

"No."

"Where did you spend the evening?"

"I got something to eat at Sprinter's Bar and waited for Santos to call from the clinic."

"Did you speak with anyone when you were at Sprinter's?"

"I talked to a couple of jockeys, Doug Whiteman and Tony Holloway, until Santos called for a ride back from the clinic. Then I left and to picked Santos up. We came back to the Ringside Hotel. Santos hadn't had dinner, so he got a sandwich, and we both had a beer, then we went up to our rooms."

"What time did you go to your room?"

"I don't know exactly. It was between nine-thirty and ten o'clock. We were both tired, and we planned to meet Sonny and have an early breakfast before we hit the road."

"Did you all meet for breakfast?"

"Yes. We met in the lobby, got some coffee and an omelet, and then drove to the clinic to pick up our horse."

"Did you see Mr. Owens after you got to the hotel and before you saw him at breakfast?"

"No, I didn't see him, but I talked to him right after Santos called. It must have been about eight o'clock."

"I think I have enough for now. Thank you for your time, Mr. Lawson, Ms. Myers."

"You're welcome," Carl and Sarah said simultaneously.

"Detective Michaels, can you tell us the cause of death? We thought Ms. McCoy fell and hit her head," Sarah pressed. "Is there some evidence to show that there were other factors involved?"
"We're waiting for the coroner's report regarding the cause of death. In the meantime, we're treating it as a possible homicide. If you think of anything that might be helpful, Mr. Lawson, I'd appreciate a call. Again, thank you for your cooperation." The detective ended the call.

Carl frowned. "Am I imagining things, or was that call not really about where I was?"

Sarah shook her head, "It isn't your imagination. I thought that same thing."

34

A few weeks passed, and Fury was making good progress. The colt was having no trouble walking, and the laceration was without any sign of infection, healing well. He had gained some weight and tolerated the daily soaks, wraps and liniments without objection.

When Sonny brought Fury back from a long walk, Jeff told him, "It's time to start turning him out for a couple of hours a day."

"Yes," Sonny agreed. "He's getting to be a handful, particularly when I get him close to the track. He wants to get out there. Are you thinking about taking him back to your place for a while?"

Jeff and Natalie had considered sheltering Fury in the small barn behind their house, where they kept Flight and Fury's dam, Natalie's mare, Felicia. The barn opened into a three acre fenced paddock.

"That's what I had wanted to do, but Natalie is afraid to leave him alone for any length of time. She said that before we do that, she wants some security cameras installed. I think the cameras would be a good idea for the barn, but extending surveillance to the far end of the property gets too complicated for me. If I move him back home, I'm going to need to fence off a smaller area near the barn to keep him close."

"Why don't you bring him over to the farm?" Sonny offered. "We have a couple of empty stalls and two small paddocks. There are always people around there, and he'd be as safe as he is at Angelina."

"That would solve the problem, wouldn't it?" Jeff mused. "Natalie spends a lot of time with him every day, so she could run in and out during the day to clean the stall and take care of feeding. I can go over to wrap his legs and check on him, if you don't mind us driving to your barn a dozen times a day."

Sonny grinned. "It won't be any problem. We usually save the small paddocks for the mares ready to foal. We don't have any that are due, so both paddocks are available. We won't charge you any board, since you'll be doing all the work."

"Let me talk to Natalie," Jeff replied. "I insist that we pay you though. You can't be doing this for nothing."

"I'll talk to Charlie tonight. He's in Utah, helping a friend with a Quarter Horse sale, but I'm sure he'll agree that the most we can accept is the cost of any supplies. After all you've done to help us out over the years, I'd consider it the simple return of a favor."

"Thanks, Sonny. It would probably be for three or four weeks. Would that work?"

"That's fine. And if you want to keep him there until he's ready to go back into training, that's fine, too. If he keeps improving the way he has been, I imagine you'll put him back in training in six or eight weeks."

"Yes, that's about what I was figuring. I appreciate your offer. As long as Natalie agrees, and I'm sure she will, I'll plan on bringing him to your place in the next day or so, if that fits your schedule."

"No problem. In the meantime, I'll let Charlie know," Sonny said. He was happy to be able to help.

That night at dinner, Jeff and Natalie discussed moving Fury to the Williams farm. She was immediately on board with the idea. "What a generous offer," she said, after Jeff explained what Sonny had proposed.

"If Fury is at the Williams's place, he'll have lots of attention. No doubt Santos will be over there spending some extra time just making sure all is well. You and I will be in and out, and with Sonny there, Fury will be even more secure than he is at the barn at the track." Natalie agreed that they could take him there the following day.

Jeff called Sonny and told him that they would like to accept his offer. Sonny said he had spoken with Charlie, and everything would be ready for them by the next afternoon.

The farm was only a few miles away, convenient for Natalie to continue to see Fury every day. She insisted on taking care of his feeding and grooming for another week, and she filled the pickup with a couple dozen bales of hay to take along.

Although it was too soon to put Fury back into training, it was important he has some exercise, particularly the way he'd been eating. While his leg continued to strengthen and heal, it was preferable to allow him to range freely for a few hours a day, instead of keeping him confined to a stall with only brief walks for exercise.

The next morning, Sonny galloped Musician around the track. The horse looked splendid, and Jeff entered him in one of the allowance races coming up. Jeff was not only Musician's trainer but also an owner in partnership with two of his clients. The four-year-old gelding tried his best every time he raced, and the partnership saved costs for everyone invested.

Sonny brought Musician back to where Jeff was standing. "What did you think?" he asked the trainer.

"Excellent job," Jeff praised. "He's moving well. I think he's ready for the race next week."

Sonny patted Musician's snout. "He really tried to get away from me when he saw that filly coming around on his outside. I'm not sure if he knew it was a girl or if he just didn't want anybody in front."

"I saw that," Jeff said. "I'm glad you let him go, rather than holding him back when she tried to pass. If he wants to be in front, I don't want him thinking he shouldn't be there. Would you mind hosing him down for me?"

"No problem. I'll get him cooled out. Do you want me to take Dancer out for a gallop later?"

Jeff nodded, "Yes, she needs to burn off some energy, if you have the time."

"That's fine." Sonny chuckled. "She's been a ball of fire lately. I like that mare, but she can be an ornery one."

"I'm glad somebody likes her. She drives Santos crazy with her antics," Jeff said. "I swear that Dancer knows how to push all of his buttons. I think she messes with him intentionally. She stepped on his foot again yesterday. Don't tell him I told you."

Grinning, Sonny said, "My lips are sealed." He turned Musician in the barn's direction, and the colt trotted back toward his stall.

Santos met Sonny at the entrance to the barn. "Natalie just ran over to the tack shop to pick up some wraps. She told me you're taking Fury to your place, for a few weeks of luxury in a private paddock."

"Yep," Sonny replied. "With all the problems they've had surrounding that colt, I'd like to do anything I can to help keep him safe and get him back on the track and racing. Natalie has helped me out a lot over the years. After I'm done here, Jeff and I are taking Fury over to his new digs."

"They're good people." Santos said. "I'll stop over later if that's okay."

"You're always welcome," Sonny told him. "Even if it's Fury who you're visiting and not me."

Then Santos moved closer. In a hushed tone, he informed Sonny, "There's a homicide detective from Laredo here. He asked me a bunch of questions about Fury's last race. He wanted to know where I was, who I talked to, and what time I left the track. After he questioned me, he asked if you were working today. I said you were out with the horses. I told him you'd be tied up for a little while, but he insisted that he'd wait. He's in the office now. His name is Michaels. I didn't get his first name."

Sonny's relaxed mood vanished. "Crap. I told Jeff I'd cool Musician out, then exercise Dancer," he stammered.

"I can take care of Musician for you. If the cop keeps you tied up too long, I'll exercise Dancer, too. She can't step on me when I'm in the saddle."

Sonny smiled nervously. "Thanks, I appreciate your help."

Santos took the reins and walked Musician around to the outside of the barn.

From all the gossip Sonny had heard circulating among track employees, he could surmise Laredo Police had questioned just about everyone who had been in Laredo on the day of the Sapphire Stakes. Police investigators had reached out to the jockeys and the trainers right away, next to the owners and all track personnel, and anyone in any way involved in the care of the horses. They still hadn't asked him about his phone calls to Angie, though, and Sonny had offered no information or explanation for those calls, but suspected that was the reason for this second interview.

Sonny walked across the shedrow to the far end of the barn to the small office. When he opened the door, a tall man, about 50, muscular and stocky-built, with a full head of steel grey hair, stood and extended his hand. "Sonny Owens?" he asked.

Sonny nodded and shook the hand of the man, who now had a weather-beaten face attached to that voice over the phone.

"I'm Detective Sergeant Michaels, Laredo Police Force, Homicide Division. I need to ask you a few questions regarding our investigation into the death of Angelina McCoy."

Sonny felt the color drain from his face. No doubt the detective noticed, too. Overcome by that same nausea he had experienced when he had first heard about Angie's death, Sonny quickly accepted Detective Michaels's suggestion to sit. Again, Sonny thought of Angie lying on the floor, possibly dying because he hadn't been there. Now he was afraid, wondering how much the detective knew about his relationship with her. If information about the affair became public, he was sure that he would lose both his marriage and, with that, his livelihood. The Williams farm had been in Vanessa's family long before he married her, and it was his primary source of income.

"Homicide Division? I thought Angie had died accidentally. That's what I've been hearing." Sonny avoided the detective's eyes.

"Where did you go, after the last race at Laredo?" Detective Michaels asked. The man projected an icy air of purpose that heightened Sonny's nervousness.

"I already talked to you about that. Our horse got hurt, and I went to the barn with him. After that, I met his jockey, Carl Lawson, and rode back to the hotel, then I went to my room and had a couple of beers and went to bed."

"Did you leave your room at all during the evening?"

Sonny nodded too quickly, sure Doug probably told of their brief meeting that night. "Yeah, I went out to get some ice, and ran into another jockey, Doug Whiteman, in the hall."

"Do you know what time that was?"

"It was shortly after we got back to the hotel, but I don't know exactly what time," Sonny hedged.

"Did you see anyone else that evening?"

"No."

"Did you talk to anyone else that evening?"

"No," Sonny said. "Wait. Yes, I did. I talked to Carl Lawson. He called to make plans to meet for breakfast the next morning."

"And do you know what time you spoke with Mr. Lawson?"

Sonny shook his head, "I'm not sure, but it would show up on Carl's phone that he called me. You can check with him."

"Can you check your telephone now for me?" the investigator pressed.

A drop of sweat slid down Sonny's forehead and into his left eye, causing him to blink. "I clear my call logs often. It probably won't show up."

"Did you clear your call logs in Laredo, or after you got back home?"

Now Sonny was sure that the homicide detective was aware of his calls to Angie. Sonny hadn't exactly lied about anything, but Carl wasn't the only one he had spoken to on the phone. He had spoken briefly to Angie, right before he ran into Doug. He cleared his call logs, almost daily, when he had been seeing Angie. That last thing he wanted was for Vanessa to notice the frequent calls listed between him and the jockey. When he learned Angie was dead, he cleared his cell phone, but not since. There was no longer a need.

"I don't know if I cleared them before or after," he lied. "I just do it every few days."

"Do you have your phone with you?"

"No, I don't." Sonny replied, which was technically true. His phone was, however, right around the corner. Before he had taken Musician out to the training track, he had called Jeff to see how far he should gallop the colt. As he disconnected the call, Musician had done a quick sidestep, causing Sonny to drop the phone on a bale of straw while he settled the gelding. Right now that felt like a stroke of luck.

"I'll check my logs later and let you know if I still have Carl's call listed," he offered. Something was telling him not to give up his phone.

"When is the last time you saw Angelina McCoy?" the detective asked tonelessly.

"It was right after the Sapphire Stakes, when she brought Nordstrom back," Sonny answered, which was accurate.

"Did you talk to her then?"

"I didn't have any time. We were pretty tied up with Fury."

"Do you recall the last time you talked to her, prior to the race?"

"I'm not sure," Sonny said. "She's a jockey, so I ran into her a lot at the track or in the barn. I probably talked to her the day of the race."

Sonny decided not to mention his text message to Angie. It had been her habit to delete most of her texts, and he hoped his wasn't an exception.

The detective had been sitting back in Jeff's office chair, relaxed and confidant as he had asked his list of questions. Now, however, he leaned forward, put his forearms on the desk, and demanded to know, "Did you have plans to meet Angelina McCoy the night she died?"

It terrified Sonny to give the detective an honest answer. If his intention to meet with Angie leaked out, the chances of keeping it a secret from his wife were slim. Angie had been exciting. She was fun and available, and made him feel like Superman, but he had never loved her. If Vanessa found out about what had been going on between him and Angie—

"Mr.Owens?" Detective Michaels emphasized, "Did you have plans to meet Angelina McCoy the night that she died?"

If he lied, it would only provide temporary refuge. Unless he could come up with another reason for their calls, the truth would come out when they reviewed his telephone records, if they hadn't been already. The police would know he'd spoken to her. They would have his voice on her cell phone and on the hotel's voice mail system. He would look guilty of a crime he hadn't committed.

Before Sonny got involved with Angie, he knew she was bad news. Everyone close to her knew it. And now he knew it. Even after her death, she was finding a way to destroy him.

"Yes," he mumbled.

"Are you saying that you had plans to meet her?" the detective leaned even closer.

"Yes," Sonny confessed. "But I didn't want anyone to know. Angie said she'd leave the door unlocked for me, but I was late getting to her room. When I was on my way, I ran into Doug in the hallway. We talked for a few minutes, and he invited me down to the bar for a drink. I told him I wasn't feeling well, and I was going to bed early. After he left, I went up the stairway to find Angie's room. I remember it was room 721, but the door was locked. I could hear the television. I knocked, but she didn't answer. I called her cell phone from the hallway. I heard it ring, but she didn't answer. Then I went back to my room and called again." Sonny's hands trembled.

Sonny reached across the desk and gripped the investigator's arm, pleading, "My wife can't find out about this. You can't let anybody know. Vanessa will never understand. I'll lose her. I'll lose everything. You can't tell anyone."

The detective's weary eyes seemed to pierce deep into Sonny's. "You were having an affair with Angelina McCoy, is that correct?"

"It wasn't really an affair," Sonny objected. "I mean, maybe you'd call it that. We spent some time together, but Angie knew I'm married and plan to stay that way. Angie and I were friends. We practically grew up together."

The detective inhaled deeply before he jerked his arms away, stood, and rounded the desk to hover over Sonny. "Sonny Owens, you are under arrest for suspicion of the murder of Angelina McCoy," he announced loud enough to carry throughout the barn. He pulled the frightened man off the chair. "You have the right to remain silent. Anything that you say can be used against you."

Sonny erupted, "Arrest? Under arrest? Murder? I didn't kill Angie. I didn't even see her." He tried to shove the detective away, but the older man must have expected the move. He took hold of Sonny's left arm and, in one motion, pulled it behind Sonny's back and painfully up to Sonny's shoulder. Michaels slipped a handcuff onto Sonny's right wrist and then raised that arm so that he could clamp the other cuff around the left.

The cold metal manacles seemed to empty all the life out of Sonny.

"You're under arrest for suspicion of murder and for resisting arrest." As he recited the required Miranda Rights, Detective Michaels shoved Sonny in front of him and steered his prisoner out of the barn.

Santos heard the commotion and was on his way into the office when Detective Michaels and

Sonny reached the doorway. Baffled, Santos demanded, “What’s going on here?”

The detective kept walking.

Sonny yelled, “He thinks I killed Angie. I didn’t, Santos. I need a lawyer. Call Vanessa. Please. Tell her this is crazy.”

Santos followed the men. “Okay, I’ll call her. Should I call Jeff, too?”

“Yes,” Sonny begged as the lawman’s hand rested on the top of the suspect’s head and guided him into the back of the patrol car. “Ask Vanessa to call a lawyer and tell Jeff I didn’t kill Angie.”

The detective harnessed a seatbelt over Sonny.

“And please tell Vanessa I love her,” Sonny wailed as the detective slammed the car door shut.

“I’ve known Sonny for a lot of years,” Santos told Detective Michaels. “He couldn’t kill anyone.”

With a curt nod, the homicide detective got into his car and drove away with his murder suspect.

35

Sarah was educating a customer about the history of the Zuni Indian fetishes. The woman was not from Quartzsite and had an absolute fascination with the carvings.

Sarah’s phone rang. She glanced at the number displayed, Jeff’s cell. “Excuse me,” she told her customer. “I apologize, but I need to answer this call." She walked away to a corner of the store, leaving the other woman alone to browse.

"Sarah. I need your help." Jeff blurted.

"Is Natalie okay?" Sarah panicked, concerned something else had happened to her friend.

"Natalie's fine. It's Sonny. He's been arrested for suspicion of murder and resisting arrest. I find both charges hard to believe, but that's what we've got," Jeff explained. "A detective took him to jail in Laredo and he needs a lawyer. Santos called his wife, and she is going to try to find someone, but I talked to her and she has no idea where to look for a criminal attorney."

"I can make a few calls for you," Sarah offered. "I don't know any lawyers in Laredo, but I'll see what I can find out and call you back as soon as I have any information."

"That would be great, Sarah. In the meantime, I hoped that you would agree to talk to the Laredo Police and see just what they have on him."

"I wouldn't be able to get any information unless I was representing Sonny," Sarah said. "I haven't done any real criminal work in years."

"I thought that, while we were trying to find a criminal lawyer, you could enter an appearance to get things started," Jeff said. "According to Santos, Sonny seemed genuinely confused that he was being arrested."

"Okay," Sarah replied. "I'll call you back within half an hour."

Sarah returned to her customer. "I'm so sorry," Sarah apologized. "Do you have any questions I can answer?"

The woman replied, "No, I think you've given me all the information that I need. I'd like to buy these." The customer placed two carved animals on the counter. Sarah carefully wrapped the fetishes and put them into a small box. One of them was a tiny horse, carved from amber.

The woman paid cash. "I couldn't help overhearing part of your conversation," she said. "Am I correct that you need a criminal attorney who works in the Laredo area?"

Surprised and embarrassed her voice had been loud enough for her customer to hear, Sarah could only think to ask, "Do you know of someone?"

"Actually, my name is Naomi Hunter, and I'm a criminal attorney." The customer offered her business card to Sarah. "I'm not from Laredo, but my office is only a couple of hours away, and I've done work there. I clerked in Laredo for Judge Simmons, and I worked for the Public Defender's Office in Los Angeles for four years. I've recently opened a private criminal law practice. If you can use some help in Laredo, I am familiar with their system. I can use the exposure, and I'll treat you right."

Naomi's statement stunned Sarah. "Have you ever handled a murder case?"

"I've handled four," Naomi declared. "The juries found three of my clients innocent, and the fourth had her charges reduced from murder to involuntary manslaughter. I can give you references, if that would be helpful."

Sarah was an excellent judge of character, and her immediate reaction to the young attorney's offer was that Naomi was trying to broaden her criminal law credentials, seeking a few more clients with that goal in mind. That translated into Sarah's opinion that Naomi Hunter would work her tail off to do her very best for Sonny. Naomi seemed young for a lawyer who had handled several murder cases, but a review of her background and experience would tell the tale.

"How long will you be in town?" she asked.

"I was planning to stay tonight, do some exploring tomorrow morning, and then drive back to California tomorrow afternoon, or early the next morning if I got caught up in something. I'm flexible." Naomi smiled. "Why don't you check me out and call me later. The business card includes my cell number."

"Thank you," Sarah said. "The man who they arrested works for close friends of mine. I know him, and everything I know about him tells me that I am right to be confident that he didn't kill anyone. I appreciate your offer, and I will make a few calls and get back to you before the end of the day."

"I'll wait to hear from you," Naomi said, and then vanished with her purchase out of Sarah's shop.

Sarah called Jeff. "You won't believe this, but I may have found a criminal attorney who is also familiar with the Laredo judicial system."

"Sarah, you are amazing." Jeff said. "How did you find him so quickly?"

"Her," Sarah corrected. "And I didn't find her, she found me. She is a criminal defense attorney who has worked in Laredo. I'll check her credentials. If her references and reputation prove legit, it might be worth going with a local, or even semi-local, attorney.

Naomi Hunter is her name. After she overheard me talking to you, she offered her services."

"I'll call Vanessa," Jeff said. "Would you be willing to be co-counsel, or at least a consultant?" Jeff asked. "I trust you and your instincts, and I know it would reassure Sonny if he knew he had you in his corner."

Sarah couldn't refuse her friend. "I'll do whatever you need, Jeff."

Two hours, and quite a few phone calls later, Vanessa, Sarah, and Naomi came to an agreement. Naomi and Sarah would be co-counsel for Sonny. Naomi would be the lead attorney and Sarah would serve as a consultant, but both would have access to Sonny and to any information that the Laredo judicial system had available. The first order of business would be to post bail.

Naomi agreed to cut her trip short and leave first thing in the morning for Laredo. Sarah would ride to Laredo with Naomi and then rent a car for the return to Quartzsite. Vanessa said she would do whatever was necessary to raise sufficient bail to get Sonny released, including mortgaging the farm.

Naomi offered to waive any hourly fee and charge a nominal flat fee, travel expenses and court costs, instead. Sarah agreed to the same arrangement, less the flat fee. Naomi admitted her reputation would benefit from the publicity garnered from what she expected would be a richly newsworthy trial, more so if a positive outcome.

Sarah didn't really need the money, and she knew her help would mean a lot to Jeff and Natalie as well as to Sonny.

Sarah and Naomi Hunter left before the sun rose on the following morning, with plans to arrive in Laredo by noon. When they arrived in Laredo, they went directly to the office of the Laredo District Attorney. Deputy District Attorney, Mark Dillinger, remembered Naomi from her successful effort to reduce charges from murder to involuntary manslaughter in the Brenda Wilkins case. But, he took twenty minutes to check Sarah's status and determine whether she was qualified to practice law in his state, before he would allow her to see Sonny.

"I have entered an appearance on behalf of Sonny Owens. We need to meet with our client immediately, and all questioning of Mr. Owens must cease until legal representation is present." Naomi directed.

After another twenty-minute wait, Dillinger advised Naomi they had cleared her and Sarah to see Sonny. "Mr. Owens was arrested based on the evidence gathered. We have proof the defendant called the deceased on several occasions on the date of her death. In addition, he left voice messages, both on her personal phone and in her hotel voice mail, at or about the time of her death. His fingerprints were found on the exterior doorknob of Ms. McCoy's hotel room. All indications are that he was the last person to see her alive."

Naomi interrupted, "Cause of death, what's the finding?"

"Myocardial infarction, believed to be induced by an overdose of the drug, Butazolidin."

"She died of a heart attack, after a drug overdose?" Naomi expressed bafflement. "Then why is my client being accused of murdering her?"

"We have reason to believe that someone else administered the drug," the prosecutor replied, in a matter-of-fact manner. "An attempt was made to flush the murder weapon, um, hypodermic, down the toilet. If the deceased was unconscious, she could hardly administer the drug herself and — "

"If!" Naomi objected. "Butazolidin is routinely used by some trainers and is easily accessible to jockeys and other horsemen. You can't discard the likelihood Angie McCoy administered the drug all by herself."

"You can make that argument in court," was Dillinger's flat reply. "The deceased placed a room service order that comprised champagne, with two glasses, and a fruit and cheese plate. She placed the order at six-fifteen p.m., but when room service arrived to deliver it, no one answered the door. The tray was still sitting outside the door when her father arrived the next morning."

Dillinger lowered his eyes to the documents on his desk. "Your client, by his own admission, was not seen by anyone after his conversation with jockey Doug Whiteman. That conversation took place at or about 6:00 p.m. on the night she died."

The deputy district attorney adjusted his glasses and leaned back in his chair, eyes shifting between those of the two defense attorneys. "You want motive? Mr. Owens is a married man. His income and livelihood depend on his employment as a partner in the Williams Boarding and Breeding

Farm. His wife and her family own the farm. It would be in Mr. Owens's best interest that his wife not discover his relationship with the deceased. Elimination of Angelina McCoy removed the possibility for Ms. McCoy to use her relationship with Mr. Owens for any leverage. That gives him motive."

"Your case is virtually non-existent," Naomi argued. "I cannot believe you are holding Mr. Owens on thin circumstantial evidence that can be easily dismantled. We'd like to see him now."

"In addition, we have the charge of resisting arrest," Dillinger justified. "I guess that's self-explanatory. Mr. Owens tried to escape when Detective Michaels put him under arrest. The court scheduled his arraignment for this afternoon. I'll escort you to Mr. Owens now if you'd like."

"Thank you," Sarah said. Naomi simply nodded her head.

At the jail, the attorneys followed a corrections officer to a compact conference room where Sonny sat at a table waiting for them. "I'll be right outside the door," the guard said. "You can press the red buzzer on the table if you need an intervention or are ready to leave."

When Sonny saw Sarah enter the room, his face lit up. He stood and blurted, "Sarah, thank you. Thank you so much for coming. I didn't kill Angie. I can't believe I'm here."

Sarah turned away from Sonny's attempt to hug her. "Sonny, this is Naomi Hunter, a criminal defense attorney. I will work with her to sort out this mess. We hope to have you out of here on bail at your arraignment this afternoon."

"I didn't kill Angie McCoy," Sonny declared sternly.

"Sarah filled me in on a bit of your background," Naomi said. She and Sarah sat at the opposite side of the table. "I've spoken with your wife. She hired me to represent you. She is very concerned about your welfare and asked me to assure you that she has absolute faith in your innocence."

Sonny bowed his head, unable to hide his shame from those hired to defend him by his loyal wife.

Naomi opened her legal pad and started to scribble on it. "Now, we need to understand what happened. Walk us through everything that occurred from the morning that you left for Laredo until you got back from the trip. Please leave nothing out, no matter how insignificant you may think it is. Anything you say to us is subject to the attorney-client privilege. Neither Sarah nor I will repeat anything you tell us and it cannot be subpoenaed. We can't afford any surprises, so please be honest and tell us, in detail, everything you can recall."

And Sonny opened up, describing all that happened from the time Jeff asked him, at the last minute, to ride along with Carl to Laredo, until they picked up Fury from the clinic and drove back home. He told them about his brother-in-law, Charlie, calling to tell him that Angie had died. He squirmed throughout his confession of his affair with Angelina McCoy and the intimate details, that they had always been very discreet, so much so that he was confident, while some may have suspected he and Angie were an item, none could be positive they had a physical relationship.

"They scheduled your arraignment for this afternoon," Naomi told Sonny. "At most, we can move for your immediate release based on the lack of sufficient evidence for probable cause. At the very least, we'll try to get you out on bail. Your wife has offered the farm to make bond if it's necessary. We'll see what we can do to get you back home, and figure out the rest from there."

Lost, Sonny could only nod in gratitude.

36

"All rise," the deputy called as the judge entered the courtroom. His legs trembling, Sonny stood with all others in the courtroom. Flanked by his attorneys, he waited for the bailiff to call his name and clasped his hands tightly to keep them from shaking.

The judge lifted a sheet of paper from the stack in front of him. "The defendant has been charged with the murder of Angelina Jane McCoy. How do you plead?"

Naomi answered for her client. "Not guilty, Your Honor."

Sonny had gone into a daze. Though he knew people speaking, he couldn't make sense of their words. '*Angie is dead and I am being blamed*' was the only clear thought in his confused and frightened mind.

After several minutes of the attorneys answering the judge's questions and arguing back and forth, Sonny was aware of Naomi's hand on his shoulder. She was smiling like an angel at him. Something good must have happened, he reasoned, but he didn't know what it was.

"We need to sign a few documents and transfer the funds, then we can get you out of here," she explained. "In the meantime, they'll take you to a holding cell, but it shouldn't be for more than an hour."

"I can go home then?" he responded, still confused.

"Yes," Naomi assured him. "Sarah will call Vanessa and let her know."

Over the objections of the prosecution, bail had been set at $50,000.00 cash. The farm was worth considerably more than that. At Naomi's recommendation, in anticipation of bail being set, Vanessa had made arrangements for her bank to wire the money to Laredo.

The District Attorney had asked for one million dollars in bail, but Naomi had successfully argued that, besides the fact that the evidence was not compelling, Detective Michaels, lacking an arrest warrant, had deliberately provoked a physical encounter with her client to manufacture a basis to charge Sonny with resisting arrest and attempting to flee so he could to establish flight risk. The ruling of so little bail in a capital murder case indicated to

Naomi that the judge was more than skeptical of the circumstantial evidence offered by the prosecution.

The younger attorney's passion impressed Sarah. Even more encouraging was the respect the court afforded Naomi, which could only be because of the lead defense attorney's past dealings within the Laredo judicial system. Naomi had even waved off the plea bargain negotiations offered by the DA, not a decision Sarah was certain she would have made.

Sonny reached his hand out to Naomi, and she clasped it in both of hers, pleased that she and Sarah had been successful in arranging for her client's release from prison.

After the money was wired, the papers signed, and Sonny freed, his lawyers escorted him through the mob of reporters shoving microphones in his face and trying to out-shout each other to get a response to their questions.

When they got to the car, Sonny dived into the back seat and slammed the door shut while Naomi slid into the driver's seat and Sarah climbed into the seat next to her.

"I rented a car to drive back to Angelina, Naomi," Sarah said. "There's no sense in you driving four hours north, then turning around and driving back again. It makes more sense for you to go home from here. Just drop Sonny and me at the airport; the rental will be waiting."

"No problem," Naomi said. "The airport is just down the road."

Sonny leaned forward to tell Naomi, "Thanks doesn't seem like enough to say. I'm so grateful for you coming here with Sarah to help me."

"Some years ago, a man was accused of raping a woman who lived in the same apartment building as he did. They charged him with rape, aggravated assault, and murder. His name was Ethan, the manager of a tack shop near Santa Ana."

Naomi adjusted the air conditioner to blast. "Ethan had left work early on the day of the crime, something that he rarely did. He called me because he'd felt one of his frequent migraines coming on and was afraid to drive. So I picked him up and drove him to his apartment. If he got home in time to take some medicine before the headache attacked in full force, he could usually sleep it away. That's exactly what he did. He'd gotten home from work about 2:00 in the afternoon. He went to bed and slept until the next morning. He didn't see anyone, didn't speak with anyone. He didn't have a radio or television turned on. There was no noise coming from his apartment."

"Vanessa gets headaches like that sometimes," Sonny said.

"The victim had been raped and severely beaten, unable to identify her assailant," Naomi continued. "But before she died, she was able to tell police that he was a sizeable man, dressed in dark clothes and wearing a Halloween mask. She didn't name Ethan, but police questioned the neighbors, including an elderly woman from across the hall who said she heard noises from the victim's apartment and watched through the peephole of her door. Said she saw a man leave the victim's apartment and, as he exited, he pulled off his mask. She said he was tall with black hair, 'kind of like' Ethan, and was wearing western boots. Ethan wore western boots."

"As some would say, with all that, why bother with a trial," Sarah quipped.

Naomi adjusted the air conditioner to a lower setting. "Ethan swore that he hadn't done it, and I believed him, but he had no verifiable alibi. Based on the old woman's testimony, and Ethan's fingerprint on a lamp in the dead woman's apartment, Ethan was arrested, and ultimately convicted. The judge sentenced him to thirty years in prison. He died there, three months later. He slit his wrists with the blade from a plastic razor that he had somehow managed to hide."

"Sad," Sonny said. "But it sounds like he might have been guilty. His fingerprint didn't get on that lamp unless he touched it. Then again, he was her neighbor, so maybe he had been in her apartment before the night she was killed. The evidence against him was all circumstantial."

Naomi nodded and cut the air conditioning back to medium. "Two weeks after Ethan's death, another woman in the same apartment complex was attacked and raped. She, however, pulled the mask off her attacker and clawed his face, forcing him to retreat. She provided a detailed description of her assailant, even his first name. Turned out to be the man who delivered for the local grocer. He lived close by and made frequent deliveries to her and to others in her apartment building. The DNA scraped from under her fingernails verified the woman's accusation. Turned out he, too, was a sizeable man, with black hair, and wore western boots."

"Damn," Sarah said.

"And he confessed to the rape Ethan had been convicted of. It was the effect of Ethan's tragic and unnecessary death that caused me to detour from environmental law to criminal defense. I'm very particular about who I defend. Every time that I win a case, I can feel Ethan smiling down on me. Sometimes I even think he guides me to the innocent. I think I was in Sarah's shop for a reason. It isn't the first time I was in the right place at the right time. As for thanks, you can thank Ethan. He was my brother."

A slight cry escaped Sarah's throat.

"I didn't kill Angie," Sonny said again. "Thank you, and Ethan, for believing me."

Through her rearview mirror, Sarah monitored the media caravan following behind. "I'm glad Ethan is part of our team," she said, reaching for her cell phone.

Naomi's eyes watered, but she smiled.

Sarah speed-dialed Natalie. "Nat, Sonny and I are on our way back from Laredo."

Before she had a chance to say anything else, Natalie repeated the news. "They got Sonny out. He and Sarah are coming home."

In the background, Sarah heard Jeff and Santos cheering and pressed the speaker button. "Looks like you've been missed," she said. Sonny chuckled for the first time in days.

Natalie said, "We've been holding our collective breaths, waiting to lear what happened. When did you leave Laredo?"

"We got out of there about fifteen minutes ago. We're on our way to the airport to pick up a rental car, but we're being followed by the hounds of the media," Sarah warned. "Can I stay with you and Jeff tonight? It has been an exhausting day already."

"Of course," Natalie replied. "Does Carl know you're on your way back here?"

"No," Sarah answered. "I haven't talked to Carl. Is he at Angelina today?"

"Yes. He's here. He found a small efficiency apartment yesterday and is considering a six-month lease so he can spend less time commuting from Desert Center. He's been helping us with the exercising while Sonny has been gone, and now a few other trainers have asked for his services. If I can find him and he's free, do you want me to ask him to join us for dinner tonight?"

"That sounds great," Sarah said

"That works," Natalie told her. "I'll track Carl down to see if he's available. I'm making lasagna."

"I wish there was a way to lose these reporters," Sarah said.

"A murder is big news in Laredo," Naomi said. "You two just scoot out quick when we get to the airport," she directed. "The news hounds will probably think you've got a flight out, but they'll need to park before they can follow you inside. Meanwhile, I'll drive to the small lot and give them a brief statement to keep them occupied while you get the rental car and take off for home."

"You've done this before?" Sarah realized more than asked.

"Oh, yes," Naomi said. "Publicity, my dear, the currency of our profession."

37

Charlie was dumbfounded when he'd heard they charged Sonny with Angie McCoy's murder. It was just like his sister, however, to deal with one crisis at a time. Sonny's situation was dire, but it was under as much control as Vanessa could provide. The next crisis was the lack of muscle to care for the farm. Vanessa couldn't do that alone; she needed his help.

He was driving back from Utah to to provide that help when Vanessa called, ecstatic to tell him Sonny was out on bail and was with her eating dinner at Natalie's house.

"That's marvelous news, Vanessa," Charlie said. "Natalie and Jeff are the best. I'm still a few hours out, but should be there in time for dinner."

"If I'd have been sure Sonny's bail would get out on bail, you probably could have stayed in Utah," Vanessa told him. "Is it too late for you to go back and finish out the week?"

Even though her world was being torn apart, Charlie was not surprised that his sister reserved a block of concern for him. "It's no problem, Vanessa. I was around for the first half of the sale, which was the most important part. Emmett can take it from there. I packed my clothes and am on the road. Turning back would be a pain in the neck. Besides that, I think it will be good for everyone if I stay close to the farm until things get straightened out."

"Thanks, Charlie." Vanessa sighed. "I don't know exactly what was going on between Sonny and Angie, but I'm sure he didn't kill her." Her voice broke.

"Vanessa," he said, "I don't believe for a minute that Sonny killed Angie, and I don't believe for a second that he would risk losing you for Angie or for anyone else. He loves you. I'm sure of that. You just hang on. I'll be home in a few more hours and we'll figure everything out."

"What would I do without you, Charlie? You've never let me down."

38

The next few weeks passed quickly. Natalie divided her time between her home, their barn at the racetrack, and the Williams Farm. Fury was recovering well. Natalie took care of their feeding and grooming daily. Jeff visited Fury every couple of days, and the vet, Leo, checked on the colt every week.

Jeff had taken one of his mares to the Williams Farm to share the paddock with Fury. He and Leo were watching Fury follow Elektra around the fence line.

"He doesn't seem to have a problem with that leg," Jeff said.

"He's coming along just fine," Leo agreed. "Leaving the filly here for a couple of days is a wonderful idea. She can keep him company and ensure that he gets the right kind of exercise before you take him back to Angelina."

"Keeping them together is as good for Elektra as it is for Fury," Jeff told the veterinarian. "I'm sure she missed having him next to her in the barn."

The two men watched the young horses for a few minutes longer. The old vet chuckled. "If I hadn't seen the x-ray, I wouldn't believe that colt had an injury. He's looking really good."

Jeff nodded. "Fury is remarkably sensible. He stands like a gentleman when I soak his leg and is patient with the liniment and daily wraps. At this rate, he'll be back in training before I expected."

"Give it another couple of weeks to be on the safe side. Then I'd start him jogging and ease him back into training." Leo advised.

"That's pretty much what I had in mind," Jeff agreed.

"I'll stop back in a few days." Leo turned from the paddock, passing Charlie as he walked to his truck.

"How is he doing today?" Charlie asked Jeff when he joined him at the paddock fence.

"He's looking better every day," Jeff replied. "Your paddock has been a perfect setup for him. One of these days, I'll figure out a way to return the favor."

Charlie shook his head. "There's no favor to return, although I would be interested in discussing a stud fee. When I compare pedigrees, it looks like Fury would be a perfect match for Resplendant."

"I don't plan to breed him for another year, maybe two, but I'll talk to Natalie and be sure we get Resplendant's name on the list for his first season. You know, bringing Fury to your farm solved a lot of problems for us. It gave Fury a quiet place to recuperate and, with all the your staff watching, it has kept him safe from whoever has been trying to cause problems for him and us. It was a generous offer, Charlie. Natalie and I both appreciate what you and Vanessa and Sonny have done to help us."

Jeff lowered his voice. "How is Sonny holding up? He has seemed distracted lately. I realize he's under a lot of stress. Natalie told me his pre-trial conference is scheduled for next week."

Charlie's face clouded. "I know, as sure as I'm standing here, that Sonny didn't kill that woman. He had a meeting with Naomi a couple of days ago. He said she doesn't doubt he's been wrongly charged, that the evidence against him is pretty weak. She acts real confidant, but that's her job. Sonny is scared. Vanessa is being supportive and trying to stay optimistic, but the whole situation is wearing her down."

"And you're trying to carry the load for everyone." Jeff said.

Charlie shrugged. "It's been a rough couple of weeks for all of us. I've got to run; lots of work to do. See you later."

"Take care, Charlie."

Jeff watched his horses for a few minutes longer and then went home for a dinner of steak, peas and baked potatoes.

"I'm going to take a shower," Natalie said after she and Jeff had finished eating and cleaned up the kitchen. "Meet me on the porch for a drink after?"

"Sure. I'll mix the drinks."

"I'm sorry we won't be going to Kentucky next week," Natalie said as she was leaving the kitchen.

"That sure would have been something," Jeff agreed. "Then again, there's always next year."

"True. There's always a chance Flight will be good enough."

Jeff wanted to lift his wife's spirits and now seemed like the time. "Flight looks superb. Did I mention that I entered her in an Allowance Race next week?"

"No, you did not," Natalie pretended to be annoyed, and then began laughing. She hugged her husband. "You schemer! Did she actually draw a post position?"

"She did." Jeff revealed. "She has been training so well. She's looking better than Fury did last year at this time. I knew you'd be a little down about missing the race next week, so Flight and I decided to surprise you."

"You did that." Natalie's green eyes reflected her happiness into Jeff's. "I didn't expect you to enter her until mid-summer. Do you think she'll do as well as Fury?"

"Flight is a repeat breeding," Jeff reminded his wife. "She has the same genes as Fury. She is showing some impressive talent. If she has his fortitude, she'll be successful. Carl will take her out to the track in the morning for a last workout before the race. In the meantime, I've got another surprise."

"Oh? It's unlikely you can top Flight's surprise race," Natalie challenged.

Jeff flapped his hand in the air. "Drum roll, please. . ." Then announced, "Leo was as happy with Fury's progress as we are. He's going to do another x-ray tomorrow and, if everything looks like he expects it to look, Fury can start jogging. That means there is a chance he can make it for the second race of the Triple Million, but almost certainly for the third."

Natalie was silent.

"I thought you would be excited," Jeff said.

"On one hand, I am, but on the other, I'd rather have him safe than famous," she confessed. "Besides that, after Fury got hurt there was no more talk of selling or partnerships. I'm sorry he got hurt, but it stopped us from fighting over his future. Do you realize we haven't fought about him once since you got back from Laredo?"

"Do you realize that we haven't fought about anything since you got back from Andrade?" Jeff added. "When you were missing, the only thing in my mind was how much you mean to me. I would rather be bankrupt and have you next to me than to be a billionaire and live without you. If you don't want to sell, we won't sell. I will never bring it up again."

Natalie put her arms around her husband and hugged his chest. "That's the best surprise you could ever have given me." Then she kissed him, a long, lazy kiss. She whispered, "And I don't mean the part about not selling."

Jeff buried his nose in Natalie's thick red hair. "Mind if I join you in the shower?"

Before Natalie responded, Jeff lifted his wife in his arms and carried her up the stairs for the first time in years.

39

Sarah traveled to the Williams Farm to meet with Naomi and Sonny whenever Naomi scheduled a meeting with their client. There was an open invitation for Sarah to stay at Jeff and Natalie's home, but she'd begun spending more and more time with Carl.

Vanessa and Charlie supported Sonny completely. Convinced of her husband's innocence, Vanessa had no doubt that he would be acquitted. Sonny's trial was docketed for the Thursday before Labor Day.

Charlie took over much of the work at the farm and encouraged Sonny to take off all the time needed to prepare for the upcoming trial. Occasionally, Charlie even filled in for Sonny at Jeff's barn. But the stress of it all had taken its toll, and Charlie started drinking heavily.

Worried about the consequences if Sonny was somehow found guilty, Charlie considered going to the Laredo District Attorney and claiming that he sold Angie a couple of vials of Butazolidin a few of days before her death. He wasn't sure if they would prosecute him for selling drugs if he made that claim, since Butazolidin was widely used by horsemen, but he couldn't imagine his brother-in-law going to prison. He didn't think Sonny would survive. Charlie knew if there was any chance the authorities would believe his story; he would need to "confess" to the drug dealing before Sonny's trial started in three more weeks.

What were the chances the real killer would be found before the trial?

Vanessa came out to greet Naomi at the door. “How was your trip?”

“Good. There was very little traffic, and I know the route so well.”

Vanessa’s laugh lines deepened, her eyes brightened, and she grinned. “Sarah got here a couple of minutes ago. She and Sonny are out back on the patio. It’s such a lovely day, Sonny thought everyone might enjoy the fresh air.”

“That sounds like a splendid idea.” Naomi agreed.

Naomi truly liked Vanessa and marveled at the woman’s ability to find a bright side in just about every situation. She had remained upbeat throughout the trial preparation. If Vanessa found out the truth about Sonny’s relationship with Angie, and it was unlikely that she didn’t, she refused to acknowledge it. Naomi followed her through the house and out onto the patio.

“Hi, Sonny, Sarah.” Naomi set her briefcase on the table.

Sonny stood until Naomi and Vanessa sat with him. “Good to see you, as always.”

“Sonny set everything up on the patio before I got here,” Sarah told Naomi. “We’ve been watching the horses playing in the field out back. I could stay here all afternoon.”

“We may be here all afternoon,” Naomi declared. “I talked to the judge again this morning. The pre-trial conference is scheduled for Monday, so we need to have everything ready to share with the prosecution."

Sarah nodded. "I guess we'd better get to work."

With Vanessa observing, the trio reviewed the lists of horsemen, the jockeys, the owners, the trainers, the grooms, the stable help and the racetrack employees. Statements had been taken from all of them, and Naomi had read and reread them many times. While the prosecution's case was nothing but circumstantial evidence, the defense attorneys had thus far come up with nothing that could negate any of it.

No one saw Sonny enter or leave his room after his discussion with Doug Whiteman. Doug's statement verified that Sonny went into his room at about 6:00 p.m., but then Doug got into the elevator so he didn't know how long Sonny stayed in his room. Doug, among others, also confirmed that Sonny wasn't at the restaurant or the hotel lounge all evening. The coroner estimated the time of death between 5:30 and 7:00 p.m. No one but Doug Whiteman had seen Sonny during that period of time.

Naomi had to convince a jury of Sonny's innocence based on one of the prosecution's primary pieces of evidence: Sonny's telephone calls, especially the message "Hey, Baby, I'm at the door. Open up" he'd left on her cell phone and "What's going on? Call me. I'm going crazy here" he'd made to her room phone's voice mail. Naomi would argue that it wouldn't make sense to call someone if the caller was in the same room. Neither would it make sense to call the room of someone who the caller knew was dead.

Of course the prosecution would counter that Sonny left those messages after he murdered her to mask his crime.

40

As usual, Jeff woke up before the alarm's buzzer sounded. He turned off the alarm so Natalie could sleep a while longer. He showered and dressed quickly, went to the kitchen and filled a mug with coffee, grabbed his keys, left the house, and locked the door behind him. The air was chilly. He was glad he had worn a long-sleeved shirt.

When inside his truck, Jeff set his coffee mug in the cup holder, locked his seatbelt, started the engine, then turned on the radio and accelerated down the driveway. Alone, he dared to *harm*onize with the late great Glen Campbell, and the two of them belted out "Wichita Lineman."

Jeff was looking forward to meeting Leo and Carl for breakfast. He had found a race where he was considering entering Fury and wanted to hear their thoughts. After breakfast, Carl was going to gallop Fury so both the trainer and the veterinarian had a chance to study the colt in motion. While Jeff was confident about his ability to see any problems, he wasn't going to take any chances. For spotting any irregularity in a horse's gait, Leo was one of the best.

When he arrived at the end of the driveway, Jeff spied a squad car to his right racing along the eastbound lane, all lights flashing and siren blaring. As he reached for his coffee mug, Jeff stepped on the brake to stop his truck and let the cop pass, but the brake pedal had no resistance and slipped down to the floor. Unable to stop his truck from rolling onto the road, and jolted by fear of being imminently broadsided by the squad car, Jeff's only option was to speed up straight across the two-lane highway, knowing a steep embankment awaited him on the other side. He leaned back into the seat, pressed his head against the headrest, and turned off the ignition just before the truck left the grassy berm and down the embankment.

The truck rolled over once before skidding to a stop at the bottom of the gully.

Upside down and coughing from the dust emitted by the air bag, Jeff first wondered if he had totaled his truck. About himself, his fingers moved, as did his arms, though his left shoulder seemed frozen. He had some pain in his right knee, but his feet and his legs worked. He was able to turn his head.

No major damage to me, he thought, as he reached to disengage the seatbelt, his hands shaking. Ringing in his ears started after he opened the door and rolled out of the truck. His knees buckled. He collapsed facedown into the narrow stream. Unable to breathe, darkness spread over him.

41

"I understand you have worked for the McCoy family for some time."

"Yes, I have." Marty told the detective.

"How well did you know Angelina McCoy?"

"I've worked for her father for twenty-six years. Mr. McCoy hired me as a kid to clean stalls. I got into some trouble and Mr. McCoy stood by me. Angie and I grew up learning to work together. My job was to take care of the horses and Angie's job to ride them. Sometimes I would ride with her; sometimes she would help out in the barn. We had a common goal to make the McCoy farm one of the best in the country."

Detective Michaels glanced about the visitor's lounge rather than at Marty as he asked, "Are you familiar with the drug, Butazolidin?"

"Yes. It is used to counter inflammation in the horses," Marty told him. He added, "I'm pretty sure Jeff Frazier uses it."

Michaels's eyes darted to Marty's. "Why do you mention Jeff Frazier? Is he the only one you know of who uses it?"

"No," Marty replied, feeling like a trapped barn rat. "Most people that work with horses use it when needed."

"I'm curious. Why did you single out Jeff Frazier?" the detective questioned.

Marty hedged, "I don't know. He's name popped into my head, that's all."

The detective looked from Marty to his notepad. "I understand that Butazolidin can be used for pain management for people."

"That's what they say," Marty shrugged. "If it works for horses, my guess is that it would do the same for people."

Irritated by the detective's comment, Marty wondered if Michaels was suggesting that Angie had been taking drugs.

Michaels confirmed Marty's suspicion. "Are you aware of Angelina using any drugs?"

"No," Marty pounded his palm with his fist. "Never!"

The detective's cell phone rang. "Michaels," he answered as he walked away and out of the lounge. A few minutes later, Marty listened to the investigator's car start and drive away.

Almost two months had passed since Angie's funeral, but old habits die hard, and sometimes, just for a moment, Marty found himself waiting for her to walk down the lane to the stable. He had loved to watch her stroll along the pathway, waving to the workers and stopping to talk to Dreamweaver when her two-year-old colt was out in the paddock.

Throughout the twenty-six years Marty Adams worked for Anthony and Martha McCoy, he became mesmerized by their daughter. Though quite a few years younger than Marty, Angie flirted with him, teased him, and always fed his ego. Angie's intermittent attention kept Marty at her beck and call. There was nothing he wouldn't have done for her.

After Angie's death, Marty made it his priority to be sure Dreamweaver was always well groomed and content. Angie had understood that Dreamweaver could never compete in the highest levels of racing, yet he was one of the very few horses, perhaps the only one, she had loved anyway.

Mr. McCoy made it clear to everyone that he would not sell Dreamweaver at any price. He would keep the colt at the McCoy farm until he died. Mrs. McCoy spent some time with the high-strung grey colt young horse every day. For Marty and the McCoys, Dreamweaver became a living memorial to Angelina.

Marty was convinced that Angie's spirit never left the farm. Sometimes he thought he could sense her come in; even feel her breath as she looked over his shoulder while he groomed the horses. Marty loved Angie.

Convinced that Sonny hadn't killed Angie, Marty was also sure that she hadn't killed herself, not accidentally and certainly not intentionally. Certain that someone had murdered Angelina, Marty had a good idea who that someone was.

As he brushed Dreamweaver, Marty imagined Angie's last moments of terror in that hotel room, unable to escape from her killer. He promised her spirit he would avenge her death.

"Good afternoon, Marty," Martha McCoy greeted. She swept past him, and into Dreamweaver's stall. Martha grabbed Dreamweaver's halter and pulled his nose down, touching her forehead to his, much the same way Angie used to greet the colt. It was the first time Marty had ever seen Angie's mother and the colt interact that same way.

"I'll be glad to take Dreamweaver out for you, Mrs. McCoy," Marty offered.

Martha had been riding horses for years, but at her age, a fall could be dangerous. Dreamweaver was what they called 'green broke.' While he was in training and could be ridden, he was not reliable. Besides Angie, only Marty had ever been on his back.

"No need. I can handle him," she said, and with a sneer, she added, "I've been riding horses longer than Jeff Frazier has been training them."

It wasn't the first time, since Angie's death, that Martha had brought up Jeff's name.

She walked the colt out of the stall and hooked him in the cross ties. Martha spoke to Dreamweaver in a whisper, while she chose a saddle and bridle. Then she asked, "Marty, will you saddle him for me?"

Although concerned for Martha's safety, Marty couldn't refuse to let her ride her own horse.

"He'll probably be full of himself." Marty warned. "I just brought him in from the paddock yesterday."

"Yes, I'm aware of that," Martha McCoy snapped at him.

Despite the colt's sidestepping and occasional buck, Marty got the saddle on him.

Dreamweaver was even more uncooperative when it came time to slip on the bridle. The colt didn't like the bit and let it be known. As soon as Dreamweaver was under tack, he flared his nostrils, pawed at the floor and then reared up as far as the ties would allow.

Without hesitation, Martha approached the colt. "Please steady him for me."

Marty tensed and got a firm hold on the bridle, ready to strong-arm the colt to keep him from bolting, when he released the cross ties.

He relaxed his grip, however, as the rambunctious colt stood still as a statue when Martha pulled herself up onto the saddle.

"He's all yours," Marty told her.

Angie's mother guided the docile colt down the path to the indoor arena connected to the barn.

Still concerned Martha might have trouble controlling the headstrong youngster, if he acted up, Marty followed and monitored the horse and rider through the glass door of the visitor's lounge.

As Martha and Dreamweaver cantered around the oval, Dreamweaver cooperated without reluctance, even changing leads on command. If Marty hadn't known it was impossible, he would have sworn that he was watching Angie, at her very best. He wondered if Dreamweaver thought his mistress was back.

While he watched Martha ride, Marty thought about another of her s that mirrored Angie's behavior. Still dark, the moon a tiny sliver in the sky, Marty arrived at the barn to get started with his chores the morning of a race. He heard a car coming up the private road and went to the barn door to check it out. Marty recognized Martha's car, and wondered why only the parking lights were on. He stayed close to the edge of the barn, and watched, Martha McCoy got out of her car, eased the driver's door closed, and quick-stepped to the house where she entered without turning on any lights. Angie used to stay out all night. She, too, would return just before dawn, in much the same manner.

Strange as it was, Marty didn't mention the incident to anyone. After all, it shouldn't be his job to carry tales. Since then, however, he paid strict attention to Martha McCoy, and the changes in her behavior. As the days passed, she exhibited more and more of her daughter's mannerisms and conduct. The usually sweet tempered, sociable woman had become demanding, moody and aloof since Angie's death, and if Jeff Frazier's name came up, Martha seethed.

42

Natalie arrived at the emergency wing of the hospital, still angry with herself for having almost decided not to get out of the shower to answer her phone. A nurse guided her to the curtained enclosure where Jeff was lying flat on a wheeled stretcher speaking with the doctor, his right leg propped up on a pillow. At the sight of his wife, Jeff moved to sit up, but the doctor put a hand on the injured man's chest and said, "You need to remain still for now, Mr. Frazier."

"I'm his wife," Natalie said, afraid to shift her eyes away from her husband. "Is he going to be alright? Is he alright?"

"I lost the brakes coming down our driveway," Jeff told her. "Almost got slammed into by a squad car. Went down the embankment. Rolled over. Police officer pulled me out of the water."

"Your husband was semi-conscious when EMT's got him into the ambulance, but he came around pretty quickly. There's a chance he suffered a concussion, so we're going to monitor him overnight. He has dislocated his shoulder and has a severe bruising, but I don't think he's broken any bones. X-rays will determine tears and fractures. There is also a two-inch laceration on his right leg, and a few superficial cuts on his forehead."

"They're telling me I will live, honey," Jeff joked. "Guess what. The cop who saved my life had my truck impounded because, when he looked at the underside, he saw someone had cut my brake lining."

Only the night before, Jeff had told her how much the thought of losing her had reminded him of how much he loved her. Now, so close to having lost him, Natalie was not about to leave her husband's side until she could take him home. Two days without a shower, she wondered if she smelled like sweat, but decided she didn't care. Natalie wasn't leaving the hospital until Jeff did. The day they had admitted him, she called to let Santos know what happened and that Jeff wouldn't be up to doing much for a while. She also asked Santos to stop by their house and take care of her mare, Felicia.

"Tell him not to worry about anything. Sonny is here now," Santos comforted her. "Between the two of us, everything will be under control."

"Thanks, Santos. I appreciate it," she'd told him. She didn't tell Santos why Jeff's brakes failed.

"Where's Jeff's truck? Do you want us to go get it?" Santos offered.

"Jeff said the police have it. But Jeff doubts the truck is salvageable. Thank God he is, though."

"No problem," Santos had told her. "Don't worry about anything. Sonny and I will have it all covered."

On the late afternoon of that second day, Jeff was discharged from the hospital. Natalie left to get her truck, only then noticing the uniformed guard standing outside Jeff's hospital room.

Natalie drove from the parking garage to the emergency entrance where Jeff, left arm in a sling, was waiting in the wheelchair the attendant had brought him down in.

With the attendant's help, Jeff limped toward Natalie's truck and eased himself in beside her. "I should stop by the barn and check on—"

"You should not stop by the barn and check on anything," Natalie interrupted. "We are going directly home and you are going to just relax with me in a tub of hot soapy water."

Jeff didn't argue, which confirmed Natalie's suspicion that he felt a lot worse than he would ever admit.

"Santos and Sonny have everything under control and told me to tell you they don't need your help," Natalie teased.

"Okay," Jeff said. He sighed and closed his eyes, thinking about how much worse the accident could have been and relieved to be on his way home with injuries no more severe than they were. Natalie needed him alive as much as he needed her to be.

At home, Natalie ignored Jeff's resistance for her help to support him into the bathroom.

"Well, my love, with your arm in a sling, I suspect you'll have some trouble getting your clothes off," she teased. "I guess I'll just have to undress you."

"I won't argue with that," Jeff replied.

Natalie poured a generous amount of bubble bath into the oversized tub and filled it with hot water before she tossed her own clothes on the floor with Jeff's. The couple got into the tub and eased themselves into the scented water.

"Maybe being stuck at home won't be so bad," Jeff murmured as he pulled his wife toward him.

43

After the bath, Jeff settled into his recliner with the day's racing program and a cup of coffee. Natalie called their family doctor and arranged for an early appointment the following day.

"I'm not going anywhere," she told Jeff. "If you're tired, you can sleep. I'll wake you for dinner."

"I'm not tired," Jeff said. Two minutes later, he was asleep.

Natalie had plenty to keep her busy at the house, but stayed close to her husband. She repeated a mental prayer of thanks he hadn't been killed.

Dinner was almost ready and Jeff had just opened his eyes when his cell phone rang. Natalie picked up Jeff's phone and motioned for him to stay where he was. It was Detective Michaels.

"I've got a couple of questions," he said. "May I speak to Mr. Frazier?"

Natalie rushed to the kitchen. "He's sleeping," she lied. "He's been through a lot, so I don't want to wake him. Can I have him call you later?"

What she wanted was to keep everybody, including the police, away from her husband until Jeff was strong enough.

"You might be able to help me out," Michaels replied. "Are you missing any equipment?"

"Not that I'm aware of," Natalie answered. "What kind of equipment?"

"Specifically, a braided rope," Michaels said.

"Fury's rope," she said. "Earlier this year, someone tried to take one of my horses. Our groom was spending the night in the barn and chased after the intruder. The guy got away, but he took Fury's rope with him. It's a six-foot lead, with a brass snap and has Fury's name woven into the top, near the loop. There isn't a lot of contrast, but you can see it."

"I've got a rope that fits that description. Any possibility there could be more than one like this, or that you let somebody borrow it and forgot about it?"

"Not a chance. That rope is one of a kind and handmade by a friend. We have a similar one for one of our fillies. Where did you find it?"

Detective Michaels hesitated before he answered. "It was in Angelina McCoy's room along with some other equipment in a duffle bag she must have carried with her when she traveled."

"In Angie's room? I don't know how she would have gotten that rope, but it wasn't from me or my husband. Can we get it back?" The detective declined her request. "We have to hold it for now as potential evidence until after the McCoy murder trial. I would appreciate it if you and your husband would keep all this to yourself for the time being."

"Sure," she said.

"I heard about your husband's accident. How is he?"

"Bruised and battered, but no permanent damage. The police said it looks like the brake line had been sliced, which caused the accident."

"I know about the brake line," Michaels revealed. "That was the other thing I wanted to discuss. A plain clothed police officer watching your husband while he was hospitalized. We didn't tell you for security reasons. I hope you understand."

Stunned, Natalie slid a chair out from the kitchen table and sat on it, "Do you really believe we are in that much danger?"

"I do. And if you don't object, we'd like to assign a few officers to monitor your residence. Based on everything that's happened, it's more than possible someone is trying to kill one or both of you. I'm guessing, but my gut connects the trouble you've had and the attempt on your husband's life to the murder of Angie McCoy."

"Thank you for everything you're doing. I sure don't object to the police watching the house."

"The security team will check in with you when they get there. They'll stay out of your way, but will keep an eye on things. In the meantime, if anything out of the ordinary occurs, call me."

44

"Your arm is still in a sling," Natalie reminded her husband. "You can't drive with one arm."

Jeff had insisted he was okay to drive to see his physician. He felt he needed to get behind the wheel of a truck as soon as possible, just as when a rider falls off his horse, he needs to get right back on to overcome any fear of horses due to the fall.

But Natalie remained defiant. She opened the passenger door and Jeff reluctantly got in. The black stain, a remnant of the brake fluid left two days before, reminded her to shine a flashlight under her truck to check her own brake lines hadn't been tampered with. Satisfied, she slid into the truck and drove.

"You got a call from Detective Michaels last night. I took a message." Natalie decided the brief drive was the perfect time to tell her husband about what the detective told her.

"Did he leave a number?" Jeff asked.

"He did more than that," she replied. "He told me they found Fury's rope in Angie McCoy's duffle bag. He knew about your brake lines being cut, too. He thinks it's all tied to Angie's murder."

Jeff released a low whistle. "Is that what he wanted to tell me about?"

"No, but I'm guessing that the local police let him know about your accident and the brake line. This is getting too scary," she said.

Natalie steered her truck from the driveway, the sight of the embankment on the other side of the road causing her to visualize the horror her husband must have felt tumbling down into it. She steered east.

"When Santos caught that guy in the barn with Fury, it upset me, but I thought it was the luck of the draw, as they say," Natalie said. "You know, I thought we just had a horse in the barn that someone chose when they wanted to steal a horse. Then, when they kidnapped me, it seemed like Fury was truly being targeted, and it meant they intended both incidents to be distractions. Someone wanted to keep Fury from racing, but didn't plan to hurt anyone."

"That's what it seemed like to me, too," Jeff agreed. "After that race in Laredo, where Fury got hurt, I figured that anyone who was trying to injure him, or steal him, would have lost interest. I was even beginning to think that Angie could be involved, but when she got killed, that theory made little sense."

"I've been trying to think of how this is all connected," Natalie said. "Now, it looks like someone tried to kill you, or at least put you out of commission for some time, and it happened just after you entered Flight in her first race."

Jeff released another low whistle. “I don’t disagree. I can't believe that we are the targets of some maniac, but it is harder to believe that this is all coincidence. I wanted to go out to the barn, but I think we should go home first. I can call Michaels from there, and then, if you want to, you can ride along to the track with me. Carl told me Sarah would be in town tonight. Why don’t you call her and see if they want to meet us for dinner?”

“I won’t be just ‘riding along’ big guy. I’ll be driving,” his wife reminded him. “Okay. I’ll call Sarah. It might be good to run all this by her and Carl and see if we can make some sense of it.”

Jeff had been thinking along the same lines as his wife, but didn’t want to worry her by voicing his concerns. He had been wracking his brain, trying to come up with a reason that someone would want to cause harm to him, to Natalie or to their horses. Jeff found himself eager to speak with the homicide detective. Maybe there was a connection between Natalie’s kidnapping and Angie’s death.

Jeff glanced at his door’s rearview mirror. A police car was following them. “I think that cop behind us is following us,” Jeff warned his wife.

“He is,” Natalie confirmed. “Detective Michaels ordered around the clock surveillance for us. After he found out about your accident, he connected the dots regarding the problems we’ve had that involved Fury. He thinks someone may try to kill one or both of us, and that it’s somehow related to Angie’s murder.”

At the medical center, the wait was about fifteen minutes before a nurse escorted Jeff and

Natalie to an examination room. The doctor assured Jeff that, while his shoulder would be sore for several weeks, there appeared to be no permanent damage.

"Yep, it was dislocated, but the ER doc just tied me down and relocated it," Jeff joked, though he recalled the sharp pain when that doctor pushed his shoulder back into place.

On the drive back home, Natalie speed dialed Sarah, who was on her way to Carl's apartment. They made plans to meet for dinner.

"It would be great to see you two," Sarah told her friend. "I'll call Carl and make sure he has nothing else planned, but I doubt that he does."

"I know Carl talked to Jeff early this morning and told him you were coming in. Jeff and I are going to take a ride out to the track in a little while, so Carl may still be there. He had planned to work Flight this morning," Natalie explained.

Sarah chuckled. "Carl really loves Fury, there's no doubt about that, but he absolutely adores Flight! I'm almost jealous."

"I thought I was the only one who saw that," Natalie replied. "Yes, he is crazy about that filly. We'll see you later. Is Champion's okay for dinner? About six?"

"Sure, see you then." Sarah ended the call.

"We're all set for dinner tonight," Natalie told her husband.

"I'm looking forward to it," Jeff said. "It's time we do a little brainstorming about this mess. I'll give Detective Michaels a call now. Maybe he has some fresh information that will be helpful."

At Champions, Jeff and Carl mostly munched on their hamburgers and fries, washed down by beer, while Sarah discussed with Natalie all the news Natalie brought to the table.

"So it isn't out of the question that our troubles could have involved Angie," Natalie said, at the same time trying to think of anyone else connected with the deceased jockey. "We need to make a list of everyone we know who had any relationship with Angie and who fits the description of the man Santos saw."

Sarah tried to chew her hamburger and talk at the same time. "If Angie had something to do with the attempted theft, and/or your kidnapping, she could very well have hired someone nobody's ever seen. But dead people don't arrange sabotaging brake lines. If the incidents involving Fury are related, she could have had a partner who decided to carry out their plan–whatever it might have been."

"So, whoever sabotaged Jeff's truck is the key, and might be the murderer." Natalie was thinking out loud now. "I doubt that Angie's death was accidental. It's possible she could have overdosed and then have fallen and hit her head, but I don't believe it."

"I could buy the fact that she fell and hit her head and died accidentally as a result, but the drugs don't figure," Sarah said. "I'm convinced someone drugged her and then dropped her to the floor to make it appear to be accidental. But what was she doing with Fury's rope? Either she had some involvement with the incident in the barn, or someone planted the rope in her equipment bag. Until we sort this out, neither you nor Jeff should go anywhere alone."

45

Sonny gave his attorneys all the information he could recall regarding the time he'd spent at Laredo and his involvement with Angie McCoy. Vanessa had not questioned Sonny about his relationship with Angie. The attorneys had been careful to avoid asking questions related to the affair when Vanessa was present. Still, sometimes it felt like there was an elephant in the room that everyone pretended not to see.

The last meeting between Sonny, Sarah, and Naomi had been the final pre-trial preparation. Naomi was confident she could mount a solid defense. Sonny was even beginning to think things were looking up, before he got the call from Santos telling him about Jeff's accident. Sonny had immediately offered to work with Santos and do whatever he could to keep things running until Jeff got back on his feet. He couldn't imagine why someone had sabotaged Jeff's truck, but wondered if the answer would lead to Angie's murderer.

"Morning, Sonny," Charlie called out, striding up to the paddock fence where Sonny stood flaking hay into the standing feeders.

"Hey, Charlie," Sonny greeted his brother-in-law. "Did you hear about Jeff Frazier's accident?"

"It's been the talk of the backside the last few days. The Fraziers sure are having some rotten luck." Charlie turned on the hose and began cleaning out the water tub.

"Deliberately cutting a man's brake lines isn't rotten luck," Sonny retorted.

Charlie stopped cleaning and stood. "Someone they cut his brake lines? The word is that he failed to see a patrol car speeding at him when he drove onto the highway, sped up to get out of the way and crashed down an embankment."

Sonny turned to face Charlie. "There's more. Cops impounded his truck. They're surveilling his house 24/7, too."

"Damn," was all Charlie could think to say.

"Jeff could have been killed. He's lucky he got away with just a messed up shoulder and a few cuts and bruises. Santos and I will run things for a while," Sonny said. "Natalie said he can't even lift the coffee pot with that arm."

A look of dread spread over Charlie's face. "I can't imagine someone would go after Jeff like that."

"So many things are happening to the Fraziers in the last three months, and with me working there, and being charged for Angie's murder, it might be a good idea to look into some security here, too."

"What kind of security?" Charlie asked.

"Some more cameras, something like we have in the foaling barn," Sonny suggested, "and a guard dog for the house. It's been almost a year since we lost that old collie, and Vanessa has wanted another dog. I'm more worried about Vanessa being here alone than anything else. I don't know what I'd do if anything happened to her, and I might not be here much longer. The trial is in a couple of weeks. What happens if they convict me, Charlie?"

Charlie patted the younger man's shoulder. "Nobody will convict you. I know you didn't kill her and the jury will know that too. I'm not sure what happened between you and Angie, but Vanesa deserves better from you. I just hope you learned your lesson. In the meantime, I agree with you about getting some more security. Let's see if we can find a dog, maybe one that's already trained as a guard dog. It makes sense to install a few more cameras, too. We should make sure Vanessa's car stays in the garage, rather than outside overnight, too."

Sonny visibly relaxed. "I'm glad you don't think I'm crazy."

Charlie chuckled. "You might be, but remember, just because you're paranoid, doesn't mean they aren't out to get you."

That made Sonny smile. "Well, this paranoid stable hand will be at Frazier's barn for a few hours. Call if you need me."

"Since you're heading to the barn anyway, would you mind stopping at their house?" Charlie asked. "Vanessa has a casserole with some biscuits she made for Jeff and Natalie. Why don't you save her a trip and drop it off at their place on your way to the track?"

"Sure, I'll head up there now."

When Sonny saw Natalie's truck in front of her house, he parked behind it. He hit the horn twice to alert Natalie, in case she was out back and didn't hear him pull in. First Jeff stepped out onto the porch, and then Natalie appeared next to her husband.

Balancing the covered tray, Sonny carefully slid out of his truck.

"Hi Sonny," Natalie greeted. "We were just on our way to check on the crew. What have you got there?"

Sonny stepped onto the porch. "Vanessa made you some dinner and a fresh batch of her biscuits to go along with it."

Natalie's face lit up. "How nice. Thank you!"

"Did you say biscuits?" Jeff started to reach for the tray with his good arm, but Natalie intervened, taking the tray from Sonny.

"Nobody can make biscuits like Vanessa," Jeff said. "Not even Nat, if she doesn't mind my saying so."

"Thanks, Sonny," Natalie said. "Come on in and eat with us. Have some coffee."

"Thanks, Nat, but Santos is waiting for me. He said the straw is being delivered this afternoon, and it will be easier to get it stowed with two of us unloading it."

"I'll help," Jeff said. "We have a big load coming in."

Sonny shook his head and stifling a laugh. "Uh, no disrespect meant, but I heard about your argument with the coffeepot. Santos and I will probably get done faster if we aren't worried about your arm falling off."

With feigned irritation, Jeff turned to his wife. "And would you be the one responsible for reporting the fact that I couldn't lift a coffee pot?"

"I am, and it's true," his wife confessed. "Your arm is in a sling for a reason. You're supposed to rest it for the next ten days and throwing bales of straw isn't resting."

"We've got it covered, Jeff," Sonny said. "Carl came over this morning, and he said he'd be back again tomorrow morning to help exercise, so other than watching the horses work, there's nothing you need to do. Why don't you take it easy for at least another day or so? One of us will call if there's any question about anything."

"What excellent advice," Natalie agreed. She knew Jeff's shoulder was bothering him. She also understood how difficult it was for him not to be able to work the way he usually did. Still, she was surprised when Jeff said, "I really appreciate it, Sonny. If you don't need me there, then I guess I'll stay here today."

Sonny stepped off the porch. "We'll be fine. I'd better get moving though. The truck should get there pretty shortly."

"Thanks again for dinner," Natalie said. "I'll give Vanessa a call a little later."

"You're welcome," Sonny replied. "She's happy to be able to help."

When Sonny turned back toward his truck, he spied something reflecting the sunlight on the ground near the parked vehicles. He wondered if might have dropped something, and reached into his jeans, where his fingers curled around the pocketknife he always carried. Glad he hadn't lost the knife, Sonny stooped and picked up the object. He was surprised to discover a farrier's pick. The etching looked familiar, as did the pick's design. Except for the letters of the name, it was the image of the pocket knife Angie had given him.

Sonny recalled what Angie had said when she had given him the knife. *I want you to have something that makes you think of me; something you won't need to hide, and that you will see every day.*

Like Sonny's pocket knife, the pick was elegant. Exquisitely etched and overlaid with silver, a name had been engraved in the overlay. Sonny wondered if he might be looking at another of Angie's gifts, and dared to consider that she'd been involved with Jeff, too.

He rubbed a drop of oil from the well-used pick. Some letters of the name were legible, but others were smooth, the engraving almost worn away. The first three letters were still clear, M A R, the next letter looked to be a T, or an L, or even a K or an S. The last letter, if there was another letter, was worn smooth.

Sonny thought about the horsemen that he knew, who would be likely to have a farrier's pick. Mark Rappaport, Marlin Thomas and Marty Adams came to mind.

Marlin was the cook in the horsemen's kitchen. While it was possible, it was unlikely that he would be the owner of the well-used implement. Mark was a possibility. He was a jockey, and it wouldn't be unusual for a jockey to have a hoof pick, though Mark was awfully young to have been able to wear one so smooth. Marty was a groom/stable hand, who worked for the McCoys.

On the other hand, it might be Jeff's. Someone might have given it to him secondhand.

Jeff had seen Sonny's pocket knife, and had commented on it, but didn't mention having one similar. Except for the brake fluid smeared across the edge, the hoof pick was clean, not tarnished or pitted, so it hadn't been laying outside very long.

Sonny returned to the porch and rang the doorbell.

Natalie came to the door. "Hello again! What did you forget?"

Sonny held the hoof pick up to Natalie's eyes. "I found this on the ground, over by my truck, and figured it might belong to Jeff or a friend of his."

Natalie took the tool from Sonny and examined it. "I wonder if Marlin dropped it when he stopped by a couple of weeks ago. No one else but Sarah has been here for a few days, except. . ." Natalie paused mid-sentence and looked timidly at Sonny.

It hadn't occurred to Sonny until that moment, and he finished her sentence, "Except for whoever cut Jeff's brake lines."

"I should call the police," she said coldly.

"I'll show you right where I found it," Sonny offered, now sorry he hadn't been more careful picking up the hoof pick. "Maybe you shouldn't handle it anymore just in case there are fingerprints and it isn't too late to save them."

Natalie immediately set the tool on a table by the door and followed Sonny to the oil stain where he'd found the pick, then she went back to the house to call the police.

Sonny decided it would be better for him if he wasn't around when the cops got there.

46

While Natalie and Jeff waited for the police to arrive, the couple exchanged ideas about anyone they associated with who had a name that began with MAR.

Detective Michaels, flanked by two police officers, found the hoof pick of definite interest. He also made a special note of the fact Sonny had made the discovery. One officer took several pictures of its original location. The other placed the pick in an evidence envelope.

"The lab will check for prints," Michaels told Natalie. "But due to its handling by both you and Sonny, I've got little hope we'll get a good print from whoever dropped that thing. Do you know anyone whose name begins with MAR?"

"Marlin Thomas is the cook at the horsemen's kitchen, on the backside of Angelina Race Track," Jeff offered. "He stopped by the house a week ago. I suppose he could have dropped it back then."

"Can you think of a reason why Mr. Thomas would want you hurt?" Michaels asked.

"No," Jeff said. "I've known Marlin for years, and frankly I doubt that the pick is his, anyway. He's more involved with food than horses."

"Anyone else?"

horse a few bites of carrots, while rubbing noses, necks and ears and calling each one by name.

Natalie was first through the barn door when she and Jeff arrived. "Coffee smells wonderful, Santos. Did Flight say she was ready to run today?"

"Flight is absolutely ready to run," Santos proclaimed. "She is going to show them all how nice she looks from behind."

"That would make my day," Jeff said. "Sarah and Carl should be here in a couple of hours. We're going to the Maverick for dinner after the races. Can you join us?"

"Sure, that would be great." Santos poured himself a mug of coffee. "Coffee is ready. Anybody interested in a cup?"

"Yes," Jeff and Natalie replied in unison.

After a few minutes of general chatter, the three horsemen went about their chores.; a normal day at the barn. Twenty minutes before the race, Santos and Jeff would walk Flight over to the paddock where Carl would meet them. Since his arm was still in a sling, Jeff would have to be content supervising the saddling, but intended to use his good arm to give Carl a leg up. It was tradition.

A race track's surface changed from day to day, and sometimes the variation in condition altered the strategy for the trainer and the jockey, so Jeff went to watch the races, and see if the track was showing any bias. Natalie stayed with Santos to take care of the stalls.

"The announcer just called for the fifth race," Natalie informed the groom. "Flight is in the sixth, so let's get ready. Jeff said he'd be back to walk her to the paddock, but in case he doesn't get here in time, I'll go over with you."

"That's fine. Flight is usually collected, but she seems to know something special is happening today," Santos said. "It will be better to have two people lead her, particularly with a one-armed trainer."

Fifteen minutes later, the sound towers blared the announcer's call for the horses that were running in the sixth race. He had no sooner finished his call then Jeff came through the door. Santos had a halter on Flight and was leading her out of the stall.

Natalie stroked the filly's neck and whispered softly, "Run fast and come home safe." Louder she said, "I'll go over now and see you two in the paddock. Sarah and Sonny are meeting me there."

"Okay," Jeff told his wife. "There are no scratches. Flight will be running with a full field."

Natalie gave her husband a quick kiss. "The little bay filly, Anmaran, is McCoys' first entry since they lost Angie. I hope she does well for them. They could use some good news."

Jeff hooked a second lead to Flight's bridle. "Peter Crawford is riding Anmaran. Carl told me that Anthony had asked Doug Whiteman to ride her, but Doug was committed to someone else," Jeff said, as hooked a second lead to Flight's bridle.

"Anmaran is Dreamweaver's half-sister. I've been watching her, and she's a nice filly. She'll be our main competition," Santos predicted.

51

When Natalie arrived, Sonny and Sarah were standing at the paddock rail, as Santos lead Flight around the small oval. "Here we go," she greeted her friends.

"She looks absolutely beautiful," Sarah exclaimed. "Carl is excited about the race today. He's crazy about that filly."

Sonny chuckled, and said, "Carl came to the barn a few days ago just to walk Flight for twenty minutes. He and Santos actually argue about who takes care of her. They're like two brothers fighting over a favorite catcher's mitt."

"She is a sweet-tempered girl." Natalie kept her eyes on Flight as she spoke. "I sure hope she'll like running in a group of a dozen."

Santos led Flight to her stall. She had drawn number 7, which Sarah believed was a lucky number for the Fraziers. Flight stood quietly, looking around, fascinated by all the surrounding activity. She didn't appear bothered by the noise of the crowd. Santos saddled her without incident. Jeff and Carl were deep in conversation, as Jeff gave the jockey a few last-minute instructions. Santos stayed by the filly's head, stroking her muzzle and whispering to her.

The track announcer called for the riders to mount. Santos gave Carl a leg up onto the first time starter. Carl took the reins, but Santos kept the lead attached and walked them to the opening onto the track where he allowed an out-rider to take over. The out-rider was an experienced horseman, riding a retired race horse. He smoothly took control of Flight and walked with her in the post parade.

Santos joined Jeff and the others at the rail, near the finish line. “She sure is behaving herself.”

Jeff agreed. “I hope that means she’s confidant and not that she’s bored.”

“How can you tell the difference?” Sarah asked her friend.

“Until she has a few races under her belt, there’s no way to know for sure,” Jeff explained. “Flight is generally well-behaved, but I thought all the excitement would have her dancing around the paddock, but she acted like a professional. We’ll see what she does next time out.”

The first six horses walked into the starting gate with only a few minor problems, which wasn’t unusual for first-time starters. Flight walked into the gate with no hesitation.

Jeff couldn’t help grinning with pride. “Way to go, Flight!”

Three more horses were loaded, but the number 11 horse was balking. The jockey jumped off the filly to allow the gate crew to try to convince her to load without his weight on her back. The gate crew locked arms, making a sling behind her to keep her from backing up, while the assistant starter tried to coax her into the gate.

“That’s Anmaran.” Sonny said. Like most horsemen who had an entry in the race, Sonny had studied the racing form and was familiar with each of the horses and their connections.

One of the gate crew draped a blanket across Anmaran's head, covering her eyes. The cover calmed her enough to allow the crew leader to walk her into the gate. Peter Crawford re-mounted the filly, and they got the last horse into the gate.

The gate flew open as the announcer called, "They're off. Fighting for the lead, it's SquirrellySuzie and LadyLiza, followed by HollysHope. JazzDancer is moving quickly on the outside. Next in line are FraziersFlight, TakeMyMoney, and PuddleJumper. It's three lengths back to Mystery, ShiningSheena and ElegantElvira, with EchosQuestion starting to gain ground on the inside, with the slow breaking McCoysAnmaran trailing."

"Carl got out of the gate nicely," Natalie noted.

Jeff nodded. "So far, so good."

The announcer continued, "JazzDancer has taken over in front. HollysHope is content to stay just off the pace. SquirrellySuzie is third. FraziersFlight is fourth. EchosQuestion is picking up the pace and here comes McCoysAnmaran. The bay filly is flying on the outside as the field turns for home."

Natalie clung to her husband's good arm. "I hope the McCoys' filly does well. After all that has happened, they deserve something positive."

"SquirrellySuzie is now even with HollysHope and they are moving together to challenge Jazz Dancer for the lead. Carl Lawson is asking FraziersFlight to pick up the pace. McCoysAnmaran is now fifth. There are two lengths back to the rest of the pack."

"Come on, Anmaran!" Natalie couldn't help rooting for that game little filly, who was gaining on the leaders with every stride.

"With a sixteenth to go, it's HollysHope, FraziersFlight and McCoysAnmaran, followed by JazzDancer, EchosQuestion and PuddleJumper. ElegantElvira is making a move, but she may have kicked into top gear a little late. HollysHope is angling out, trying to hold on, as Carl Lawson guides FraziersFlight to the inside, saving ground. McCoysAnmaran is still gaining. She is half a length behind Fraziers Flight, as Hollys Hope fades to third. They are at the wire and from last to first, the unofficial winner is McCoysAnmaran, a first-time starter owned by Anthony McCoy. In second place, also starting for the first time, it's FraziersFlight. ElegantElvira got up for third, and HollysHope finished fourth."

Jeff and Santos jumped over the rail and onto the track to meet Carl and Flight and walk them to the winner's circle. Jeff never relaxed after a race until his horse was safely back from the track and settled in the stall.

Natalie, Sarah and Sonny were clearly excited at the way Flight and Carl had run the race. Sonny was the first to speak. "That was a darn good race."

Natalie gave Sonny a hug. "I am so proud of her. She sure didn't act like a first time starter, but after the start, neither did Anmaran. With that break, it would have been no surprise if Anmaran had stayed dead-last. She made up a lot of ground awfully quickly. What a lovely filly she is."

"That's true, but Flight just kind of slipped into second gear and cruised. I don't think you saw what she's capable of doing, and Carl was smart not to push her too hard the first time," Sonny told her. "Carl can tell us more, but I'm impressed with that little girl, and I suspect you'll find a few others are, too."

The three of them joined Jeff and Santos to walk Flight back to the barn. Carl dismounted, unsaddled Flight, and then left for the weigh station. From there, he would go to the jockey's room to shower and change. Flight was his final mount for the day. He and Sarah planned to stay for the last couple of races before they met Jeff, Natalie, and Santos for dinner.

While Jeff, Natalie and Santos walked Flight back to the barn, Sonny and Sarah were going to the Clubhouse to get something to drink and wait for Carl.

Flight danced and pranced. She acted happy and not tired by her seven-furlong dash from the gate to the finish line. Jeff could not have been more pleased with her performance. Sometimes the way they race is more important than where they finish. This was one of those times.

They had turned from the track when Jeff heard someone call his name. He stopped and looked over his shoulder. Anthony and Martha McCoy were approaching.

"Go on ahead," Jeff told Santos. "We'll meet you at the barn."

Anthony shook hands with Jeff and Natalie.

"Congratulations on an excellent race." Natalie said.

Mr. McCoy gave Natalie a friendly hug, "Thank you. That's quite a filly you've got there, too."

Jeff returned Anthony's smile and included Martha in his gaze as he shook Anthony's hand. "Thank you. We were pleased with her performance, but Anmaran looked fantastic. She overcame that slow break like a veteran. When she found her stride, she certainly covered the ground. With a clean break, she might have won by three lengths."

Anthony's eyes lit up. "Thanks, Jeff. We have high hopes for Anmaran."

Martha McCoy, who was usually quite sociable, said coldly, "High hopes are often dashed." She turned and walked away.

Anthony looked momentarily uncomfortable. "Martha is having a hard time these days. Best of luck with your filly." Then he turned and followed his wife.

Nobody noticed Marty, who was standing off to the side, silently watching the exchange.

Jeff draped his arm over Natalie's shoulders. "I guess the win is bittersweet for the McCoys," he said. "Angie would have been riding Anmaran today."

"Yes," Natalie answered. "I can understand her not wanting to stay and talk."

Santos and Flight were ambling toward Barn 17, when Jeff and Natalie caught up with them.

"She sure seems content," Jeff commented. Flight had stopped to nibble at the grass along the edge of the fence.

Santos seemed distracted.

Jeff added, "She handled the race well, exactly like her big brother."

Natalie looked up at her husband. "Well, let's get her home and see if she'll eat. It's about time to feed everybody again, anyway. Carl and Sarah are meeting us in a couple of hours. I asked Sonny and Vanessa to join us. He said he'd call Vanessa and let me know if they can make it."

52

Natalie went home to shower and get dressed for dinner while Jeff and Santos were finishing up with the horses. Shortly after she left, Jeff thought that Santos seemed distant. He had been distracted since they left the paddock. "Is everything okay, Santos? Is there something that I need to know about?"

Santos replied, "I was thinking about something, but it's probably nothing. There's no worry about Flight though. She looks fine to me."

"Okay," Jeff said. Maybe Santos was tired. It had been a long week, with the groom working double duty since Jeff's accident.

Santos finished filling the bins with fresh hay, before he blurted, "Before the race, Charlie was in the paddock helping with Anmaran. We were talking, and she reared up. When he turned to keep her head down, I saw a wide scar across the back of his wrist."

Jeff didn't understand why Santos would find that disturbing. "Charlie used to be a boxer. Between that and his time in the Army, I imagine he has more than one scar."

"I know, but when I saw the scar, it reminded me," Santos stammered. "The man who tried to take Fury had a mark on his wrist, at the edge of the glove. It could have been a scar. That man was big, like Charlie, and he was agile. He moved quickly for someone of his size. He moved like a boxer, like Charlie."

Jeff stopped and peered into Santos's eyes. "Are you sure?"

Santos nodded. "If it wasn't Charlie that night, it could have been his twin. I don't know what to do."

"I don't want to accuse him, but. . .."

Baffled, Jeff wanted to reject what Santos revealed to him. Charlie? Not Charlie. But if Charlie was the thief in the barn that night, could Sonny, Charlie's brother-in-law, have been in on the scheme, too? But Charlie and Sonny were his friends. He didn't want to believe they would turn on him. Jeff was sure Santos was mistaken. And so, for now, he shoved those awful notions to the back of his mind.

"Let's sleep on it," Jeff said. "Besides, Charlie will probably have a perfectly acceptable explanation, proof he was nowhere near the barn that night. I hope he does. We just have to wait and find out."

"Yes," Santos said. He forced his gloom away. "Tomorrow is soon enough to do that. Tonight is a celebration for Flight." Santos felt better now that he had told Jeff. They would figure it out tomorrow.

53

Detective Michaels shuffled through the pages of his open folder, sometimes pausing to study a document, seemingly oblivious to the police officer who sat on the opposite side of the table in the interrogation room.

Irritated by Michaels's sporadic humming, Derek asked nervously, "What is this all about?"

Without looking up from the paperwork, the detective began, "Officer Adams, do you recall responding to a call from Santos Velasquez about the attempted theft of a grey horse owned by Natalie Frazier?"

"Yes, I do," Adams responded.

"Is this a copy of your report?" Michaels slid a document across the table to Derek.

"It was early morning," he replied, looking at the paper in front of him. "Yes, it says here it was 3:35 a.m., when I got there. Velasquez didn't get a good look at the perp, and the perp got away. The horse was fine, nobody was hurt. I took the report, talked to the people in the barn, and filed the paperwork. Never heard any more about it."

"According to your report, an identifiable rope was stolen on the night of the attempted theft. Do you recall that?"

"Yes, I made a note of it. I remember they said the name was on it, but it was hard to see. Kind of strange, huh?"

"What is kind of strange?"

"Strange that somebody would put a name on a horse's rope, if you can't see it. Did you find the rope?" Derek asked, relaxing.

"What I find strange is what Velasquez said, when I questioned him. He told me about a glove the perp had dropped. He said he turned the glove over to you the night you responded to the incident."

"I already explained to Chief Robbins," Derek said. "I stopped at Dora's Donut Hut for coffee on my last break, but when I got back to my car, the glove was missing. I think the perp followed me and stole his glove while I was inside Dora's.

The detective pursed his lips and made a humming sound before he said, "What I think is strange is that a criminal would follow a police officer to try to steal evidence. Even stranger to me is that you never mentioned any glove in your report, or the theft of the glove from your vehicle."

Derek scratched his right ear. "Okay, like I told Chief Robbins, I realized I'd be in trouble for leaving my patrol car unlocked while I was away from it. Since it was gone anyway, I didn't include anything about it in my report. I shouldn't've reported it. I'm sorry."

Detective Michaels leaned against the back of his chair and stared into Derek's eyes. "You're sorry." He lowered his eyes to the folder and shuffled again through the documents, finally sliding one out.

"We recovered the horse's rope from a duffle bag belonging to Angelina J. McCoy."

"So did you find the thief?" Derek asked, relaxing again. "I wasn't involved in the investigation after I turned in my report.

"Then I'll let you in on what we uncovered," Michaels offered, almost smiling. "We know that, at some point, Jeff and Natalie Frazier handled the rope. Santos Velazquez would have used it frequently during his employment for the Fraziers. Sonny Owens helped with the Frazier horses often enough that it's probable he also would have used it. We know the decedent handled it, since we found it at the scene of her murder. It was in her duffle bag. What if I tell you we got a clear partial on the brass snap and it belongs to none of the above?"

Derek responded hesitantly. "Then I'd say the print would likely belong to the horse thief."

"Yet, how did the stolen rope get into McCoy's duffle bag, could she have innocently picked it up somewhere? Did the thief give it to her, or plant it to frame her? Was she involved in the plot?"

"That's a question you need to figure out," Derek said. "I'm just a cop, not a homicide detective."

Detective Michaels read aloud from a document pressed between his fingers, "At some point in time, Charles Theodore Williams, former United States Army Lieutenant, had the lead rope in his possession. His right thumb print, identified from his military file, was on the base of the snap. The print is partial, but still about three-quarters complete, with twenty-four matching points and three area matches."

"Well, there you go. You've got your thief." Derek said, as he rose from the chair. "Do you need me for anything else? My shift starts in a couple of minutes."

"How well do you know Charles Williams?"

"I don't. Never met the guy."

Michaels continued to read to Derek from the report, which verified Sonny Owens was married to Charles Williams's sister. They worked together at the Williams Farm, but there was no indication that Charles had worked for the Fraziers. "There are, however, numerous statements that put Williams in Laredo during the weekend of the murder."

Derek shrugged. "So, go get him. I've got to go or I'll be late."

"Just one more thing." Michaels said confidently. "The state police sent us a report about some evidence recovered with regard to Mrs. Frazier's kidnapping."

Derek felt sweat begin to pop out on the back of his neck. He shifted his weight from one foot to the other.

"The crime lab got some good prints off of a water bottle one of her kidnappers gave Mrs. Frazier on the day she was kidnapped. They found two partials near the top of the bottle and a full index on the bottom. You can imagine how it surprised us to learn those prints belong to Derek Adams, one of our own Chino police officers."

Derek's eyes darted to the door, but there was nowhere to run. He dropped back into the chair.

"And how long have you worked for the Chino Police Department?"

"Fifteen months."

"Where did you work before that?"

"I worked night security for Angelina Racetrack."

"How long did you work security?"

"I was there for almost five years."

"Were you acquainted with a lot of the horsemen at the track?"

"Sure."

"You're a sociable guy. Did you make some friends, talk to a lot of people?"

"Some."

"Did you have a personal relationship with Natalie Frazier?"

"No."

"Did you know Angelina McCoy?"

"I talked to her a couple of times. My brother works for her family."

"Did you have a personal relationship with Angelina McCoy?"

"No."

"Were you acquainted with Charles Williams?"

"No. Okay. I mean, I know who he is. His family is a big deal in Chino."

"Did you kidnap Natalie Frazier?"

Derek's face changed from an irritated shade of red to a terrified shade of white, when he answered in a high-pitched voice, "What?"

Detective Michaels closed his folder, crossed his arms on the table and leaned forward. "Can you explain how your fingerprints got all over bottle of water given to Natalie Frazier from one of her kidnappers?"

Derek's face changed to a paler shade of white. "I think I want a lawyer."

"You can have a lawyer, Officer Adams," Michaels replied. "If you are making a formal request, our discussion stops now. If our discussion stops now, I'm prepared to arrest you for the kidnapping of Natalie Frazier."

"As I'm sure you are aware, after your arrest, you will be arraigned, and if found guilty, you'll be facing at least ten years in a federal prison. You realize kidnapping is a federal crime, right?"

Defeated, Derek asked, "And what if our discussion doesn't stop now?" He'd been around long enough to figure the detective had a deal to offer. Since a corrupt cop is a black eye for the entire department, they'd keep things quiet, if they could. If he provided enough of the right information, he'd still lose his job, but might avoid prison.

"You'll tell me everything you know and everything you suspect–everything–about Natalie Frazier's kidnapping, the attempted theft of the horse, and the sabotage of Jeff Frazier's truck and Angelina McCoy's murder."

"What will happen to me?" Derek asked, using the shirt cuff of his uniform to wipe the sweat from his forehead.

"If you are cooperative, and everything checks out, I'll talk to the DA and recommend he lets you plead to lesser charges. What those charges will be is up to the District Attorney. But whether you cooperate or not, as of right now, you are under arrest for the kidnapping of Natalie Frazier. Do you need a telephone?"

"There's an apprentice jockey, Mark Rappaport. He rides at Angelina, though he's pretty young to have worn the etching off so smoothly."

"We don't really know him too well," Natalie told him. "He seems like a nice enough kid. He stopped by on a couple of occasions and offered to exercise our horses. We didn't take him up on the offer because we use full-time riders."

"Another person we thought of is Marty, from Anthony McCoy's barn." Jeff said. "I can't think of his last name, but he's a heck of a likeable guy and a hard worker. He's helped us out on a couple of occasions, and he's been around a long time."

Michaels got back on his feet. "Okay, we'll follow up on these leads and let you know if we find anything. In the meantime, keep your doors and windows locked."

After the lawmen departed, Natalie asked her husband, "Do you really think it could have been one of the horsemen who tried to kill you?"

"No, I don't," Jeff answered. "Heck, we don't even know if the letters are someone's first name. It might belong to someone whose name has nothing to do with the engraving. It could be someone's last name, a company, a horse, or anything."

"What about David Marsico?" Natalie suggested. "His last name could fit the inscription, and he's a thoroughbred trainer. It wouldn't surprise me if he carried a well-used hoof pick."

Jeff was slow to answer. "I know how you feel about David, but I can't imagine him being in any way involved. Then again, I can't imagine anyone we know being involved. We should give his name to Detective Michaels, though."

Jeff felt certain that the pick belonged to whoever cut his brake lining. He was also convinced that no matter who it belonged to, the owner's name would come as a surprise.

47

While Sonny drove to the racetrack to meet Santos, he called Naomi and informed her about what had happened.

"Are you sure it belongs to Marty Adams?" the attorney asked him.

"No, I'm not positive, but the name would fit, and it's a good bet," Sonny insisted. "Angie gave me a pocket knife with a similar overlay. She had my name engraved on the knife, very much the same way the name is engraved on the farrier's pick I found. The problem is that I don't want to tell them about the pocket knife. I don't want Vanessa to find out I got the knife from Angie, but if the hoof pick is Marty's, he's the one who dropped it. That's why I'm calling you."

"I understand," Naomi said. "Let's wait a day or so and see what the DA comes up with. Did you ever see Marty use that particular tool?"

"Not that I recall," Sonny replied.

"Is there any reason that Marty would want to hurt Jeff?"

"Not unless he thought Angie's death somehow involved Jeff," Sonny said. "Marty always took care of things for Angie. He's worked for the McCoys for a lot of years."

Naomi cleared her throat before asking, "Could Jeff have been involved in a relationship with Angie?"

Now Sonny's head was spinning. Was it possible? A lover's quarrel? Or what if Jeff finally had enough of Angie's racetrack antics? Sonny ran through the details about that night. He remembered that Jeff had watched the race with Natalie and Sarah. There was enough time for Jeff to drive to Laredo, arrive within the time frame in which Angie had died, and return home before anyone realized he had been away. His wife would never testify against him, and Sarah was Natalie's best friend.

Sonny thought back, Sarah was awfully quick to represent him when they charged him with murder, and all three: Jeff, Natalie and Sarah, came to his defense. Each of them insisted they were certain hadn't killed her, like they knew something they couldn't tell him.

Abruptly ashamed for even considering Jeff's involvement, Sonny shook his head, "No. I can't imagine Jeff looking at any woman but Natalie. Besides, Jeff wasn't in Laredo that night. That was the same day Natalie disappeared."

"Okay," Naomi replied. "I expect Michaels to contact you and ask where you found that tool, if you recognized it, or if you can tell him who owns it.

There's no reason you can't say that Marty comes to mind, but you'll need to tell him why. If Michaels asks anything other than specifics about where you found the pick, tell them I've told you not to discuss anything without either Sarah or me being present. There is a chance you will need to tell the authorities about the resemblance between your pocketknife and the hoof pick and I realize you'd prefer not to mention your knife. We can keep it quiet for now, but the situation might change. If it comes to that, I'll arrange a conference call to expedite matters and you can answer any other questions then."

Sonny agreed.

"Was Marty in Laredo over the weekend Angie died?"

"I can't say for sure," Sonny told his lawyer. "I didn't see him, but that doesn't mean he wasn't there."

"I'll go over the list of the people interviewed and see if his name is on the list. In the meantime, keep me posted."

When Sonny got to the barn, the delivery wagon was pulling into the parking lot. It was loaded with bales of straw which had to be stacked in the far end of the loft. Sonny was grateful the grain elevator would transport the bales from the wagon to the loft where he and Santos could easily arrange them. It wouldn't take long to finish the job.

Sonny hoped Charlie would be there when he got back home. Charlie was the one-person Sonny knew would always give him an honest answer, and also the one person, besides Vanessa, who he could trust with his life.

After the bales were all unloaded and stacked, Sonny filled Chaser's dish with food and poured fresh water into her water bowl, while Santos swept the loose straw from the steps to the loft.

"Thanks for coming out this afternoon," Santos told his friend. "I'm glad we can keep things running smoothly for Jeff and give him a chance to get himself in shape again. It's still hard to imagine that somebody tried to kill him."

"I know what you mean," Sonny replied bitterly. "Jeff is one of the good guys. It makes no sense for somebody to go after him like that. It seems like all Jeff's problems have something to do with Angie. If I got to the bottom of that situation, maybe I'd figure out who killed her and get my life back."

Santos stopped sweeping and walked across the barn to where Sonny was filling the water buckets. "I know you wouldn't have hurt Angie. Everybody knows that. I don't think anyone believes you killed her. You just hang in there and trust Sarah. She won't let anything happen to you."

"Thanks," Sonny said.

When they finished the barn chores, Santos said, "I've got a feeling it might make sense for me to stick around tonight."

"Chaser will be happy about that," Sonny told him. "I can stop back later tonight if you want some company."

"Appreciate the offer, but I'll be fine. I've been staying more often anyway, and everything I need is in the fridge or the coffeepot."

With a slight wave of his hand, Sonny left for home.

When Sonny walked into the kitchen, Vanessa and Charlie were chattering about unique breeds of dogs, and whether it would be better to get a puppy or a trained young adult. Charlie opted for the latter, while Vanessa leaned toward a puppy.

Sonny joined them at the table and offered his opinion. "Under the circumstance, it would make more sense to get a dog that's trained and ready to protect the house."

"Under what circumstances?" Vanessa asked.

Sonny realized he had incorrectly assumed that Charlie explained his reasoning behind the sudden urge to move a four-legged family member into their home.

"With the problems that have been going on with Fury, and now Jeff's truck being messed with, not to mention that jockey being killed in Laredo, I decided a little extra security would be a great idea," Sonny explained. He didn't mention the fact that since the possibility also existed that he would spend much of the rest of his life in prison, he wanted to be sure his wife wasn't alone.

"These incidents are all connected, aren't they?" Vanessa prodded.

"It sure seems likely," he answered. "Keep in mind that we frequently keep a horse or two for the Fraziers, and that Fury was here while he was recovering. If somebody is after them, and somebody sure seems to be, I'd say we have reason to take some extra precautions."

Charlie covered Vanessa's hand with his own. "I agree. We should also get a few extra surveillance cameras. It wouldn't hurt for you to put your car in the garage at night, too."

Vanessa looked from her brother to her husband. "You two are serious, aren't you? Okay, I'll make some calls tomorrow." Wanting to end the scary talk, Vanessa said, "Dinner is almost ready. Sonny, would you check the roast for me, please? I'm going out to put the car in the garage."

When Vanessa departed the kitchen, Sonny opened the oven and pulled out the roasting pan, set it atop the potholders his wife had spread on the counter, and then rejoined Charlie at the table.

"There's something I need to talk to you about, before Vanessa gets back," he said just above a whisper.

"What's up?" Charlie asked.

"When I dropped dinner off, for Jeff and Natalie, and was on my way back to the truck, I found a farrier's pick on the ground. It was at the edge of where the brake fluid leaked out of Jeff's truck. It's made just like my pocket knife, and it's engraved the same way. I gave it to Natalie. She called the police."

"That should be easy enough to trace," Charlie reasoned. "What was engraved on it?"

"There's a partial name. It starts with MAR and the next letter is tall, but worn. It might be a T, or an L, or a K."

"That makes it a little tougher to identify, but not so difficult. You said it's like your pocketknife," Charlie said. "Where did you get yours?"

Sonny didn't hesitate. "From Angie."

Charlie took a deep breath and slowly exhaled. "I see the problem."

"I'm betting the pick belongs to Marty Adams. I called Naomi and told her everything. She said basically that if the police ask, I will need to be up front about where I got my knife. If that happens, how will I explain it to Vanessa? I told her the knife was a gift from one of Jeff's clients."

"There's really no reason you need to tell anybody about your knife," Charlie told him. "It has nothing to do with the tool you found, unless you make it have something to do with it."

"But it would probably show that the pick came from Angie. It may connect the person who lost it to Jeff's brake lines being cut. That might even help my case," Sonny argued.

Charlie nodded. "If it comes to that, we'll figure out a way to deal with Vanessa. Similar gifts could also indicate that you and Marty were both involved with Angie. Throw jealousy into the mix and it gives the prosecution a motive for you murdering your Angie."

Charlie wondered if he should put his story together about selling the drug to Angie. He was sure his brother-in-law hadn't killed her, but the more time passed, the stronger the case was shaping up against Sonny, and Sonny seemed to be doing more harm to his case than good.

48

"I agree that there has to be a connection, and it goes back to the attempted theft of Frazier's horse, but I'm no longer convinced now that Sonny Owens is the killer." Detective Michaels paced back and forth in front of the conference table, as he reviewed the evidence with the Laredo Deputy D.A. Mark Dillinger.

"Everything still goes back to Sonny Owens," Dillinger insisted.

"He's having an affair with McCoy but he works for Frazier and has access to the horses and the equipment. He was in Laredo, at the request of Jeff Frazier, only because Frazier's wife was missing and Frazier needed to get back home to Chino. Is it another coincidence that McCoy was racing against Frazier's horse, the same horse that someone tried to steal and who was injured by McCoy's action? Next we have the telephone calls to McCoy's room and her cell phone. Did he go to confront her about the accident on the track? Could he have been upset because she was responsible for the horse's injury, or on the other hand, because the horse wasn't injured badly enough? Were they working together to try to stop Fury? If so, could they have been at odds about how far to take the attempt? Where was Sonny when Natalie Frazier was abducted? He, of all people, would have known her schedule, her veterinarian, and what buttons to push. Now, we located a rope identified as belonging to Frazier's horse, Fury. How did Angie McCoy get that rope?"

"We know that she didn't take the rope from the Frazier barn, since Velasquez told us that the intruder was the one who grabbed it," Williams countered.

"So, she either took it from someone else, or somebody gave it to her, or even left it in her equipment bag to throw us off. Did she find the rope, realize where it had come from and confront the person who had it? Could it be that nobody realized the rope had a name woven on near the loop and the rope was used and passed through several hands? Does the possibility exist that the thief planted it in the McCoy barn and Angie was the last person to use it?"

"Look, here's how I see things." The deputy district attorney bore down, "Sonny Owens and Angelina McCoy were involved in an intense relationship. McCoy wanted her competition out of the way, and Owens had the ability to get that accomplished. He tried to get the horse so that he could dispose of him, but he got caught in the act. Thinking only about getting out of the barn, he hung onto the rope when he took off. Since stealing the colt didn't work, they kidnap the horse's owner, who is also the trainer's wife. The reason they do that is so everyone will be frantic and they'll scratch the horse in Laredo, but that doesn't work. They go through with the race. Owens's luck holds and he's sent to take care of things in Laredo, which allows him to connect with McCoy. But, she takes things a step too far, and the horse gets hurt, which wasn't on Sonny's radar, and so he confronts her about what happened. She doesn't want to talk to him, but he calls and nags until she finally agrees. Then she threatens to pin everything on him and he decides to end the threat permanently."

Although Michaels had been the one who arrested Sonny, he was having second thoughts. "It bothers me that Sonny Owens doesn't seem to fit the description that Santos Velasquez gave the police.

Besides, how could Santos not recognize the man he works with daily, even from behind. And Sonny surely knew that the horse's rope had his name woven on the side. He would have returned it or destroyed it. He may have been in on some kind of conspiracy, but I don't think Sonny is our horse thief, and based on some recent evidence, I'm not convinced he's our killer."

"What recent evidence?" Dillinger mocked.

"Jeff Frazier was in an accident a couple of days ago. His brakes failed because of a sliced brake line. There was a puddle of brake fluid where the truck had been parked, and Sonny Owens found a farrier's pick at the edge of the oil. The pick has what looks like a name engraved on it. The first three letters are MAR, but there's a fourth, and it looks like a fifth letter worn almost smooth. The lab will try to enhance the remnants of the etchings, but I'm not hopeful they'll have much success. Since there are a few people who work around the track and whose names would fit, I plan to go out and talk to those boys myself."

"Anything else?" Dillinger asked flippantly as Michaels turned to leave.

The detective turned back. "As a matter of fact, there is." He reached into his coat pocket and pulled out a photograph. The picture showed a clear bag containing an empty water bottle. "The state police found this in Natalie Frazier's truck, after she escaped from that barn. Their lab lifted prints from it. Natalie's prints were on the bottle, but so were those of one of our Chino police officers, Derek Adams."

49

The Track Bar was crowded with horsemen and fans. Marty and Charlie had been sitting together at the bar for two hours, both drinking heavily.

"I have an idea you might be interested in," Marty told Charlie.

"Oh? What idea?" Charlie was on edge. He had never fully trusted Marty Adams, and without Angie to keep Marty in line, Charlie wished Marty wasn't still working at the McCoy farm.

"I'm sorry that things didn't go the way she planned." Marty said in a conspiratorial tone of voice. "I'm sorry that things didn't go the way she planned," he repeated groggily.

"What are you talking about?" Now Charlie knew he'd made a mistake by not leaving, when Marty joined him at the bar.

"I heard they found Fury's rope in Angie's room," Marty said. "Now, you and I are the only ones who know how Angie got Fury's rope."

"Angie was around horses all the time. She had lots of ropes," Charlie scoffed.
Marty burped. "Anthony was telling me about it. The rope has Fury's name braided into it near the end loop. If you didn't know to look for it, you probably wouldn't see it. Angie didn't."

Marty had been with the McCoys for a lot of years, and to some extent was Anthony's confidant. So Charlie didn't doubt Marty's claim that Anthony told him about the rope.

"Jeff Frazier killed Angie," Marty said. "That's what Mrs. McCoy thinks, anyway. She thinks Frazier went to Angie's hotel room in a rage when Fury got hurt, might have accused her of trying to steal Fury or even kidnapping Natalie, and when Angie fought back, he killed her."

A jar of peanuts was sitting on the bar. Charlie considered reaching into it, grabbing a hand full, shoving them down Marty's throat, and watching him choke. "Marty, you're going off the deep end here. Jeff wasn't in Laredo the night Angie died. It isn't even an absolute certainty that she was killed. She died of a drug overdose. It could have been accidental."

Marty's eyes became menacing. "Angelina was no drug addict. If you're so sure Jeff didn't kill her, and Sonny didn't do it, maybe you did."

Charlie glared at Marty and said through clenched teeth, "Are you out of your mind? Why would I have any reason to kill Angie? Our families have been friends for decades."

Marty burped again. "Look, there are lots of questions being asked all over. I wasn't in Laredo when Angie was killed, but if I happened to come up with some helpful information, the cops'd probably listen."

Now, angered, Charlie brought his nose to within a fraction of an inch from Marty's. "What exactly are you saying?"

Marty took another swallow of his beer, some dripping from the corners of his mouth, before he rambled on.

"I'm saying Derek got moved off patrol duty onto the desk, and they kept asking him questions about what happened to the glove Santos gave him the night Angie's plan fell apart. All he told them is he don't know what happened to the glove. He said he stopped for coffee at the donut shop, and somebody must have got in his squad car and stole it, but they don't believe him because he never wrote about the glove in his report. The union can keep him on the desk for a few weeks, but Derek knows he's going to lose his job, or worse."

"He can't be the first cop that missed something in a report," Charlie said.

"But what he missed went missing," Marty slurred, "and Derek's planning to leave town. Meanwhile, $25,000.00 will make sure he holds up to the heat they're putting on him. He'll forget I told him you tried to steal Fury. He already forgot about me being ready to load the horse into the trailer. Look, Derek's family. He'll need that money to tide him over until he can leave town and find another job or maybe even as bail money. I know you can come up with the cash, so save yourself a headache and pay up."

Charlie's jaw tensed and he felt the heat of his blood pressure rising. "You're drunk. First you accuse Jeff of murder, then you try to blackmail me to save your worthless brother's ass. What about your involvement? You've admitted you had a trailer ready to load up a stolen horse. Nobody would believe you if you said I tried to steal Fury, and Jeff was back here the night Angie was killed. He couldn't have killed her."

"I got alibis. Angie give 'em to me," Marty claimed. "Of course, I might tell them that you and Angie were an item, until she took up with your brother-in-law. You were in Laredo the night she died. If Sonny didn't kill her, maybe you and Jeff were in it together."

Marty didn't flinch when Charlie grabbed him by the shirt collar and whispered, "You are a crazy fool. I should knock your head off and bury it in Dreamweaver's manure pile. Ridiculous though they are, you better hope Jeff never gets wind of your accusations."

Marty laughed. "An extra $5,000.00 will make me forget you put your hands on me."

Charlie released Marty's collar.

"Think about it," Marty yelled as Charlie stormed away. "If Derek goes down, you'll be going down with him. He won't rat on me. And he'll say you're lying if you finger me over Fury. That's two words against one."

Charlie didn't bother answering. Now he was certain who owned the farrier's pick that Sonny had told him about, and that would get Marty arrested for something more than being a horse thief. Attempted murder sounded right. His brother wouldn't be able to give Marty cover for that.

50

Santos awoke to the soft rumble of Chaser's purring. She was curled up on his shoulder with her chin just below his ear. Through the window in the loft, Santos saw that the sun was beginning to peek up over the distant mountains. He reached across his chest and stroked the soft, grey bundle of fur. She responded with a quiet meow and snuggled closer to his neck. An early riser, Santos was eager to be up this morning. Today was Flight's first race.

"Come on, Chaser. We've got to get moving and get the horses fed."

As if understanding, the little cat yawned and stretched, then walked the length of Santos's body before she hopped off the cot. She looked back over her shoulder expectantly. When Santos's feet hit the floor, Chaser dashed down the steps from the loft, no doubt waiting at the bottom for Santos to arrive and fill her dish with food.

The barn was quiet until Santos turned on the light. First there was some rustling, which came from a few directions, then a snort or two, followed by a hoof pawing at the stall floor, and a whinny that could only have come from Flight.

"Okay, ladies and gentlemen. Breakfast is on the way," Santos promised, while he was getting Chaser's food. He kept up a steady stream of conversation throughout his morning routine. He had been spending more nights in the barn since the night he interrupted the horse thief, and the horses liked his presence as much as he enjoyed being with them.

Knowing that Jeff and Natalie would probably be getting there before too long, Santos made a large pot of coffee. While it was brewing, he got a bag of carrots from the fridge and made his way down one side of the shed row and up the other. He gave each

"Okay. I'll tell you what I know," Derek said. "But I had nothing to do with Angie's murder or with Jeff Frazier's truck. I was just the look-out when Charlie tried to take the horse. I didn't kidnap Natalie Frazier, but Angie told me the plan. I was supposed to monitor the radio; in case something went wrong. Angie told me Charlie Williams was going to snatch Natalie. I don't know anything else."

Detective Michaels slid a yellow legal tablet and pen across the table to Derek. "I'll step out while you write your statement." He looked down at the notes he'd made of Santos Velasquez's morning phone call to him, closed the folder and carried it out with him. He waited outside the interrogation room for Derek Adams to finish his statement, eager to get away from the crooked police officer and arrest Charles Theodore Williams for the kidnapping of Natalie Frazier. He was sure Charlie Williams was the second kidnapper, but he needed more proof. Derek's accusation was based on what Angie told him. While the detective believed Derek was telling the truth about Charlie, it was hearsay.

54

"That was a nice little dinner celebration last night, don't you think?" Jeff put the bread in the toaster, then poured his wife a cup of coffee.

Natalie agreed. "It was. I'm sorry Sonny and Vanessa couldn't make it though."

"Santos sure did a good job of calling the race. I don't know how he did it, but I think he remembered every step Flight took from the time he handed her over to the out-rider."

"Isn't he amazing?" Natalie replied. "Then he insisted on staying at the barn again tonight. You know, Fury has made us a little more money that we've expected. Let's take Flight's second place earnings and build a private room upstairs in the barn for Santos. He spends so much time there. We can do a half wall with windows, so he can see down into the barn without leaving the room. It would be more comfortable than that cot sandwiched between the bales."

"I think that's a great idea," Jeff agreed. "And it really shouldn't cost that much. We can do most of the work ourselves. I'm sure Santos will insist on a cat door, so Chaser can go in and out."

Natalie laughed. "Of course he will."

Jeff shrugged his left shoulder a few times. "My shoulder has progressed a lot more quickly than I expected. It's still a little sore, but I've already gotten a lot of the strength back in my arm. The doctor said I won't do any damage as long as I keep the heavy lifting to a minimum for a few more weeks. I can scrub and feed and clean stalls. Santos and Sonny have been hauling the water buckets and tossing the bales down and handling all the heavy work."

Natalie rolled her eyes. "I want your guarantee that I can trust you to allow them to continue to do the heavy lifting, when I'm not there to watch you."

"You've got it," he said. "Do you want your eggs scrambled or fried?" Wondering if he should tell Natalie what Santos had said, Jeff decided to wait until he had a chance to re-visit the conversation, just in case Santos had second thoughts about what he saw. "Are you still coming out to watch Elektra?" Jeff asked.

"Absolutely," she said. "I want to see how Flight is acting this morning."

55

Charlie steered his truck onto the McCoy Farm and to a stop in front of the barn. He had to see Marty and get things settled once and for all. Before he opened the door to get out of the vehicle, some motion in the rear-view mirror caught his eye. He could have sworn Angie was in the paddock with Dreamweaver.

He didn't see anyone when he walked into the barn, so Charlie called out, "Hello."

"What do you want?" Marty responded from one of the stalls at the far end.

"It's Charlie. Can we talk for a few minutes?"

Marty stuck his head out over the gate. "I'll be done here in about a minute. I'm cleaning her last foot."

Charlie had always had a certain amount of respect for Marty, because of the care he gave the horses. Marty was known to be a perfectionist when it came to grooming, and he was a fanatic about the horses' feet.

No more than another minute passed before Marty came out of the stall with a hoof pick in his hand. Charlie wondered if the tool was a replacement for the one that Marty had lost under Jeff Frazier's truck.

Marty held the pick like a switchblade which gave him a threatening appearance. "Got your attention yesterday, did I?" Marty asked warily.

"You got my attention, but not because you're right. It's because you're crazy," Charlie replied. "I don't have the kind of money you want and I can't get it. We mortgaged the farm to get the money to pay for Sonny's bail and for the attorneys. I'm broke. All I can give you is $5,000.00 when we sell Mariah's yearling in a couple of months. Instead of blackmailing me, why not call this a good faith effort to put the past behind us and move forward? It's the best I can do."

"Not good enough," Marty rebuffed Charlie. "You need to do better than that. That detective called me about forty-five minutes ago looking for you, so you don't have much time to figure something out. Murder puts a man away for a long, long time."

"Murder?" Charlie stepped closer. "I don't believe you."

Marty grinned. "No, he didn't say that. But you're so certain your brother-in-law is innocent and that Jeff Frazier didn't kill Angie, some people might think you were the one who killed her."

Charlie was tired of Marty's insinuations and accusations. He could fee his anger building. In an attempt to quell the rage, Charlie took a deep breath, exhaled, and repeated the process. It didn't work.

Two quick strides brought him within inches of the other man, and one right cross caused Marty's legs to give out from under him. Dazed, Marty looked up at Charlie in shock. Charlie was reaching for Marty again when he heard footsteps behind him. He turned only to be overcome with horror as he met the ferocious stare in Angie's eyes, just before she crashed a shovel against the left side of his head.

With a stabbing pain above his left ear, and watery eyes from the blow, to his head, Charlie staggered to his knees. It took him a few seconds to realize he had mistaken Martha McCoy for her dead daughter.

Marty hollered, "Get out of here, Martha. Call the police."

Alarmed at the disturbance, the horses snorted and stomped. One of the mares started kicking the wall which encouraged another to join in the rebellion. Furious, not only that Charlie had hit him but also that the horses were frightened, Marty threw himself onto the larger man, throwing Charlie off balance and back onto the floor of the barn. Using his weight and mustering all the strength his arms would give him, Marty pinned Charlie's shoulders to the ground.

"Martha is calling the police. When they get here, I can do two things. I can tell them what I know and what I suspect. Of course, I'll spin the tale a bit. My only job was to get a horse loaded in the van that night."

"You'll end up in jail for sure," Charlie sneered.

Marty forced a mirthless laugh. "I'll take my chances. I might even be able to convince them I didn't know I was loading a stolen horse. I was just a loyal employee doing what Angie asked me to do. On the other hand, I can save us both a lot of grief, and tell them this was nothing but a disagreement between friends, and we'll talk again later. You decide."

With the police summoned, Charlie was in no position to negotiate, and his head was aching from Martha's attack. Using the substantial power in his legs, Charlie rolled to the right, pinning Marty to the ground.

"Angie used a lot of people to do her dirty work, and I know she used you, too. Before she died, she was using Sonny. Angie was a user her whole life. She did what she wanted to get what she wanted. She didn't keep it a secret that you were supposed to drive Fury to Andrade, either. When Santos caught me in the act, Angie's scheme disintegrated, and I didn't get paid. I'm broke, Marty. That's why I agreed to take Fury in the first place. Angie promised a major payday, and we needed it for the farm."

Marty gasped. Almost suffocating under Charlie's weight, he wheezed, "Loading a horse onto a trailer isn't kidnapping. Besides, I would have brought Fury back in a couple days, claimed I found him lost along a road. Nobody was gonna' get hurt. But you're in a lot deeper if I tell that detective that you were the one who snatched Natalie."

"What?"

"Derek told me they found his prints on the water bottle he tossed into the stall with her. They know at least two people were involved and Derek won't ever give me up."

Stunned by Marty's threat, Charlie tightened his fingers around the Marty's throat. "So, your brother dropped my name, huh? And you expect me to pay him to get out of town?"

And then he saw the shadow of the shovel, but too late to stop it from crashing against his skull for the second time.

His full weight dropped on top of Marty. Charlie would not be getting back up.

Martha helped Marty get out from under the unconscious man. "Are you okay? I called nine-one-one. They said somebody is on the way."

The police arrived several minutes later, and Marty told them his story. He and Charlie disagreed about a breeding agreement, and they got carried away. Asked if he wanted to press any charges, Marty said he didn't.

Charlie remained unconscious, even after an ambulance arrived and while they transported him to the hospital.

56

"Has the entire world gone crazy?" Sonny asked rhetorically.

"Something sure is crazy," Sarah responded. "Why on earth would Charlie go to the McCoys' farm and get into a fight with Marty? It makes no sense."

"I agree. The police wouldn't tell Vanessa anything except that there had been some kind of altercation and Charlie was in the hospital." Sonny told his attorney, just as his telephone rang.

"It's Detective Michaels. Should I answer?"

Sarah reached for the phone, "I'll answer."

Sonny eagerly slid the telephone into her hand.

"This is Sarah Myers," she said.

"Sarah, Kyle Michaels here. I'm about fifteen minutes away. I appreciate you arranging this meeting with your client on short notice. "Based on some of the evidence that has surfaced, I have a few questions for Mr. Owens."

"No problem as long as it doesn't take too long," Sarah told the detective. "Vanessa called to let Sonny know her brother was in an accident at the McCoy Farm. An ambulance is taking him to the hospital. Vanessa is on her way now. Sonny and I want to meet Vanessa there as soon as we can.

Fifteen minutes later, Sarah welcomed Detective Michaels as he stepped onto the Fraziers' front porch. After getting the details about Charlie's transport to the local hospital, the Laredo detective spent the next half hour asking Sonny about the relationship he had with Jeff and his handling of Fury. Sarah had no problem with the inquiries, and Sonny answered honestly.

"You said Santos is the one who primarily cares for Fury, but is it unusual for you to handle him?"

"Not at all," Sonny replied.

"Would that include taking him out of his stall?"

"Sure."

"Besides you, Santos and the Fraziers, who else would lead Fury in and out of the barn?"

"Carl might take him out once in a while, and I guess the vet or the farrier might move him into the stall, but Jeff is usually right there with them."

"Would you say that you and Mr. Frazier have a friendly working relationship?"

"Absolutely. Jeff and I are friends. He's the boss when we're at the barn, but he brings his horses to our farm to board or to turn out. Our families have worked together for years."

"That's all the questions I have. Thank you for your time."

Sarah walked the detective to the door. Sonny joined her as she watched him drive away. She said, "I have a feeling that those question were because of finding Fury's rope. Maybe he's finally figured out that he needs to look somewhere else for the murderer."

Kyle Michaels was finally convinced that Sonny was telling him the truth, not only about his relationship with Jeff but also about the night of the murder, and his connection with Angelina McCoy. What he wasn't quite able to figure out was how Marty figured into the mix. The farrier's pick Sonny found at Frazier's place appeared to belong to Marty.

But what was the motive for a barn worker, who worked for the McCoys, to want Jeff Frazier or Angie McCoy dead.

57

The ambulance stopped outside the emergency entrance. Charlie regained consciousness as two attendants slid him out of the vehicle and into the hospital. He closed his eyes to gather his thoughts, but felt like his brain was underwater. Ideas were swimming around his mind, but he couldn't quite grasp them. What had Marty told the police? Had he told them the truth about Angie's scheme, or lied about it? Had he suggested Charlie was involved in Angie's murder? With a little luck, maybe he told them nothing. But why did Kyle Michaels want to see him? He figured he'd know that soon enough. His thoughts faded into darkness.

The EMTs wheeled Charlie into an examination cubicle and stayed with him until a doctor arrived.

"Good afternoon, I'm Dr. Engels."

Charlie forced his eyes open and started to sit up, but a wave of nausea swept over him. Dizzy, he decided to stay flat on his back.

"Can you tell me what happened?" the doctor asked.

"I'm not sure exactly," Charlie answered. "I drove over to McCoy's to get together with Marty about a business matter. We argued, got into fight, and he hit me with something, knocked me out cold."

Then Charlie noticed the blood covering his left shoulder and upper arm. "I guess he split my head pretty good."

Nodding, as he removed the temporary bandage the technician had applied, Dr. Engels said, "Scalp wounds bleed pretty heavily. It looks like a few stitches might be in order here. Are you dizzy or disoriented?"

"Both, along with a heck of a headache," Charlie told him.

After several more questions and an examination, the doctor said, "I'm going to stitch that laceration, and keep you here overnight."

As if on cue, the curtain to the examination cubicle slid aside and Vanessa walked to her brother's side. Charlie's head and left arm covered in blood, reminded Vanessa of the many injuries he'd gotten in his younger days. A laceration, from his eyebrow across his temple almost to his ear, had already discolored the area below his eyes. It would be deep purple before long. Though generally level-headed, Charlie's temper could be wicked, and as a kid, he had competed in his share of fist fights, before channeling his aggression into the boxing ring.

Vanessa shook her head, "Charlie, what happened? Are you all right?"

Charlie nodded. "The doctor is getting me fixed up."

"And you are?" the doctor asked Vanessa.

"Vanessa. I'm his sister."

As he finished stitching the wound, Dr. Engels said, "We'll set you up in a room as soon as we can. In the meantime, I'll leave you with your sister."

When they had a room arranged for Charlie, Vanessa followed a nurse who wheeled him through the corridors, into and out of an elevator, and down a seventh floor hallway and into his room.

Charlie had only been settled into his hospital bed a few minutes when Detective Kyle Michaels walked in.

"I have a couple of questions, Mr. Williams."

"Is this necessary right now?" Vanessa asked. Before Michaels answered, she turned to Charlie and said, "If you aren't feeling up to it, the questions Detective Michaels has can wait until tomorrow."

"It's okay. I can talk to him."

"If you're sure you'll be alright, I'll go on home, and let you two talk. I'll be back in a few hours and keep you company, Charlie."

"Bring some of those muffins back, please." Charlie said, with an enthusiasm he didn't feel. After Vanessa departed, he turned his attention to Detective Michaels. "Other than a lousy headache, I'm fine. Ask away, detective."

"Did you ever work for Jeff Frazier?"

"We have a working relationship. I've helped him out when he needed it. Once in a while he sends a horse over to the farm. When Fury got hurt, we kept him for a few weeks."

"Did you help with Fury before, or during the day of the race in Laredo?" Michaels was firing the questions rapidly.

The rope, Charlie thought. *He's trying to connect me to the rope.* Charlie answered, "No."

"Did you ever have possession of a braided rope, belonging to Jeff Frazier?"

"I could have. We move horses back and forth, and sometimes the equipment gets moved with them." Charlie replied.

"Are you aware of an attempt to steal one of the Fraziers' horses a few weeks ago?"

Charlie nodded, "Everybody around the track knows about it."

"Where you were at the time?

"I have no idea," Charlie replied. "From what I've heard, it happened in the early morning hours. If I was home, I was sleeping. I can check my calendar when I get back to the farm and find out where I was that day. I've been doing some travelling lately."

"Did you see your brother-in-law on the day of the Sapphire Stakes in Laredo?"

Charlie thought a minute before he said, "I remember talking to him, over the phone, but I don't think I talked to him face to face while we were there. He was busy getting ready for the race, then taking care of his horse afterward. I saw him down on the track after the race, but I wasn't close enough to talk to him."

"Are you aware of any intimate relationship between Angelina and Sonny Owens?"

"No."

"Did you see Angelina McCoy, after the races, on the night of her death?" Detective Michaels asked.

"No."

"Did you have an intimate relationship with Angelina McCoy?"

Charlie's head was spinning. "At one time, I did. That was a while ago, though. Angie and I had known each other for a long time. Can we finish this later? My head is pounding."

Detective Michaels said, "Just one more question. How did your fingerprint find its way to the snap on the rope that was stolen from Jeff Frazier's barn the night an attempted horse theft was interrupted?"

"How the hell would I know," Charlie snapped. "I've been in that barn many times. I must've handled every rope in the place one time or another. No more questions. I need a nurse to give me something for this headache."

He had left police headquarters to make an arrest and was leaving his suspect's hospital room having made none. Though he believed he had sufficient evidence that Charlie Williams was a horse thief, Detective Michaels was in no hurry to arrest him. He would allow Charlie to get the medical care required and talk to him in a day or so. He decided to drive out to the McCoy farm, where he would have a less than friendly discussion with Marty Adams.

58

Marty stood in the visitor's lounge, watching Martha ride Dreamweaver in the training arena. Anthony McCoy was working in the office, when Detective Michaels knocked on his open door. McCoy directed the detective to the arena and called Marty to tell him that Michaels was on his way to see him.

"Good day, Sir," Marty greeted.

The detective showed Marty a photograph. "Does this hoof pick belong to you?"

Marty took the picture and immediately recognized the farrier's tool. "No, it isn't mine."

"Have you ever seen it before?" The detective asked.

It was one thing not to mention the pick's owner but another to flat out lie. Marty considered himself to be many things, good and bad, but he would never admit to being a liar. "Yes, I have."

"Can you tell me who owns it?"

With a slow nod, Marty replied, "Yes. It belongs to Martha McCoy."

The detective's irritation became obvious as the blood rushed to his face. The day had not been what he expected. Not only did his anticipated arrest of Charles Williams not occur, but Michaels's certainty that Marty Adams owned the recovered pick turned out to be wrong.

He pressed on. “What is your relationship with Charles Williams?”

Marty wondered if the investigation had been told about his fight with Charlie earlier in the day. “Charlie and I have known each other for years. We don’t always agree on things, but we always work it out.”

“What did you disagree about this morning?”

Marty slowly shook his head before he answered. “I’m not sure exactly. We argued about a couple of horses and a breeding agreement. Charlie can be a hot head and I guess I can be, too. Things got out of hand. I got in the last punch.” He figured that sounded close enough to the truth.

“Mr. McCoy said that Mrs. McCoy was here, with you. Is she the one riding that horse?”

“Yes,” Marty replied. “She’s about finished now.”

“Would it be all right if I wait for her here?”

“Sure,” Marty told the detective. “I’ll tell her you’re here.” He turned on the intercom and announced, “Martha, that detective from Laredo wants to talk to you when you’re finished.”

Martha signaled that she heard, before she slowed Dreamweaver and walked him out of the enclosure.

“She’ll walk him across to the barn,” Marty said. “Come with me. We can meet her there.”

The two men walked in silence.

Martha McCoy rode Dreamweaver down the path toward the barn. Marty met her at the door. She gracefully slid from the saddle and gave Marty the reins. “He’s behaving so well,” she told him. “I plan to try to have him ready for the show at the end of the year. He is a gorgeous colt, isn't he?" She turned to Michaels. "Hello, Detective. Please come up to the house."

"Good afternoon, Mrs. McCoy. I only have a couple of quick questions. I don't mind staying out here and enjoying the weather."

"Fine with me," Martha responded. "What can I do for you?"

Detective Michaels showed her the photograph. "Do you recognize this?"

"Yes, I do. It's mine. Thank you, so much. I noticed I'd misplaced it a week or so ago. Where did you find it?" She seemed genuinely pleased that he had found her pick.

"Do you have an idea where you might have lost it?"

"Somewhere between the house and the barn, or maybe at the track, I guess." She shrugged. "I noticed last week that it was missing. I tried backtracking, but I'm really not sure when I dropped it. I used to use it daily, when I rode in competition, but for the last several years, I've gone weeks without needing it. But it does have sentimental value to me. I'm so happy it's been found. Thank you."

"Have you been to Jeff and Natalie Frazier's house any time in the past few weeks?"

Martha paused. "No, I saw them at the racetrack a couple of days ago, but I haven't been to their house. Why do you ask?"

Michaels nodded, "Your tool turned up at Jeff Frazier's place. Someone found it next to a puddle of brake fluid that had leaked from his truck. Someone cut the truck's brake lines."

"Well, how in the world. . ." She stopped, as if suddenly realizing what the questions meant. Obviously insulted, Martha eyes narrowed and her tone turned chilly. "And you came here thinking that I dropped it, when I cut the line so that Jeff would be hurt? Listen to me, young man, someone killed my daughter, and it's your job to find out who murdered her. Anthony and I have cooperated every step of the way in your investigation, and you dare to accuse me of a crime. Now, you go out there and find my daughter's killer."

She moved past the detective, but, over her shoulder, instructed, "If you have anything more to discuss, you can speak with Anthony." She walked quickly to the house without looking back.

Detective Michaels strolled back to his car, not certain whether he had truly offended Mrs. McCoy or if she was simply a good actress. He did, however, find it difficult to picture her crawling under a truck to slice through a brake line. Of course, he'd seen stranger things in his career.

The long drive back to Laredo gave Kyle Michaels plenty of time to ponder what he had learned that day. The pieces of the puzzle were coming together, but he was having trouble figuring out how Jeff Frazier's accident fit into the mix. Although the attack on Jeff might be completely unrelated to the murder, he found that possibility doubtful.

Standing under the window in the barn, Marty had heard most of the conversation between Kyle

Michaels and Martha McCoy. Martha carried that hoof pick every day, and she had lost it sometime in the past couple of weeks, exactly as she said. Marty was certain, because he had found it at the edge of the paddock. He put it in his vest pocket, intending to give it to Martha the next morning when she came to see Dreamweaver. He had been irritated with himself for dropping it somewhere before he saw her. Marty had searched his truck and had looked all around the barn and the grounds trying to relocate it. Now he realized that it had slipped from his pocket when he slid under Jeff's truck at 3:00 in the morning.

Martha learned that Fury was doing well and would be back in training soon. She told Marty what she'd heard and confided that she wished there was a way to delay Fury's racing comeback, or even end it, which would benefit Nordstrom. With Nordstrom recognized as the champion that he should be, Angie's dream would be realized. Anthony had entered Nordstrom in the Triple Million, and after he won the first race of the series, there was a good chance he'd win the second and third. But that good chance would be greatly reduced if FraziersFury came back in training in time to run in any of those races.

As if that wasn't reason enough to keep Jeff's horses off the track, Angie's mother had her heart set on racing the filly, Anmaran, named for Anthony, Martha and Angie. A winning season for Anmaran meant putting the McCoys back on top. Even though Angie hadn't lived to see it, she would be remembered as the top jockey for the top thoroughbred farm. Martha wanted that for her daughter.

A full sister to Dreamweaver, if Anmaran became a champion, it would reflect on Dreamweaver, Angie's darling. But Jeff's filly would be competing head to head with Anmaran, the same way Fury competed against Nordstrom. Martha couldn't bear that defeat. Marty sympathized with Martha. He didn't want Frazier's Flight to become the McCoys' new nemesis. With Jeff out of the way for a while, the chance that would happen diminished.

Like Angie always said: the end justifies the means. If it took a little inconvenience to the Fraziers in order to give the McCoys a boost, Marty saw no reason he shouldn't make that happen. Even if Jeff didn't murder Angie with his own hands, and Martha still thought he did, Angie would never have gotten involved with horse stealing or kidnapping. It was Jeff Frazier's fault, and he deserved to suffer.

59

It was dusk when Vanessa got back to the hospital. Charlie would be restless, but she understood that he had been hit harder than he realized. If the doctor wanted him to stay for observation, she'd do her best to keep him occupied, so he didn't decide to check out prematurely. With a thermos of strong coffee, and some biscuits and fresh jam, Vanessa strolled into his room to cheer him up.

Charlie was sitting up in bed, looking out the window, when his sister came in. "You are right on time, Vanessa. I'm better now. I can get my things and head on back with you."

Not surprised, Vanessa told him, "No. I'll spend a couple of hours with you drinking coffee, munching on biscuits, and talking about horses until you go to sleep. I'll be back in the morning to take you home." She'd been this route before. Charlie was a tough guy, but Vanessa was stubborn and usually convinced him to see things her way.

"But I really am much better, Van," he said.

"And the reason you're getting better is that you're resting. Please, Charlie, spend the night. There's nothing you'll do at home besides sleep, and you might as well sleep here where they can check on you in case something goes wrong. You have six stitches, and two black eyes. Marty hit you pretty hard."

Vanesa slid a chair over to her brother's bedside and sat, waiting for phase two of the argument, but Charlie was quiet. "Do you want to tell me what happened this afternoon?"

He hesitated before saying, "I'm not sure. Marty and I started talking about breeding one of McCoy's mares, and we disagreed about the sire, and—"

"Charlie, that's nonsense. There is no way in heaven or on earth that you and Marty Adams would get into a fist fight over a sire for Anthony McCoy's mare. Either tell me the truth, or tell me you don't want to discuss it."

He blurted out, "I'm in trouble, Vanessa, and Marty knows it."

It was common knowledge that Marty had been in prison for burglary years back, but Anthony had gone to bat for him, and Marty had been paroled early. Marty's loyalty to the McCoy family was intense and genuine, but his disdain for most others was almost as earnest.

Vanesa asked, "What kind of trouble? How can I help you?"

After a deep breath, Charlie began at the beginning. "It all started when Angie decided she wanted Frazier's grey colt, Fury."

Step by step, Charlie outlined the situation, from Angie's anonymous offer of purchase, through Nelson Dickenson, to her promise of one-hundred-thousand dollars to Charlie if he 'borrowed' Fury for a quick romance with her mare.

"Angie wanted me to take Fury from Frazier's barn and get him into the trailer where Marty was waiting to drive him out to his grandfather's abandoned ranch in Andrade. I would meet them the next day, help get Fury bred to Angie's mare, and a few days later, Marty was to return Fury, claiming to have found him wandering along a backwoods road. Angie would register the foal as Dreamweaver's."

"And by breeding him, Angie would not only have the potential for a top notch foal but also make Fury much more difficult to handle on and off the race track?" Vanessa said.

Charlie nodded his head, "Exactly. No one would have understood why his temperament had changed, though they might have figured it out, knowing he had been gone for several days."

He told his sister about Angie's attempts to keep Fury from racing, by having Natalie kidnapped.

"Angie wanted me to help Marty kidnap Natalie and take her to the ranch. She figured, with Natalie missing, Jeff would scratch Fury from the race," Charlie confessed. "But I told her there was no way I'd be involved with any kidnapping. I know, right then I should have called the police, but I was guilty of attempted horse theft and Angie threatened to tell the cops, ready to call me a liar and ready with an alibi if I turned on her. And well, Van, I was in too deep, and I didn't do anything to stop her."

Vanessa nodded sadly.

"I took Fury's rope by accident. After I got away from Santos, I realized I was still holding it. I was afraid to just drop it, so I took it back with me and gave it to Angie as a souvenir. Stupid, huh? We didn't see Fury's name woven within the braiding."

Charlie told Vanessa about Marty's threats and his blackmail attempt, and that he had gone to McCoy's farm to confront Marty, and that Marty blindsided him before he could leave.

She sat quietly listening to the details of what had happened over the course of the past few months. When he stopped talking, she asked, "How did Sonny get involved in all of this, Charlie?"

Charlie answered quickly, "He wasn't. He didn't know anything about any of it. He still doesn't."

"But he was involved with Angelina McCoy, wasn't he?" Vanessa whispered.

"Sonny and Angie got along okay," Charlie said. "They kind of got thrown together at the track, the way a lot of people are. I can't tell you that nothing ever happened between them. That's between you and Sonny. I will tell you that if anything went on, it had nothing to do with you. Sonny loves you, Vanessa. There's not a doubt in my mind about that. I also know that Sonny didn't kill Angie. That's a fact."

Vanessa had to ask the question. "How do you know, for a fact, that Sonny didn't kill Angie?"

Charlie looked straight into her eyes. "Because, I did." His eyes filled with tears, and he said, "I was never going to let Sonny go to jail."

Charlie's words hit Vanessa like a fist in the stomach. For several minutes, neither of them spoke. Charlie turned his gaze from her and observed as the sky turn from twilight to darkness. Vanessa watched him, while thinking of Sonny, and wondering how she could save both her husband and her brother. She thought she should hate Charlie for what he had put them all through, but she loved him, and she saw that right now he hated himself more than she ever could.

Vanessa stayed with Charlie all night, sleeping fitfully in the chair in his room. She was very much afraid of what he might do, now that he had told her what had happened. Vanessa knew Charlie better than he knew himself. She was certain that he had monumental feelings of guilt, which explained his recent, sometimes distant behavior and his heavy drinking. She was concerned that he might be suicidal.

The next morning, Dr. Engels pronounced Charlie fit to be released. Vanessa got his clothes from the closet and waited out in the hall while he dressed.

"Let's get something to eat before we go home," Vanessa suggested as an attendant wheeled Charlie into the elevator.

"I'm not hungry," Charlie said. "All I want to do is get back home."

"I'm not hungry either," Vanessa admitted, "but we need to figure out what we're going to do, and it might be easier to talk about it before we get back to the house."

When they got outside, the valet brought Vanessa's car to her and the attendant assisted Charlie into the passenger seat. Vanessa wanted to go to a special, secluded place to continue the conversation with her brother.

Vanessa called Sonny and told him she and Charlie had a few things to take care of, but that she'd be home later that afternoon. She and Charlie drove out to a small lake where they used to swim when they were kids.

"What do you want to do, Charlie?"

"I guess I need to find a lawyer. Michaels has my print on that snap, which clearly puts the rope in my hand, at some point in time. That doesn't prove murder, but it goes a long way toward attempted theft of the horse and the would-be horse thief is the one who took the rope. Once that word gets out, it's more likely that Santos will associate me with the guy he saw from the back. Even if he doesn't, he gave a pretty good description the night he saw me, and I obviously fit the description. Without a credible theory as to how the rope got from my hands to a thief's hands to Angie's office, I'm pretty well done." Charlie had been awake most of the night and was resigned to the fact that he was going to be eventually charged with murder.

"When they arrested Sonny, I thought about telling the police that I sold the drug to Angie. Then, I remembered that I got rid of the syringe and didn't leave the vial in the room. She would have needed both, if she had injected herself, so it didn't make sense to go that route. I figured if I had to confess to keep Sonny from jail, I'd do it, but there didn't seem to be any way his case could go to trail, and no way to prove him guilty. It's been driving me crazy watching what you and Sonny are going through. I came so close to confessing, but I can't imagine spending years locked in a cell. If Sonny got off, and I wasn't arrested, I figured it would be over, and I could live with that."

Though resentful of what her foolish brother had knowingly put them all through, Vanessa loved him. She understood his dilemma. "Sonny's trial date has been set for three weeks from now. Sarah and Naomi are relatively confident that a conviction is unlikely. I won't repeat what you told me to anyone, but if Sonny is convicted, you'll need to come forward."

"I'm so sorry, Vanessa." Charlie had thought that eliminating Angie would be good for Sonny and for Vanessa. He never imagined that his sister's husband would be arrested and put on trial for a murder he, not Sonny, committed, or even that he would ultimately be held accountable for his actions.

"I'm going to wait until I'm arrested before I call a lawyer. Unfortunately, I might not need to wait very long."

They stayed at the lake for a couple of hours; they talked and reminisced. After vowing to deal with whatever came at them together, they went home.

60

Three days later, Detective Michaels planned to arrest Charlie Williams for breaking and entering, and felony burglary, as a result of the fingerprint on the snap and Santos's statement identifying him as the suspected intruder. Charlie, not surprisingly, refused to talk to the detective again without an attorney present, so Michaels could only rely on their discussion at the hospital, until he arrested Williams.

In the meantime, Detective Michaels questioned Santos about the identity of the man he confronted in the barn. Santos said he was big like Charlie, and it could have been Charlie, but the more he thought about it, he couldn't swear that it was. Jeff Frazier confirmed that sometimes they transferred horses between the Frazier barn and the Williams farm, and that it was quite possible Charlie used Fury's rope on one or more occasions.

Vanessa and Sonny said that Charlie had been at home with them the night of the attempted theft. They went to bed about 11:00, and Vanessa said she would have heard Charlie if he had left the house. Based on the information available, the detective held off on the arrest, but he wasn't done with Charles Williams just yet.

Although he still suspected Charlie of being involved with Derek Adams in the kidnapping of Natalie Frazier, he couldn't prove any connection. Derek swore he was only the lookout on the morning of the kidnapping, just as he had been the lookout on the night of the attempted theft of the colt. He was to monitor the police channel and make sure that neither the thief nor the kidnapper was interrupted. Derek confessed to involvement with Angie, who he testified was behind both incidents, but said he dealt only with her and had no information about anyone else's involvement. As for his fingerprints on the water bottle, he claimed he gave the water to Angie and made her promise to give it to Mrs. Frazier so she would have water when she woke from the sedation. Michaels didn't believe him, but the Chino Police opted not to pursue it. In exchange for Derek's statement, and with no way to refute it, the Chino Police Department allowed the policeman to resign; his career as a police officer ended.

Throughout the investigation of Angie's murder, the police had concentrated on the horsemen involved in any way with the race at Laredo, and anyone with a working relationship with Angie. Charlie wasn't associated with the race and didn't have any relationship with Angelina McCoy. He had only been questioned briefly. By his own admission, however, Charlie did, at one time, have a personal relationship with the jockey. The detective wondered how personal it was right before her death.

Early in the investigation, Michaels interviewed some of the hotel staff who were working close to the time of Angie's death. One of the hotel maids remembered seeing a man walking down the hallway on the 7th floor, at just after 6:00 p.m. She'd told Detective Michaels she'd spoken briefly with the man. She remembered the time because her shift started at 6:00. She had given Michaels a description of the man, but it was too vague to be of much value. The detective had shown her pictures of Sonny and Santos, among others, but none of the pictures were of the man she saw in the hallway. Detective Michaels planned to talk to the lady again. This time he would take a different set of photographs, one of which would be a picture of Charlie Williams.

"Thank you for taking the time to talk to me again, Miss Reynolds," Detective Michaels said to the young housekeeper.

"It's not a problem. How can I help?"

"When we spoke a few months ago, you mentioned talking to a man in the hallway. near room seven-twenty-one. I have a few more photographs I'd like to show you. Are any of these men the one you saw that night?"

He gave her the pictures, and she pointed to Charlie, without hesitation.

"This is the man," she said. "He smiled at me and spoke briefly, such a nice man," she told the detective.

The maid's identification of him, along with his relationship with Angie, past or present, was enough to warrant Charlie's arrest as the prime suspect in Angelina's murder. Although it didn't seem like much, when he looked at the big picture, Detective Michaels was certain the rest of the puzzle would come together.

The detective, accompanied by the local Sheriff's Marshall drove to the Williams farm, and placed Charles Williams under arrest, for murder. Charlie offered no resistance. Vanessa called his lawyer. They transported him to Laredo to await arraignment.

At the arraignment, he pled not guilty. The judge was skeptical of the evidence of Charlie's guilt and granted the same cash bail that he'd previously set for the now exonerated Sonny Owens. Vanessa again used the farm as collateral for the bail, determined to keep Charlie out of prison for as long as possible.

Based on the new evidence and Charlie's arrest, the Laredo District Attorney withdrew the charge of murder against Sonny. The D.A., however, made it a point to withdraw it without prejudice, so they would be able to refile the murder charge should evidence of Sonny's complicity surface. Vanessa was torn between devastation and celebration. If found guilty, her brother was on the road to spending the rest of his life in prison, but her husband appeared to have escaped what could have been the tragedy of an innocent man convicted.

61

Natalie greeted Carl and Sarah at the front door with a broad smile. “Hi there. Jeff will be the chef this evening. He picked up some salmon for the grill. I’m in charge of vegetables. Santos will be here in a little while.”

The couple accepted a glass of wine and the four friends relaxed on the front porch, catching up on everything that had happened since they were together the last time.

“Have you heard anything more from the police?” Sarah asked.

“No,” Jeff replied. “They discovered that the tool Sonny found belongs to Martha McCoy, but the problem is that anyone could have found it and dropped it, either accidentally or on purpose. She claims to have lost it a couple of weeks before Sonny found it.”

“Detective Michaels said they weren’t successful in finding any full fingerprints on it,” Natalie added. “Too many people handled it, and the prints were stacked and smeared. There was one partial, but it wasn’t enough to narrow down for a match. He said it would be enough to suggest that a suspect could have handled it, but not enough to prove that he did.”

“I can’t picture Martha McCoy crawling under your truck and cutting your brake lines,” Carl said.

“I can’t either,” Jeff agreed.

"What's happening with Sonny, now that they dropped the charges?" Natalie asked Sarah.

"The investigation is still open, so it is unlikely but still possible that the D.A. could refile them. The evidence against Sonny was all circumstantial. The evidence pointing toward Charlie is more direct, but certainly not a slam dunk."

Carl said, "I was talking to Peter Crawford last night. Peter is Anmaran's jockey. Well, he told me Marty made a comment after Anmaran won that race that bothered him. Peter, Marty and Anthony were talking. Anthony told Peter that, except for Flight, he hasn't seen a two-year-old filly anywhere that shows as much promise as Anmaran. Marty had been drinking and supposedly said that Flight's career will end the way Fury's ended. Keep in mind, we haven't formally announced that Fury will race again."

"I wonder what he meant by that?" Natalie asked.

"Peter said he asked Marty that question," Carl continued, "and Marty claimed that Peter misunderstood him. He said he meant that she was a nice filly and would have a good career ahead. Peter said that he just let it drop. That race in Laredo has been the talk of the jockey's room more than once," Carl confided. "Fury is a local favorite and everybody is looking forward to seeing him race again. Angie caused a lot of trouble over the years. People remember that."

Natalie said, "I don't know if you heard about Sonny. He talked to Santos this morning, and said he was sorry to leave Santos without help, but he wanted to give him a heads up that he wouldn't be coming back. Then he called Jeff and said that, under the circumstances, Vanessa needed him at the farm full-time and he wouldn't be able to continue to work for us."

"I told him that I was sorry to lose him," Jeff said, "but that I understood, and that if he found he had time on his hands, I'd appreciate him giving me a call. He's having a hard time with Charlie's arrest, even though it got him off the hook."

They saw Santos driving up the road.

"Santos is really upset with Charlie," Jeff told them. "He told me he was always certain of Sonny's innocence and that Sonny had no idea what his brother-in-law was up to. Meanwhile, he said he'd talk to a few people and help me find a replacement for Sonny."

Jovial, as usual, Santos jogged from the truck to the porch, smiling and carrying a homemade pie. Although he didn't bake often, when he did, Santos made the best pies ever. Offering the dessert to Natalie, Santos said, "Your favorite, peach!"

Both Natalie and Sarah blurted, "Yum!"

"Jeff, I found somebody interested in working a few days a week to help with the horses," Santos said. "His name is Johnny Baker. He works at the animal shelter, but they moved their location and now it's a ninety-mile round trip drive for him. He's looking for something closer, and he really wants to talk to you. Johnny's a likeable kid and a hard worker. I've known him since he was a baby. His mother is a good friend."

"Thanks, Santos," Jeff told him. "Can you ask him to come by the barn tomorrow morning?"

"Sure can."

"I can help out a few hours here and there," Carl said. "Let me know what you need. I don't mind mucking out stalls now and then, either."

Santos gave Carl a thumbs up. "If you do all the exercise riding, and some of the cooling out, I can take care of most everything else, until we get someone else hired."

"That should work out," Carl agreed. "By the way, Jeff, have you decided to enter Flight in that Two-Year-Old Stakes race you were thinking about?"

"As a matter of fact, I entered her today. The race is in two weeks. We'll have to see if she draws in."

The five friends spent the rest of the evening eating Santos's pie and talking and planning for the upcoming races.

62

Sitting in a jail cell in the Laredo County Prison, Charlie had had all the time he needed to think about what he had done and what he still had to do. Bail had been set and Vanessa made arrangements to post the necessary amount. It amazed Charlie that, despite everything, she and Sonny were so ready to help him.

The guard came to Charlie's cell. "The paperwork is done. Your attorney is waiting for you out front, and you'll be out of here within half an hour."

Charlie went through the motions for his release from prison, but his thoughts were on what lay ahead. Thanking his attorney for everything, Charlie made arrangements to meet with him later in the week to review the next step in the criminal proceedings, even though didn't plan to keep the meeting. Vanessa was waiting to drive him home. When they got into the car, she said, "You need to understand Sonny is trying hard to act like there's nothing wrong. He's angry about your attempt to take Fury and he will never admit it, but I know he suspects you killed Angie. He'll be fine, but he needs some time. I will do whatever I can to get our family through this."

"I understand. I'll give Sonny some space," Charlie promised.

"Sonny quit his job with Jeff Frazier. He said it was because he thought it was time he worked at our place full time, but I know it was really because he's afraid of what people think of him." Vanessa said. "Whether you are convicted or exonerated of the charges you're facing; it will take a while to get over this."

They were quiet for much of the lengthy trip home, lost in their individual thoughts. When they were driving up the road to the farm, Charlie said, "I'm going to take a drive out to Goat Rock." That was the place he always went, when he needed to relax or escape for a few hours or even a few days. "Are my keys in the truck?"

Vanessa nodded. "It's getting late. Why don't you wait until tomorrow morning?"

"No, I'd rather get there tonight. I've got a change of clothes and my diving gear in the truck. I'll get something to eat later and find a room for tonight. I've got my phone if you need me. Thanks for everything, Vanessa. I'm so sorry for all the trouble I've caused you and Sonny."

Vanessa hugged Charlie and said, "We'll work everything out. This farm is your home. You'll always have a home with us here."

With tears streaming down her cheeks, Vanessa watched her brother get into his truck and turn back down the driveway. To her knowledge, she was the only one who knew for certain that Charlie was the killer. She had not told Sonny, nor had Charlie, but she believed that somehow Sonny knew. Vanessa wondered if she would ever see her brother again.

Charlie's truck was always packed for an excursion. Clothes, tools, money and hiking boots were among the supplies he kept stored in the toolboxes of the three-quarter-ton four-wheel drive. It was a four-hour trip to Goat Rock Beach. The rocky beach, in Sonoma County, known for its steep drop off, treacherous undercurrents and tremendous waves, also had a few sightings of great white sharks. Except for an occasional wanderer, the beach remained deserted. That's what Charlie liked about it. It was a perfect place to think.

Charlie appreciated everything his sister and his attorney were trying to do, but he was a realist. Even with a plea bargain, Charlie was facing years in prison. He had decided as soon as the cell door locked behind him, when he was taken to the Laredo Jail, that once he got out he would never go back.

He had one stop to make, and then a detour, before he turned north to Goat Rock.

Marty was the only one who used the McCoy's red and white horse trailer, so Charlie knew Marty had used it to transport the mare to the farm in Andrade to wait for Charlie and Fury. Charlie also knew, for all Marty's faults, he was a stickler about caring for the horses, and always kept a full set of grooming tools in the trailer.

The idea came to Charlie when he was in the hospital, only six days ago. Charlie drove to the track and walked to the back of the barn where Marty stored the trailer. Charlie ripped the front page from an old newspaper that was in the truck and took it with him as he unhooked the back gate on the trailer and went inside. There, as he remembered, was a pegboard, with a host of grooming tools, and a couple of pocket knives, all of which would have Marty's fingerprints all over them.

Using the newspaper, Charlie plucked one of the pocket knives from the pegboard. It was the one he had seen Marty use regularly to cut the twine on grain bags and bales of straw. Carefully folding the paper around the knife, Charlie left the trailer, closed the back door and returned to his truck. He had one more stop.

Charlie turned south toward Andrade. He was on his way to the farm where Natalie had been held, and where Marty had been waiting that night. When he got to the deserted farm, Charlie drove to the old farmhouse, rather than to the barn. The police tape, from the investigation into Natalie's abduction, was still visible at the barn door.

He opened the front door of the house and dropped the knife on the doorstep. He closed the door. Then, using a pen, he slid the knife to the edge of the door where he positioned it so it stood on end, not obvious to a casual observer. He returned to the truck and continued south. The first gas station Charlie saw was the last one before the Mexican border. Charlie pulled a small blanket from behind the seat, folded it into a rectangle and slipped it under his shirt, sliding the bottom edge into the waistband of his jeans. He put on a hat and put a handful of loose change into his left shoe to encourage a realistic limp. Satisfied that his disguise was the best he could do on short notice, Charlie hunched his shoulders, went into the store and purchased two pre-paid cell phones from the uninterested attendant.

When he got back to the truck, Charlie was pleased to see that he had a telephone signal. He dialed nine-one-one.

He stuffed the edge of a bandana into his right cheek, then dialed nine-one-one.

"Nine-one-one, what is your emergency?"

Charlie responded with his best Spanish accent, "I was passing by the old farm on the road to Los Algodones and saw a man carrying a body over his shoulder. I don't know if it is a dead woman or if she is sleeping, but she didn't move. He tossed her into the back of a truck."

"Where are you now, sir?"

"I'm a quarter mile past the farm, driving toward Los Algodones. I stopped on the side of the road to call you."

"Is the man still at the farm?"

"He dumped her in the truck and went back inside the house. I drove on past, but didn't see him come past me."

"What kind of truck?"

Charlie gave a vague description of a grey pickup.

"Can you describe the man?"

"Not really. He was wearing a hat and the woman on his shoulder covered his face."

"An officer is on the way. Can you drive to the gas station at the crossroad just before the border and wait for him there?"

"Yes."

"What is your name?"

"My name is Billy Martinez."

Charlie disconnected the call and pulled the cloth from his cheek. A trace would show the call came from the location he'd told the operator. Between the accent and the bandana, there was no way his voice was recognizable. Confident that a thorough search of the farmhouse would result from his claim, there was no doubt the police would find Marty's knife.

Charlie couldn't make up for what he'd done to Jeff and Natalie, but he could provide the authorities with some evidence that Marty had been at the farmhouse. Kidnapping carried a stiff penalty.

Charlie turned north toward Goat Rock Beach. Four hours later, he opened the window and, after first wiping it clean of fingerprints, tossed the cell phone he'd used to call the police.

Three hours after tossing the phone, Charlie checked into a Bed and Breakfast. He used his credit card so his whereabouts would be clearly documented.

Charlie awoke before dawn. Careful not to make any noise and wake his hosts, he left his room and drove to the north end of the beach where swimming was prohibited. Vanessa would be upset, but she'd be okay. His sister was the beneficiary of a substantial life insurance policy she didn't know anything about. Years ago, Charlie had purchased it so that his sister wouldn't lose the farm if anything happened to him.

Vanessa knew where he kept all of his important papers, along with the information about his bank accounts. She knew where to find his passwords and the names of a couple of army buddies who would always be willing to help if she ever got into some kind of trouble. She'd find the policy there. Properly invested, it would provide enough income to pay them back for his bail, and to pay for the upkeep on the farm, now that he wasn't there to help.

Charlie was sorry for the hell Sonny and Vanessa had gone through because of the crimes he had committed. He concluded, however, that taking Angelina McCoy out of their lives was almost a fair exchange.

Charlie took all but twenty-three dollars out of his wallet and stuffed it in his pocket along with the emergency cash he kept in the truck. He checked the contents of his backpack, although he knew exactly what was inside: a multi-function pocket knife, half a dozen protein bars, a water filter, two changes of clothes, a jacket, a hat, a sleeping bag and a tarp. He added his pre-paid cell phone, swim trunks, hiking boots, a sweatshirt and a half a dozen bottles of water. He wrote a note to Vanessa, dated it, and folded it in his wallet.

Van, I'm sorry for the pain that I've caused. I can't live my life in a cell, and so I'll end it before that happens. Everything I have is yours. Sometimes the end does justify the means. Please understand. Love, Charlie.

Next, Charlie wrote a letter to Homicide Detective Kyle Michaels at the Laredo Police Department. He explained the details of Angie's plan to take Fury, transport the colt to Andrade, and breed him with her own mare, claiming the foal as Dreamweaver's, but then to return him unharmed. He admitted his attempt to take the colt and that Marty was waiting with the trailer. Charlie also outlined the details of Natalie's kidnapping. Angie told him that, at her direction, the Adams brothers were supposed to keep Natalie hidden long enough to have Fury scratched from the race. He slipped the chronicle into his wallet next to the letter to his sister.

Charlie grabbed his backpack and his diving gear, and then locked his keys inside the truck, along with his wallet and cell phone.

He walked to the edge of the cliff.

63

Three days later, Vanessa answered the door to face Detective Michaels.

"Mrs. Owens," he said sadly.

"It's about Charlie, isn't it?"

Michaels nodded. "Some diving gear was found hung up on the rocks. Charlie Williams's name was etched on the tank. His truck was parked near Goat Rock. The local police noticed it hadn't been moved for a couple of days and ran the plates. The name matched. Ocean rescue is out there now, but it's being called a recovery operation. I'm so sorry."

"No." Vanessa said.

Sonny had seen Michaels's car and was trudging toward the house. When he saw Vanessa's face, he knew why the detective was there.

"He wasn't answering his phone," Sonny said. "We expected him back the day before yesterday."

"There was a note in his wallet." Michaels told him. "His truck has been towed to the county lot. I'll need you to come down to the station and I can arrange for the police at Goat Rock to turn everything over to you."

Vanessa nodded. "If he had been convicted, he wouldn't have survived in jail."

64

Kyle Michaels closed the file on Charlie Williams. He'd driven to Chino when he got the call from the Goat Rock Police about the letter Charlie left for him. Charlie committed suicide. He'd written a note. They found his wallet and phone in his abandoned truck. His diving gear was scattered among the rocks. There were sharks in the area.

Vanessa read and re-read the letter that Charlie wrote to her. Although he was gone, he would always be with her. She was not surprised that Charlie had taken out a life insurance policy, but was shocked at the amount. The money was more than enough to pay off the bills, with a substantial amount left over.

Jeff and Natalie said they wanted to continue their association with the Sonny and Vanessa and the Williams Farm, and Vanessa agreed that their relationship was a good one.

Anthony McCoy was blindsided by the allegations against Marty. When the details of Natalie's abduction came to light, both he and Martha were devastated. To find that Angie had been involved in theft, deception and quite possibly sabotage on the racetrack overwhelmed them. Anthony told the detectives that it almost seemed like their daughter died a second time.

Anthony called Jeff Frazier and apologized for his daughter's behavior. Jeff accepted Anthony's apology and assured him that it was his intention to move forward and not look back. They talked about bloodlines and the possibility of combining them, with consideration given to breeding Fury to one of the McCoy's mares, perhaps even Anmaran. Neither of them realized that in so doing, they would be carrying out Angie's last wish.

65

Jeff and Natalie joined Santos, Johnny, Carl and Sarah at Carl's apartment for an afternoon barbeque. They had gotten together to celebrate Johnny Baker's addition to the team and to put the problems of the past six months behind them.

Fury was fit and ready to race. While his injury had prevented him from competition in the Million Dollar Derby, it wouldn't stop him from pursuing what could still be a very successful racing career. Nordstrom won the Derby, but had lost as the favorite for the second race of the series. IvoryPrince beat him by a length. Fury was being conditioned for the third race in the Triple Million Series, and everyone expected an exciting finale.

Flight was looking every bit as good as her older brother. Jeff had high hopes for her chances in the Triple Million Series in the upcoming year. In her second race, Flight finished first. Anmaran, had competed in a different race, and was also a winner her second time out. The two fillies would undoubtedly meet again, and the owners were looking forward to a friendly rivalry.

Santos missed having Sonny around, but was happy Jeff had hired Johnny Baker. Jeff and Johnny hit it off right away, and the new stable hand interacted well with the horses. Flight and Elektra had already become attached to him. Santos had begun teaching Johnny the all the skills involved in thoroughbred racing. They were looking forward to the Breeders Cup Races.

66

Only an hour before sunrise, the glint of moonlight peering through the trees illuminating the woodland floor of the Oregon forest. When a breeze floated through the branches, there was an illusion of candles flickering from above. It created enough light to allow the fugitive to travel unhurriedly through the dense brush and avoid the vines that sought to wrap around an ankle and topple him to the ground. He couldn't afford to be injured, neither could he risk traveling during the day. Caleb Jones was on his way to Alaska, to meet up with an old army buddy, a musher who raised sled dogs. Caleb liked dogs. He supposed caring for them might be something like caring for horses.

He figured winning Yukon Quest or the one-thousand mile Iditarod would probably be something like winning a Breeder's Cup Race, or maybe even the Million Dollar Derby. He'd talk to Walt about that when he got to Shaktoolik. In another life, Caleb

Jones had been Charlie Williams. When Charlie died, Caleb was born.

67

Kyle Michaels opened the file on Charles Williams. He recalled the call from the Goat Rock Police. Charlie committed suicide. He had written a suicide note, and a letter addressed to Detective Michaels. They found his wallet and phone in his abandoned truck. His diving gear was scattered among the rocks. There were sharks in the area.

The detective didn't believe any of it. Charlie Williams was out there somewhere, on the run. But why would he run if he hadn't killed the jockey? And where would go? Who would he run to?

Michaels thumbed through Williams's military record, thinking about his own days in the Marines. He thought about the friends he still remained in contact with from those years, friends who would do anything for a fellow soldier. No doubt Charlie Williams had friends like that, too.

###

Made in USA - North Chelmsford, MA
1194454_9781975790127
11.16.2020 0758